3. 23. 18

WHISKEY SHARP

JAGGED

LAUREN DANE

WHISKEY SHARP

JAGGED

HQN™

ISBN-13: 978-0-373-79940-4

Whiskey Sharp: Jagged

Copyright © 2018 by Lauren Dane

Recycling programs
for this product may
not exist in your area.

This one goes out to all the badasses with an aftermath story. Big or small, you survive. You make it through and serve as an example to the rest of us. Thank you.

Author Note

While Pioneer Square and SoDo are two very real neighborhoods in downtown Seattle, I've taken some liberties. Added some buildings, renamed a few, as it helped flesh out the characters and their stories. Still, Pioneer Square is every bit the former home to bootleggers and the criminal element partly responsible for the face of the city today.

CHAPTER ONE

LINES ON THE PAGE. Each sketch, each movement created a world she was responsible for. A world whose rules she made. A world whose rules they obeyed.

For a control freak like Rachel, it was as good as the talk therapy she'd been in for the last three years. It freed her. Gave her the ability to effect change on multiple levels.

And she didn't need to hunt serial killers or carry a gun to do it.

It was also a hell of a lot safer.

Sleep often eluded her, but the creative fire that had ignited into fierce existence in the wake of the events that had shattered her entire life four years ago rarely did. So when she couldn't find rest, she could always find art.

Her music wasn't so loud she missed the ping of her phone, indicating a text.

I'm in my driveway. Your light is on. Are you still awake?

Her pulse kicked at the sight of his name on her phone's screen. Vicktor Orlov. Heard the words in his voice in her head. That accent, a sexy Russian lilt though he'd been born in the United States. Growing up in a houseful of Orlovs and various relations with heavy accents had been close enough, she figured.

And it worked. Like really, *really* worked. It didn't hurt that he also happened to be gorgeous. Sinfully sexy. Funny. Super smart. He worked with his hands so he had great forearms. One of her favorite parts of a man.

Over the years Rachel and Maybe had lived next door to his parents, he'd come to be an acquaintance. And since her sister had gone and fallen in love with his cousin, Rachel and Vic had gone from acquaintances to friends.

And the door had been opened to something else. Something *more*. The possibility of what *could be* hung between them.

She considered not replying. He wouldn't know either way. He was messy. She couldn't keep him in a tidy box marked Friend. Not any longer and certainly not if she went and texted with him at three forty-seven in the morning.

Couldn't sleep. Working instead. Why are you up so early? Hot date that went late? Just enjoying stalking my window like a creeper?

It was a joke, or she wouldn't have said it. His house sat on the curve of their street, so from his front window and driveway he could see the side of the house Rachel's bedroom was on.

I run a bakery. I'm usually up by four thirty most days. Today I switched with my mother so she could accompany Evie to a doctor's appointment. I start work in about half an hour or so.

Ah.

He always smelled really good. Like bread and cake and just a smidge of vanilla. She wanted to take a bite. Or a lick. Something of the sort.

Vic made her tingly and warm and sometimes he made her want things she didn't need.

And yet, she found herself responding because she liked him—more than she should—and around Vic she was less alone. And maybe closer to being a normal person again who did things like have crushes and went out on dates with hot bakers.

Save me a loaf of black bread. I'll drop by later this morning to pick it up on my way to work.

Then she'd be able to get some food and look her fill at him while she did it.

That'd most definitely give her workday a fine start.

I'll save you two and throw in some salmon. But you don't need to come get it. I'll be done by eleven. I'll drop it by your house when I go home.

A flush washed through her. She'd be alone in the house by then.

It wasn't that having him in her house was bad. It was that he was dangerous for her constitution because she wanted to jump on him and ride him like a stallion.

Which would be a bad idea. Probably.

Possibly.

Not that she planned on avoiding it. The having him in her house part. The riding like a stallion was still in the fantasy stages.

Okay. Thanks, she typed back.

It wasn't like she had no self-control. She could say hello and look at his butt and flirt and it would be fine. She was a grown woman!

And, since this was just a conversation in her head, she could admit that maybe she wanted something to happen with him. They had chemistry—major chemistry—and she got the feeling, given the way he moved, that he knew his business when it came to a woman's body.

She went back to her pad but instead of the drawing, all she could think of was Vic and those shoulders of his. Wide. Not linebacker wide, but solid and strong. Capable. She liked that.

In fact, she was bummed she'd agreed to let him bring the bread to their house because she realized he probably looked ridiculously hot when at work. She bet it was pornographic just watching him knead bread. She already had watched him in her kitchen doing things and gotten a little swoony.

Yeah.

Her phone pinged again.

How often do you have trouble sleeping?

That was a very long and complicated subject and one she didn't want to get into via text, in the middle of some flirting.

I get most of my best work done after midnight.

Truth.

He sent her a selfie. One of his brows was raised and he wore a smirk. All parts south of her hairline went on alert. She'd be keeping that picture of him. Just for reference. Or something.

He was *unf*-worthy for sure. He was just so fucking much. Hot hot hot.

Hm. What's that face for?

Other than licking and kissing. Perhaps even a nuzzle of that spectacular beard.

That's my I don't believe you face. As for sleeplessness, I have some tea that might help. I've had bouts myself. What time do you leave for work?

Rachel frowned again and then forced herself to relax. That line between her eyes was getting deeper due to what her sister called glowering. Whatever it was called, it was going to make her look old if she didn't stop it.

She'd rather think about how Vic's waist nipped in, creating some sort of inhuman pizza shape of gorgeousness from his shoulders to his other parts, like his penis.

His cock was probably commensurate with his overall size. Which meant big. And what sane gal didn't like that? Well, if she liked dick in the first place—and Rachel most assuredly did.

Her little sister, Maybe, had been giving more *get it, girl* messages when it came to Vic over the last weeks.

Maybe, with all her glitter and snarling punk rock. Her sister was a little bit of the best parts of all sorts of things and she blurted weird stuff all the time.

It was one of her finest qualities because you always knew where you stood with Maybe. She didn't play games and she loved and protected Rachel as if it was she who was the oldest, not Rachel.

Hello? Did you fall asleep? he texted.

Before she'd gone off on some fantasy about his body, he'd asked her a question, hadn't he?

I'm leaving at a quarter to noon so I can catch my bus.

Rachel liked taking the bus. It forced her out of her comfort zone to be around people in such close quarters. Every time she managed to make it through without freaking out or getting even slightly uncomfortable she began to believe she'd truly be better at some point. And it cost a crapton of money to park in Pioneer Square.

Some days she drove or rode in with Maybe and Alexsei, who both worked just a block away from the tattoo shop, but that day she'd planned on busing into downtown as her sister and her sister's boyfriend were headed in earlier than Rachel needed to be there.

I have to go back downtown this afternoon anyway. I'll be at your house by eleven thirty. I'll make you brunch and give you a ride to work after. Turning off my phone now as I'm headed out the door. See you later today.

Oh! The cheek! Rachel stared at her phone a few moments and then, with a smile, she tossed it to the bed and took up her pen once more.

THERE WAS FROST on the front lawn as Vic pulled away from his house and headed toward the bakery his family had run for the last thirty years. It crouched right at the southern edge of downtown Seattle most locals referred to as SoDo.

The location meant their business was heavy with commuters and downtown workers at their lunch hours when they wanted to pick up one of the bakery's *runzas* for a quick meal. It also meant they were closed by three and on most weekends.

The bakery was pretty much always busy. A constant stream of customers, punctuated by rushes, meant the place was either full of customers, or all the employees were busily setting up for the next round of things to do.

As jobs went, it was a good one. Kept him busy. Paid his bills and enabled him to keep a hand in the family business along with his sister and parents. Gave him the space to keep an eye on everyone and make sure they were doing okay. Especially in the wake of his brother's death when the family had all but fallen apart.

He pulled into one of the two parking spots that came with the building and unlocked the back door, turning on the lights in the smaller prep kitchen before heading down into the heart of the bakery where the big ovens lived.

This was a place he knew. A place he'd been part of—and had been part of him—since before he could walk. As much a home as the place he'd slept at night.

He knew the slight warp on his favorite pastry scraper. The way the lights made the stainless steel worktables gleam. He hung his coat on the second hook, replacing the clean apron his mother had left on her way out the afternoon before.

First he turned on some music. Phantogram's "You're Mine" came on and smiling, he began to make dough.

He'd done it so many times it was second nature. Muscle memory as he dumped the yeast into the flour.

The ancient mixer was still there because despite its age, it worked perfectly.

As the place began to hum and the dough took shape he allowed himself to think about his exchange with Rachel.

Want roared through him. He'd had a thing for his parents' mysterious and broken next-door neighbor for well over a year by that point and over the last few months their friendship had deepened to the point where he'd truly gotten to know her better.

And now he was pretty sure he was already half in love with her.

At first he'd thought she was stuck-up. But he'd come to realize a lot of what he'd perceived as standoffishness had to do with anxiety and a bit of fear. The longer she and Maybe had lived in Seattle, the more she'd begun to settle in, the less anxious she appeared to be. And thankfully he saw way less fear in her eyes—especially when she looked at him—over the last year. She was taking her life back, pulling herself from the dark place she'd been. It was like watching a phoenix.

Just a few days past, Rachel's father had burst into her home and threatened to institutionalize her under a conservatorship and keep the sisters apart. Their burning resentment of Maybe, and the overly controlling parenting of the oldest, Rachel, had boiled over into what Vic believed was a death blow to the parent-child relationship for both Richard Dolan's children.

And as hard as it had been to see Rachel's heart get broken by her parents, it had been the way she'd stood up for herself and her sister that had been the last sign Vic had needed.

Rachel was strong. Fierce. Independent and utterly capable. This was a woman he could pursue in earnest without worry. He'd wanted to give her time and space to heal and to grow to trust him.

In truth, he hadn't been ready either. Not ready to step into something he knew without a doubt would be serious. But he'd been in her kitchen as her father had been railing about something ridiculous and the desire to protect her had been nearly overwhelming. In that moment *everything* had shifted. He hadn't felt this way—this powerfully—for a woman in a long time.

He saw her so clearly, saw the beauty of the strength at her core, he knew there'd be no peace for his heart until he kissed her. And more, though that was down the road a ways. Knew too that he was ready to dedicate the time and attention a woman like Rachel and a relationship with her would deserve. She needed spoiling and he was the guy to deliver.

She called to him. Something inside him stirred every single time he saw her. Her eyes and the shadows there. Her flaws and the way she powered through and did what needed to be done, even when the cost was written all over her face. All of it comprised the whole of her. The whole, fascinating bundle of gorgeous contradiction.

He'd been thinking about her so hard he didn't even hear his dad come in until he spoke. "I'm getting too old to be out of my bed on a cold dark morning."

An oft-repeated thing from his father, who'd most likely be happily kneading dough right where he stood just then until he was ninety-five.

"I told you to sleep in today. Nicklaus is coming in soon." Nicklaus had worked at the bakery for fourteen years and he was Vic's right-hand man. He normally did the first shift, getting the dough started before the second crew—including Vic—arrived at five. Bread would be in various stages of the process, proofing, baking, second rise, resting and once done, put in wire baskets Vic was sure were older than he was to hang on hooks at the top of the stairs to be brought to the counter.

His aunt Klara ran the upstairs with his mom and they made up the last shift that started at six thirty. Evie usually came in around six. Her specialty was the sweet dough. Together with their father, they'd make *vatrushka* with apricots, a particular favorite of their customers, along with cinnamon rolls and the other sweets that they'd sell over the course of the day.

Every single employee of the Orlov Family Bakery was truly family, including Nicklaus, who was a second cousin. For a long time Vic had appreciated that, but hadn't *understood* just how important it was. And then Danil had died and without the support of his extended family Vic was sure they wouldn't have gotten through it.

His dad slung on his apron, tying it around his waist with a satisfied grunt. Vic didn't bother to point out the freshly brewed pot of coffee. His father was old school. He had coffee with cake and black tea with everything else.

"Your mother was up. She's in fine form. Bossing the dogs around. I got out before she started on me too." Though he sounded grumpy, Vic knew it was an act. His parents had a real, deep and intense connection. They could fight, that was also true, but they'd drawn closer each time they'd been hit with tragedy as well as when times were good.

His sister, Evie, had said once that they were spoiled by that example and would never accept anything less than a love like that.

He agreed. Vic felt *settling* was for pizza and music when on a road trip. It was definitely *not* for love.

While getting his tea, Vic's father switched the music from Vic's choice to Stevie Wonder. Vic hid a smile and kept working. His father was the senior member of the staff and the family. He got to make the musical and television choices. This was his edict for all of Vic's and Evie's lives.

"I'm going to ask Rachel Dolan out," Vic said, forming high, round loaves on the long worktable.

"You'll lose your heart to that girl," his father murmured as he stirred sugar into his tea.

Surprised and not entirely sure what his dad had meant, Vic said, "I like her. I have for a long time now. But I knew we had to be friends first. She's not going to do me wrong."

His dad grunted a laugh. "Not my worry." He switched to Russian, which Vic knew was his dad's emotional language. "She is fragile and yet resilient. That draws you. You are easy to laugh. Easy to lend a hand. But she is not easygoing. She comes with heartache and sadness."

"So do I," Vic said.

His dad nodded again. "It's why you two are drawn together. You want to fix things. Make people happy. You always have. Our little sunshine child, your mother says. But here, with your Rachel, you can't fix what's broken with her. You have to live with that and so does she."

Hard, he understood, to sit by when someone you cared about dealt with the sort of pain Rachel toted around.

"One step at a time. First dinner and maybe a movie."

"Tell me, why now?"

There wasn't any judgment in his dad's tone. His parents liked the Dolan sisters a great deal. But he wanted to understand. Which is why Vic had brought it up, because he knew his dad would give him good advice and a pep talk that might or might not include an actual kick to the seat of his pants.

Just in case, Vic always kept a safe distance for escape.

He told his father about the scene he'd witnessed at Rachel's house just a few days prior. Explained how he'd felt, how much he'd wanted to burn things down to protect her, even as he'd admired her strength and spirit when she stood up for herself and her sister.

"I just knew I wanted her to be mine. I looked at her and she was hurting and it *meant* something to me. I wanted to fix it. Assure her she was everything her father told her she wasn't." And because she'd let him stay to witness the whole scene, it had also felt like she'd opened the door up into a far closer and more intimate relationship.

His father glowered. He adored Maybe with all her vibrant color and noise. Every time she came over to his parents' place, his dad would brighten. They'd already begun to see her as a daughter and had definite opinions about how the Dolans treated their children.

He stabbed a finger in the air before he put his tea aside and began to work. "I don't like those people. How they upset their daughters!"

What'd been revealed during that terrible scene was very private. But he knew Maybe would be all right with him talking to his family about it. He told his father about how Rachel and Maybe's dad blamed their youngest daughter for being repeatedly sexually propositioned and stalked by one of his coworkers. Told him about how devastated Rachel had been that her sister had been so abused and hurt. The guilt he knew she would never let go because she hadn't protected Maybe.

His father cursed a long stream in Russian. Not loud. No, when Pavel Orlov got pissed, he got quiet. He bellowed when he was happy instead.

Vic merely nodded at his father before continuing. "They want to control Rachel. Take away something she needs to make her dependent on them. If they succeed in taking her freedom, we'll fight for her. She can't be caged." She'd been at the mercy of someone else when she'd been kidnapped and Vic knew she'd break if it happened again.

"You make sure she gets the papers to protect herself," his dad told him.

"She's supposed to call Seth to get his advice." Seth was his cousin Cristian's fiancé. He was a cop with the Seattle Police Department so he had good information and given the way Seth was, he'd walk her through the process. "I'm making her brunch later on today so I'll make sure she does it then."

"You be careful too. The father is dangerous. It would be good if they leave Maybe alone now. It's Rachel they want. But if they can't get it…"

Richie Dolan had a temper. One laced with threat and menace and Vic didn't like it at all. He was the type of man who probably bumped shoulders with other men to assert some sort of dominance.

Vic didn't underestimate that threat. But he damned sure bet Dolan underestimated his children and their resilience.

"I am. I promise," Vic assured his dad.

CHAPTER TWO

RACHEL STOOD IN her closet, looking at her clothes. Annoyance warred with delight. It'd been a while since she'd dressed up for a man for more than just a few weeks of sex and then moving on. That was easy. A mask, a costume that spelled out the limits and boundaries of the interaction.

Sexy in a generic sense.

But Vic wasn't some dude she'd bounced on a while. He was someone she knew and liked. Someone who came over to her house on a regular basis. A guy who'd seen some of her most private stuff aired out.

God. *She shouldn't do anything with him.* Just stay friends. If they started something and it went bad it would be awkward. And she really liked the Orlovs and his cousin was living in her house, sullying up her sister. Gah!

So much energy buzzed just under her skin. Had been since she'd gotten out of bed and tried to pretend it wasn't a big deal that he was coming over and making her food and giving her a ride and being all helpful and nurturing and it was really insanely hot and comforting and he was sexy. So sexy and he wanted her. Her!

"Going off the rails here," she murmured to herself.

Of course she was naturally going to try to talk herself out of getting into anything romantic with him. It was dumb and risky, just as she'd reminded herself.

And of course she was going to do it anyway.

He made her dizzy and sort of sappy and dumb and really horny. She wanted to see what it would be like. To have something with him, to give the zing a chance. She wanted to let herself feel all this really good stuff.

BY THE TIME he showed up at her door she'd managed to get the eyeliner on both sides into pretty respectable wings and given the goofy look on his face when he checked out her tits, the choice of the snug T-shirt she'd worn over a long-sleeved Henley was a good one.

"Hi." He smiled at her, all gorgeous teeth framed by his beard. Sometimes she let her cheek brush it when he hugged her. And she wondered what it would feel like against the sensitive skin of her neck. Or the inside of her thighs.

Holding up an armful of packages, he thrust a huge bouquet of flowers at her. "I bring food and flowers in tribute."

Rachel took them, pausing to breathe in the scent of the pink-tipped cream-toned roses he'd given her.

"Good morning." She stepped back to let him come inside, taking a surreptitious sniff of him as he passed.

Yum.

She led him into the kitchen, where he began to unpack the haul he'd brought. Trying not to show how giddy she was that he'd brought her such pretty flowers, she made busy with trimming the stems and arranging them in a vase she placed in the center of the kitchen table.

"Thank you for the roses," she said, shyness in her belly.

He turned, approaching her slowly until he'd backed her to the counter, his body shy of touching hers. "You deserve roses."

The shyness in her belly turned to butterflies.

"I do?"

He nodded and then, shocked her into total stillness as he dipped and slid his lips over hers. Tasting. Sipping.

He backed up just a little before he got close again, this time sliding his tongue against her lips and into her mouth when she opened on a sigh of pleasure. The heat of him blanketed her, along with his scent, and she had to exercise all her self-control not to rub against him.

One last kiss, this one with a nip of her bottom lip. "I've been waiting a long time," he murmured, gaze searching hers. Looking for fear? Hesitation?

She went up on her tiptoes and kissed him quickly, one last time, chasing that query from his eyes.

"I hope it was worth the wait," she said, trying to sound saucy.

He smirked. "It was."

She smiled. "Good. I concur. On the being worth the wait, that is. Coffee?"

"Yes, that'd be great. Omelets okay?" he asked.

Nodding, she poured them both a large mug, leaving his near where he'd begun to assemble the ingredients for their meal.

"You know where the milk and sugar are if you want some." She indicated the sugar bowl.

"My mother says I'm sweet enough on my own," he told her.

Snorting, she rolled her eyes and went back to looking at him, enjoying the tingling left after that kiss.

"You do pretty well in that department, I must admit."

Visibly pleased, he shrugged, not at all bashfully. He was just so damned self-assured. Easy with himself as he moved around her kitchen.

"I've decided we should go on a date. First dates can be weird, even when you already know the person. So I propose this to be our first date so when I take you out, it can be the second date and we don't need to be nervous. Naturally there'll be flowers because, as I mentioned, you deserve them." He nodded as he began to assemble things in a fashion her love of order found very sexy. He poked around in the cabinets until he found what he needed and got about his business.

She sat back in her chair, utterly charmed. Damn it, why did he have to be so sexy and funny? So emotionally well adjusted and stuff? The whole of him was utterly irresistible.

It'd been hard enough when he was aiming all that charm at others. But over the last several months he'd turned it on *her*. Making it clear what his intentions were. Even as he never pressed for more than she was comfortable with she couldn't deny the chemistry between them.

He'd pushed his sleeves up, exposing ridiculously sexy forearms, and then washed and dried his hands. He stood, giving her his profile, his features exposed because his hair—acres of thick, gorgeous hair, nearly shaved at the sides but long on top—was captured in a ponytail at the back of his head. He usually wore it that way when he worked.

It should have been douchey or bro-something. It was
hot. Slightly messy but that was because he'd been up
since four working on that upper body she got a little
dizzy when she looked directly at. Like the sun.

"When you turn on the taps you go all the way, don't
you, pretty boy?"

"Too much?" he asked, knowing she wasn't going
to agree.

"It's impressive."

"Impressive is good." Cocky, he raised a shoulder
slightly.

"That remains to be seen," she told him, teasing.

His laugh was one she hadn't heard from him before. Low and lusty. It made all her hormones stand
up and cheer.

"I'm very competitive. It means I tend to get very
focused when I'm trying to hit something out of the
park. Get your rest."

It was Rachel's turn to laugh. Flirting with him felt
good. And she couldn't deny the curiosity about just
what he'd show her to *impress* her.

"Do you want ham or turkey?" He pointed at the cutting board with his knife.

"Ham is good. Thanks."

Silence lived between them for a bit as he cooked,
filling the kitchen with some really good scents. It
wasn't uncomfortable. Being with him rarely was.

"Busy morning at the bakery?" she asked.

"Even my mother was pleased with the business
today. She's a hard taskmaster and has very high stan-
dards when it comes to what she considers a successful day's take."

Rachel laughed. Mrs. Orlov was one of her favorite

people. Though small in stature, she was a big presence. Especially within her family. A force to be reckoned with in her community.

She only hoped to one day live as boldly as her own person as Irena did.

As he made the food, she hopped down and began to slice thick pieces of bread to be toasted. Pretty much daily throughout the last several years, she'd eaten bread created in the Orlovs' ovens. It had given her roots. A sense of place in her new life.

And at least a few more pounds.

"I brought fresh butter," he told her, indicating a wax paper–wrapped square on the counter.

Fresh bread and butter brought to her by a gorgeous man? She must have done something pretty awesome in a past life.

"I also brought some of the tea I texted you about earlier today. Drink it an hour or so before you want to go to sleep." He paused. "How are you feeling? Aside from the sleeplessness that is. I haven't seen you in person since Sunday night."

Embarrassment flooded her. "I'm *so* sorry. I can't believe you had to see all that. We invite you over for a meal and then act like assholes."

He looked up, anger on his features a moment. "You don't apologize for that. I told you Sunday. Everything that happened was from your father. Don't insult me with apologies." He made a sound. A distinctly Russian thing his whole family tended to do when they got annoyed or impatient. A *bah!* of a sound.

It made her smile. She saluted him. "Okay then. I'm feeling tired. Worried, I suppose. But pissed off is the dominant emotion."

"Did you call Seth about a protection order?"

"I called someone else. A friend of a friend. I used to be in law enforcement, remember? I have a meeting with an attorney tomorrow." Though if Washington was like most other states, getting this order would be difficult because her father hadn't physically threatened her.

But if an official body like a court told her father to leave her alone, he would. It would be the underline of authority he'd need to truly back off.

It hurt to know she was going to take an official step to keep her parents away from her. Hurt to know she *had to*.

He'd gone to the stove, the omelet now in a skillet.

They worked in the kitchen, stepping around one another to complete their tasks and she realized he didn't evoke the need to step away. She didn't think about how she'd take him down if he ever tried to hurt her. Not anymore anyway.

They were alone in her house and he was half a foot taller and she trusted him not to use that against her.

It made her feel just a little more human, a little more okay every time she was able to take a step back from that dark pit she'd been in for so long. She was more person than wounded animal in a trap.

THE WANT, THE need to put his mouth back on hers rode him hard. She was more than he'd thought even just an hour before.

Now that he'd tasted her there was no going back. No *unknowing*. Part of her lived in him now and he liked it.

He hadn't planned to kiss her that morning. He'd wanted to wait until their date. But well, she'd been there and looked at him with that fucking gorgeous face.

It had been better than he'd imagined it could be. The connection between them sparking to life.

Sexy. So sexy his skin seemed to buzz just being near her.

She placed a pitcher of juice on the table, nudging it his way.

"You're a good host," he told her as they sat.

"You did everything. All I had to provide was a table and some plates. I think I win." She shook her head as she peppered her food. "And I also have to admit Alexsei is the one who grocery shops most often so I can't even take credit for the juice."

This private Rachel was one he craved. She was open with those closest to her. He loved it when she teased him. Her dry sense of humor had been a delight to discover. And the sexy flirting, a new addition to their interplay, had been a really great surprise.

"I bumped into Evie at the grocery store yesterday. She showed me pictures for a tattoo she wants," she told him.

He withheld—barely—an eye roll. His sister was trendy. She had the latest shoes and clothes and now wanted a tattoo. But she was so picky it had been at least a year since she came up with the idea of getting one and hadn't pulled the trigger on it because she couldn't choose.

"It's nice that you're so close with her," she said.

"She's a pain in my ass with shit taste in men." He shook his head. "But no one makes a cinnamon roll like her so I suppose we're stuck with each other." His little sister was the heart of their family. Especially since Danil had died.

"Little sisters are the best. Don't tell Maybe I said so. I like to keep her guessing."

Vic snorted. "I'm fairly sure your sister already knows you have a soft spot for her."

"Someone needs to," Rachel muttered.

Vic reached across the table and squeezed her hand, surprising them both. But she smiled, squeezed back and then pulled away.

"So. Our second date. What should we do? Dinner? Movie? Drinks? All three?" he asked.

She looked at him awhile. Not speaking. He looked back, wanting her to see he was serious.

"I'm weird."

"Huh." He cocked his head a moment. "I was not expecting that. Like at all."

She laughed. "I'm told I can be unpredictable."

He leaned closer, pleased at the way her pupils grew larger as he did. "I like unpredictable." He took a bite, thinking over what else to say. "Are you trying to warn me off? List your supposed negative attributes so I'll see you're not worth my time? Because after those kisses I should warn you it'll take more than you telling me you're weird. In case you hadn't noticed, my whole family is weird."

She paused and he watched what had to be a dozen thoughts flit over her features. So expressive when she decided to share that part of herself with him.

He *challenged* her.

It made her feel like he knew she was strong enough to own her shit. So he called her on it because she was worth the energy.

"I'm just saying I come with a lot of baggage." She

shrugged. He was an excellent cook. The eggs were buttery soft, the saltiness of the ham a perfect addition.

He eased back, eating once again, but keeping his focus on her. "You're attracted to me. We have some major chemistry. Are you saying I'm imagining it?"

She was a lot of things but she wasn't a liar. Not even to herself.

"No. You're not imagining it. Zing." She waved a hand between them, indicating their attraction. "We've got it big time."

His smile sent a shock of desire through her. "All right, that's established. So why hesitate about coming out with me?"

"To be clear, I'm not hesitating about going out with you. I just wanted to be clear up front that I'm damaged goods."

He sat back to take her in, all feline and powerful. He moved like music, caught her up in him like magic.

"You're not damaged, Rachel. You've had life happen to you. And some of it was a nightmare."

A nightmare she wasn't entirely done with. Some scars never healed.

Most people wanted to *save* her. Pity her while being fascinated by the gruesome details.

He just *was*. When he was around her, he expected nothing more than what she wanted to give. She'd never really given thought to what it might feel like to be doing this slow dance into romance with someone like him.

Easy. Alluringly so.

"Look at you having such an intense discussion in your head." He began to eat again.

She could have told him it was too risky. His cousin

was now living in her house. Utterly besotted with her sister who adored him right back. Vic also happened to be close as brothers with Alexsei so if things went very badly between them it would impact pretty much every aspect of their lives. His parents lived next door, along with his sister. He only lived half a block up. They saw one another at the various events the bakery had booths at, as well as at the barbershop Alexsei owned and Maybe worked at too. Which was four minutes door-to-door from the tattoo shop Rachel worked at.

But she didn't say any of it. Because he knew all that already.

"It's just dinner. We can work our way up from there. If you were going to try to talk yourself out of it, you should have done it earlier," he added.

"You're right." She snapped free of her internal argument and snorted. "Fine. I just want to be sure you're going into this realizing what you're doing."

"I always know what I'm doing, Rachel. I'm deliberate. I always have been. I've wanted to go out with you for quite a long time," he said in an infuriatingly calm voice.

She tore off a piece of toast and jammed it into her mouth, chewing a while before finally asking the question that'd been nagging at her. "So why now? What changed from yesterday? Or the day before?"

She couldn't deal with pity. Not from him.

"I let you have yesterday because after that fuckery on Sunday you needed a break. I also knew you and Maybe took the day off to hang out and I left you alone. But Sunday is when I knew. I'll give you all the reasons why when you're ready to hear them."

"When I'm ready to hear them?"

"That's what I said. Tell me, how is work?" he asked, changing the subject. She began to demand he tell her but hesitated.

"Busy. Lots of people like to get ink around Valentine's Day."

"Romantic gestures they'll have to get covered up in a year?"

"I thought *I* was jaded," she said.

He blushed and she couldn't help the way it moved her.

"I'm not jaded. I can see the appeal of getting ink for your sweetheart. I know several people with horror stories, but they'd have horror stories either way, I suppose. The bakery does a brisk business for Valentine's Day too. This year Evie is making heart-shaped *vatrushka* and she uses strawberry in the center."

Oooh! "Did you bring one of those? It doesn't have to be shaped like a heart as it's already a pastry and I'd just eat it anyway."

"I didn't. For our second date, I'll bring you some to go with the roses."

That the normally easygoing Vic was coming back to the second date thing clued her in to the fact that he also could be like a dog with a bone when it came to getting what he wanted.

Damn it. Every second that passed he just got sexier.

Thankfully, since she wanted it too.

The moment stretched out between them as they finished brunch. Rachel tried not to jump up to clear off the table and clean the kitchen, telling him since he cooked she'd clean. It gave her some physical space and something to do while she processed the way he made her feel.

Vic eased back, watching her. Giving her silence but not taking his focus away. Once he'd fully stepped into her world, he apparently wasn't going anywhere.

Which, she had to admit, was a nice thing. She wanted to be wary of it. Look for ulterior motives. But… he wasn't that guy.

"Ready to go? I took what I needed to drop off next door on the way here so I can take you straight in. My mom isn't home or I'd take you over there first," he added.

"Really?" A flush of happiness hit that Irena wanted to see her and say hello. Vic's mom had become more and more involved in the lives of the Dolan sisters.

Actually, it was more that Rachel and Maybe had been involved in *their* lives. The Orlovs and their wonderful, giant, loud family who'd begun to treat them as if they were family too.

"Yes, really. She likes you and Maybe. You listen to her stories and let her teach you things in her kitchen. That means a lot to her."

It was totally mutual. Being able to hang out in Irena's kitchen had been a reasonably new experience in her life. Rachel loved it there. Vic's mom knew so much about so many things and was always happy to share her expertise. She was hilarious and nurturing and in general, a lot of fun.

"It's the other way around. She's always so patient even when I'm terrible at something." Rachel grabbed her things and made one last check to be sure the stove was turned off before they headed out.

Vic said, as they reached her front door, "It's what moms do." It must have been her snort in response because he paused and then said, "What they *should* do."

Even though he'd reassured her that she had nothing to apologize for after that scene with her parents, it still embarrassed her that he'd witnessed it.

She used the excuse of locking her door to get herself together again. But when she turned, he was there, a hand out to stay her.

"Wait," he murmured as he bent to zip her coat. "Don't want you getting cold."

It was so unexpectedly sweet it knocked her off balance a moment. "Thanks," she managed to say right before he gave her a quick kiss. Right there on her front porch.

His hand, warm and sure, sat at the small of her back as he steered her to his car and opened the door for her.

On the way to the south end of downtown that made up Pioneer Square, where Ink Sisters was located, she could have told him she didn't need a ride to work. She could have driven. She could take the bus and still make it on time.

But the truth was, she wanted to spend more time with him. He smelled good and it was really cold and parking was expensive.

And she wanted to be able to be honest about her life with someone other than Maybe and their best friend, Cora.

He lightened her mood just by being around. Accepted her without expectations that felt like a burden.

"If it helps any, my mother is bossy and nosy and insufferably meddlesome sometimes," Vic told her, surprising a laugh from her lips.

It used to feel sort of rusty when she laughed. Like an old hinge on a door not often used. But it didn't feel like an act to laugh with him, didn't feel unnatural to guffaw or snicker.

"I may have noticed that a few times," Rachel told him, deadpan.

HE DUG HER sense of humor. Dry and sarcastic with a sense of darkness he undeniably clicked with.

"What time do you get off tomorrow? For our date." He figured it was time for another pass at nailing down details.

She blushed, ducking her head slightly so her hair slid to partially screen her face. "Tomorrow is Wednesday so I'll be done by seven."

"I'll drop by the shop at seven, then, to pick you up. I'll drive you home and then you can come to my house when you're ready."

"I'm fairly sure you must have gotten this bossiness from your mother. I can just get home and meet you after that. Or we could go straight to dinner from Ink Sisters."

"I know you can. I'll pick you up at seven tomorrow night but I'm sure I'll see you before that." He hoped.

He pulled to a stop in the loading zone in front of the shop.

He wondered if she was going to argue and then wondered whether it would be a disappointment or not if he had to coax her into the plan. Coaxing her was rather pleasurable. And her crankiness was hot.

"Fine," she agreed at last. "Thanks for brunch and the bread delivery. And the ride."

"Wait just a moment," he told her, reaching back to grab the bag he'd placed there for her earlier. "Shortbread cookies made this morning. Just in case you get a craving for something sweet later."

Her mouth curved up into a smile before she leaned in to quickly brush her lips over his and scrambled away and out of the car. She held the bag aloft. "Thanks for these too."

With a grin, he waved before heading back into traffic once he got an opening.

NEEDING TO TALK to Maybe immediately, Rachel hurried through the shop to the back where the lockers were.

"He gave me cookies," Rachel told Maybe over the phone the moment she answered. She was so giddy she was past being embarrassed at how giddy she sounded.

"Who gave you cookies?"

"*Vic!* He came over and made me food and then grilled me sort of and then he told me we were going on a date. Our second one. Which we are tomorrow night and I'm not sure how it all happened. He's very smooth and possibly he mesmerized me with his forearms. Maybe, have you seen the man's forearms?"

Her sister laughed. "Took him long enough. I honestly was beginning to wonder if he was ever going to jump to it or if I was going to have to manufacture something to get you together. Jeez. And of course I've seen his forearms. They're like art. They need to be appreciated."

"So say we all," Rachel told her. "It'd be a crime not to."

"So you have a date. A second date, which means you declared brunch a date, which means there was at least some smooching today. Tell me everything right now," Maybe demanded. "Did you do below the underpants stuff? Or is that what the second date is for? Probably second date."

Rachel laughed so hard people in the shop most likely heard. "He made me food and kissed me stupid and gave me a ride to work and when we got here, he handed me a bag of cookies. You know, if I wanted something sweet today. It's pretty hard to resist," she admitted.

"So don't. Why resist at all?" Maybe's voice had softened.

"Well, you're right. I'm not going to."

"Duh. Save me two cookies. I want to hear every last detail about the brunch but I've got to run, my client is here. Don't tell Cora first or she'll lord it over me forever."

The sisters had been close, but in the years since she'd been kidnapped, they'd become best friends. Without Maybe, and then later, Cora, Rachel wasn't sure she'd have made it through some pretty rough spots as she recovered.

The three women had a deep bond and connection that included plenty of teasing and ass-kicking along with the love and support.

"I'll tell her you said that. She's going to ask me what happened the minute she comes in."

"She'll understand. Tonight how about we catch up on some shows, eat pizza and hang out? You can fill us both in then. Alexsei will be here until ten and then he and Vic are having drinks afterward so we have plenty of alone time to gossip," Maybe said. "I gotta go. Love you. See you tonight at home."

CHAPTER THREE

CORA SMIRKED AS she dumped off her bag and coat before coming through to the kitchen where Maybe was.

"I can't believe you wouldn't let her tell me about the brunch. What if something of a sexual nature had taken place?" she said, pointing at Maybe.

Maybe said, "If something of a sexual nature happened she'd have made me come to the shop this afternoon. Or she'd have called you to meet her at Whiskey Sharp before she was due in. Crybaby. Pizza should be here in like ten minutes. I called when I got home."

Cora hugged Maybe quickly before she got them all glasses, filling them with ice for the root beer she'd brought along.

"What are we watching tonight?" Rachel asked as she got plates down from the cabinet.

Maybe took one of her hands and tugged her to the couch, where she sat, Cora across from them perched in the big chair. "While we wait for pizza you need to tell us what happened with Vic."

"Well, he texted me. I told you both about that. And then he waltzes in and smells all good, like bread. Seriously, it should be a cologne, right? Anyway, then he kissed me! And gave me flowers." Rachel indicated the overflowing vase on the table. "And he cooked. Not just toast or an Eggo. An omelet!"

"Back to the kissing," Maybe said. "We really don't care about eggs."

"He's a really good kisser as you might have imagined. He tastes good. The beard is soft and smells nice. Self-assured. Confident. All signs point to really knowing his way around a lady's best parts."

Maybe clapped her hands over her mouth, eyes comically wide. Cora stomped her feet as she whooped and Rachel just shook her head at the two of them.

"And I'm pretty sure he was happy to see me, if you get my meaning, and I know you do because you are both women of loose morals."

Cora wiped a sarcastic tear from the corner of her eye and then flipped Rachel off.

"So, was he like *really* happy to see you? Like big guns happy?" Maybe asked.

"Proves my point. Floozies, the two of you. I assume you're inquiring about the size of his equipment?" Rachel asked, faux pearl-clutching.

"Of course we are. So? Is his dick big or will he try really hard to make up for it in other ways?" Maybe snickered.

"He won't need to make up for anything. I mean, it was like laundry day or something because he felt like he had a few rolls of quarters in his pocket."

The three of them dissolved into laughter for a little while.

"Anyway. Like I said, he's a very good kisser. He's got a great body. He's smart and funny and I don't know, it's easy to be around him. He's our carb connection and your boyfriend's bestie so there's that risk if things go south. But he makes me feel all this really wonderful stuff. You know?"

The pizza arrived so they filled their plates and settled in on the couch to continue the conversation.

"I do know and I'm in total support of it." Maybe shrugged. "It's good to see you taking this step. Letting yourself have some romance."

"It's not like I've been a nun since Brad and I broke up," Rachel told her sister.

Cora said, "No. But that wasn't romance. That was casual—but prudent—sex. You had these long-term fuck friends but none of that was about anything more than sex. Which was all you wanted and so yay for you because fuck pretending a lady doesn't need some sex to clear out the cobwebs and be living our best lives and stuff."

"You've always been happier in a relationship. Even back in high school," Maybe said. "You just never had the right guy. Vic though? He's another level. He's the kind of person you deserve. Who'll give you the energy and focus you deserve. And he's a grown man. He doesn't need saving or taking care of. If things don't work out, it's not going to be weird."

Cora said, pointing at Maybe, "Yes to all that. He's gorgeous. He clearly knows how to kiss and he's got a big dick. This is all very good. He brings you flowers and bread. He's definitely worth a second date. Now, not to be a buzzkill or anything, but what's up with the situation with your parents? Maybe said you two are seeing someone about it?"

"We're meeting with an attorney tomorrow," Rachel said. "We'll file for a protection order against Mom and Dad both. Keep them away from Ink Sisters and Whiskey Sharp as well as the house. He needs to have it underlined that we don't want anything to do with him and that we won't tolerate any more of this threatening crap."

No one was going to cage her ever again.

WHICH IS WHAT she said to her attorney as she and Maybe sat in front of her the following day.

Sarah, their lawyer, nodded. "First let's talk about the conservatorship. His chances are pretty dismal. You're gainfully employed. You're physically healthy and working on your mental health. We'll get your therapists here and back east to file evaluations. I'll do it up front so we can be ready when the requests for them come.

"At this point, given your stability, there's no reason to assume you can't handle the day-to-day decisions in your life. I know it's easier said than done, but I want you to try and remain calm about this. I can handle most of it without either of you needing to be there. That'll save a lot of time and he can't use the system to force you to see him. Sometimes that's enough. Once that avenue is closed, a lot of jerkoffs will lose interest."

"I hate that he's just doing this to try to control me and harass Maybe," Rachel said.

"It's not an unusual thing for an abuser to do. It's a classic move." Their attorney shrugged. "I don't much like bullies so I'm going to have a delightful time thwarting him." She put aside one folder and opened another. "As for the protection order, I don't think you've got the grounds with your mother so I'd suggest holding off. With your father, we might be able to get some leverage with feeling threatened. He's big, he's come to your home uninvited. He's threatening your independence. It's enough we can at least get a temporary order. Some guys back off and don't contest the order after the temporary expires after two weeks."

"He'll contest it. He's very into authority. The court is an authority. If the court tells him not to do something he feels entitled to do, he'll contest it because he won't want a judge to feel he's an abusive guy. And he'll contest it because he won't see himself as harassing anyone, merely being a good parent," Rachel said.

Their attorney tapped her pen against the pad on her desk. "That could very well be. I just wanted you to go into the process understanding it and what your chances might be."

They moved to outlining some next steps and an hour and a half later, she felt a little bit better about her future and her ability to protect it. She'd taken some of her lost control back, steadied herself with it and now she'd keep enjoying her life because she'd earned every day.

HE TRIED NOT to rush, but it was hard because now that he'd allowed himself to openly want her, it was like he couldn't hold it back.

"Slow it down, dude," Evie bitched at him. "You go showing up over there an hour early and she's going to think you're a creeper."

"I have things to do before I go pick her up. It's rush hour anyway and I don't want to be late or have to hurry."

Generally, he tended to be really mellow about most things. It took a lot to get him riled up. But he hated to be late. Probably because his family was always so big and had so many moving parts that they tended to have been late for everything.

But his mother had volunteered him—without even

asking him first—to go with Evie down to Pike Place Market to pick up fruit for the bakery. And naturally his sister had wanted to stop at Beecher's for cheese and then she'd hauled him across the street, pointing at the florist's shop. "Give her flowers."

"I was going to," he muttered. But this place did have really nice bouquets, especially for the season.

"Where are you taking her?" she asked.

"Le Pichet," he said, grabbing a huge bouquet full of color. The pick-me-up, especially as it had been a dark, wet and cold winter, would be a good thing. And it enabled him to spoil her more.

Evie nodded, clearly impressed with his choice. He had a feeling there was a hedonist inside Rachel and he wanted to lure her out. Good food, good wine, flowers, pastries, Vic wanted to fill her life with treats and delights of all kinds.

"Excellent choice, especially for an early date. She's going to know you won't be taking her to gross chain places where everything has a punny name."

He withheld a curled lip because that was what she was trying to get from him. Little sisters.

Back at the bakery, his mother made him have a cup of tea with her as Evie packaged up the heart-shaped *vatrushka* he'd promised to bring Rachel the day before.

"I don't need to tell you to be nice to her. You have wonderful manners," his mother told him. "I don't need to tell you anything because you're a grown person, a man who is kind and will do the right things."

She nearly always knew the exactly perfect thing to say. A lot of people—himself included—bitched about their mothers, but his was pretty wonderful. And supportive.

THE SHOP HUMMED with talking and the buzz of the tattoo machines as clients got their ink done. Rachel's neck was a little sore as she'd spent several hours on a half sleeve, bent at an awkward angle to get the lines laid just right.

But the work had been really good and she was proud of it, so the sore neck was worth it. Finley, her boss, Cora's big sister and the owner/operator of Ink Sisters, plopped down in Rachel's chair.

"When is the hot Russian coming to get you?"

"In about twenty minutes. I really could have gone home and met him there." She shook her head with one of those *what can you do* movements.

"Sure you could have. He knows that too. But he wanted to drive you. That's nice. It's not like he's unaware that you can handle yourself and your commute. He wants to take care of you."

He did. That's really what it was. So sweet and sexy. "I bought a new sweater today. I'm so stupid."

"Why? Because you want your tits to look nice on your date? Girl, stop. Of course you do. There's nothing wrong with you. Stop looking for problems."

True. She had enough as it was.

Finley continued, "He's cute. He's nice. He has good manners, a job, a house. And he likes you. For you. This is all good. And, by the way, you did amazing work today."

"Yeah?" Rachel asked, grinning. She admired Finley's talent so much, and that she'd been such a wonderful mentor and so supportive had been one of the major reasons she'd been able to make a real go at tattooing.

It hadn't been easy. Rachel was good with paper and pen. Or pencils, chalk, paint, whatever. She was artistic.

Not something she'd really pursued earlier in her life, but in this new chapter, it had been part and parcel of every day.

But paper wasn't skin. And at first it'd been a challenge getting past the fact that she was permanently changing someone's body and the cost of a mistake was huge. She *hated* making mistakes.

Finley had repeated that some artists took longer than others to hit their stride, but that once Rachel trusted herself to do ink, she'd be headed that way. Fear was holding her back from her real potential.

It had taken a while. Trust, especially of herself, hadn't been easy. But once she'd taken the leap it had made all the difference. Trust in herself had unlocked something, had enabled Rachel to connect with the work she did on a whole new level.

"It'll definitely go up on the wall with your other birds." The best of the shop's tattoos were placed on the wall in the small waiting area as examples of the kind of work they did. It would give her some extra attention, which meant more clients.

"Excellent," Rachel said, not bothering to hide how proud she was. Pride in yourself when you did your best was a good thing. That was one of her mantras and one day she might actually believe it.

SHE MADE IT a point to be outside at the curb right at seven. Over the years, Rachel had taken note of how punctual he was. Generally amiable, he got agitated when everyone lagged or made him wait.

He pulled around the corner and frowned when he saw her. It didn't stop him from double parking to let her in, though.

"I said I'd come in and get you," he told her once they were headed home.

Though Rachel knew what he meant—that he wanted her to wait inside so he could come to the door—she couldn't seem to stop herself from acting like she didn't. Just to get a rise out of him. "You did come and get me. That's how I came to be in your car at this very moment."

"You should have waited for me to come in and get you," he said in a grumbly tone.

"Well, that's silly when I can just take a few steps out the front door so you don't have to try to find a place to park. We're not teenagers on a first date and you parked at the curb and honked your horn."

"Sometimes I think you argue because it pleases you," he said and it made her laugh.

"I think you're too used to how easy your life is. You're pretty and charming so everyone just gives you what you want. You don't know what to do when anyone won't go along."

"If everyone did that, life would be better. It's not too much to expect," he told her, the laughter in his tone obvious.

That was the difference between his sort of bossy and what her parents were trying to do. It was why he was charming and they were being abusive.

Funny how she knew that and yet it still caught her up.

It puzzled her but she put it away as Vic pulled up at her place.

The lights were on inside so Maybe and Alexsei were already home. Rachel had thought it was nice to have her sister's boyfriend around. Maybe had brightened even more since they'd become an item. She was more confident—if that was possible—and steadier. Love suited Maybe.

If for no other reason than the fact that he made Maybe happy, Rachel would have liked Alexsei. But he'd become an awful lot like a brother since he'd moved in. And it meant Vic was at their house a lot more too.

"I'll be back to get you in half an hour. We have dinner reservations," he told her before he drove the half block to his driveway.

"Okay then," she muttered to herself as she let herself into the house.

Jesus, hot Russians everywhere. Alexsei stood in the kitchen with Maybe and one of the various cousins, Gregori, who was a fancy-pants megastar artist. His girlfriend, Wren, also an artist, sat at the table with a glass of wine.

They all greeted her with smiles and hellos when she moved through the room on her way to her side of the house. "Hi, all!" she said as she kept going. "Gotta run!"

Maybe was at her door two minutes later. "What are you going to wear?"

"Sweater, trousers, boots. It's fucking freezing out there." Rachel tossed off the layers of T-shirts and tanks and swapped out for the beautiful smoky gray cashmere sweater she'd splurged on after they'd left the attorney's office earlier that day.

"But cute underwear, right? I mean what if something happens and you two want to throw off some clothes and you're wearing something old and gross?" Maybe said as she dug through a nearby drawer.

"I don't wear old and gross panties!"

"Okay, but you've got like, underpants to be viewed

by the outside world and then those you save for your period."

"I promise not to wear my period panties on my date, Maybe."

Her sister tossed a hot-pink bra and panty set her way and then shook her head. "Never mind, not those. The color is too bright and you'll be able to see through the sweater. Hmm." Maybe pawed through her stuff some more before finding a similar set in an icy blue with a triumphant hoot.

Rachel knew her sister well enough to just put on the things she'd procured. The bra was one of those extra perky ones so it mounded up all that lady-flesh nicely at the neckline of the sweater.

"Go eat dinner with your boyfriend for god's sake and stop pestering me," Rachel said, batting Maybe away from her hair.

"Just let me get to the back. It's sticking up."

Finally she just let her sister fuss as she managed to reapply her lipstick after brushing her teeth.

"I want to know every detail," Maybe said in a stage whisper as they heard the noise downstairs that indicated Vic had arrived.

"So everyone keeps telling me. This is dumb though. He's your boyfriend's BFF!"

"Shut up and go break off some of that. I'll be waiting up and don't argue because it won't matter." Maybe pushed her down the hall.

"Bossy bitch."

"You got that right."

CHAPTER FOUR

Vic pulled her chair out and leaned in, taking a sniff at the back of her neck. "You smell like jasmine," he said, joining her.

"It's one of my favorite scents."

His too, now.

"How was your day?" he asked her once they'd ordered and the wine had arrived. The small dining room was absolutely packed and he wondered if she'd be all right with that, but she didn't seem to be having any difficulty.

He warred with himself over protecting her and leaving her alone and respecting however she wanted to handle herself. It was his nature to want to take care of people. He'd always been that way. But Rachel was a whole new problem. A whole new situation to try and figure out.

"It was weird. Saw an attorney. Then we went to the courthouse and got a temporary protection order for my father. We have to go back for a permanent one in two weeks after my dad gets served. That'll be oodles of fun."

He clinked his glass to hers. "You're doing what you need to, to protect yourself. Not fun, but necessary."

"It's a huge waste of my time and it pisses me off."

He sat back and took her in. "Okay then. Good." He

got the feeling she'd fight better and harder if she was pissed off. And what they'd done to her and Maybe was provocative and naturally she was upset.

"He's a retired cop. He knows how to work the system. My attorney wanted me to be prepared. I hate that I have to be. Seth called to check in on me, which I thought was nice."

"Once the Orlovs consider you family, you can't escape us. Even fiancés and next-door neighbors," he told her with a smile. "You think he'll fight you on this." It wasn't a question.

"Yes. He's used to being obeyed. When we lived on opposite sides of the country and I was doing what he expected me to everything was fine. For me anyway. He and my mother were abusing Maybe and I didn't know how bad it was."

She ran a hand through her hair, exposing the delicate shell of her ear, and a nearly insurmountable need to touch it with his mouth hit him square in the head.

Thank Christ the charcuterie showed up so he had something to do with his hands—and mouth—before he hauled her close enough to do it.

"I heard the whole thing. On Sunday with your father," he clarified. Her father had shown up angry, ripe for a fight. He'd savagely ripped into his children, trying to pit one against the other so he could control his eldest. So that he could jettison the youngest. Richie Dolan was a poor excuse for a human being and a shit father. "You can't blame yourself for that. We talked about this yesterday morning."

"No. You said I didn't have anything to apologize for when it came to you seeing how my dad acted. Not that I didn't protect my baby sister."

Shadows then in her gaze and he knew she'd remembered those three women who'd died in that basement chamber of horrors as she'd been waiting, wondering when her time to die would come.

"Can I admit something?" he asked. He had to lean close to be heard because the place was full of noisy, happy diners. It lent a sort of privacy that even a more empty restaurant couldn't offer.

She turned, her face close enough that he could really see her eyes. The amber fringe of color around the pupil. "Yes," she said.

"Sometimes I'm not entirely sure how to talk about certain things with you. Not because you're fragile or because I pity you. But I don't want to stumble into something that brings up bad memories. So I apologize in advance for the times when I'm going to put my foot in it."

She swallowed and then nodded. "You didn't. Stumble into something. It's always with me. What happened. It'll never completely go away and that's how it is. So yes, I didn't protect Maybe from my father and I didn't protect those women Price killed before they found me. But they're not the same thing anyway."

She busied herself with food awhile as they drank wine and were just together, but silent.

"I think he will fight. I think he will try to pull strings. I think he will hurt Maybe to get to me. I think he underestimates me and how far I've come. And I think he overestimates how good he was at his job when he compares his skills to mine," she said at last.

Vic nodded his head. This was good too. She wasn't going to let this stop her from living the life she'd worked so hard for.

And it was really fucking hot when she got mad and a little violent.

"Yeah? You were a hot shit FBI agent looking all tough and sexy as you brought down the bad guys. Your sister has sung your praises more than once."

"Maybe is good for my ego." Rachel shrugged. "I was good at it. Better than he ever was. And that never occurred to me until this mess. I was just glad they were proud. I simply had no idea that to them pride was such a poisonous thing. But he wanted to put me and Maybe in enemy boxes and all he managed to do was put himself there instead."

"Is there no going back? Nothing he could do to fix this?" Vic knew it was easy to be in his place and make judgments about what she should do. He thought Richie Dolan was bad for his daughters. Toxic. He'd done and said things that seemed impossible to get past. But sometimes families did.

"I don't think so. I can forgive a lot. But what they did to Maybe? And what they're trying to do to me now? Take away my freedom. Cage me? No. And that they don't seem to understand why that's a problem? I feel like they should know me better. But I guess I didn't know them very well either. No. There might be a time when I could be in the same room and not want to punch his face, but I don't think I'll ever be happy to see him again. He broke something important and some things can't be fixed."

"Some *people* can't be fixed. He's an adult. A parent. He makes his own choices. No one can look at you now and think you're not in control of your own life, Rachel."

"I'm outraged, you know? Like, how dare he try to

do this to me? He's disrespecting me and my life. My friends. My sister and best friend. Their daughter!"

He rather liked seeing her this way. Not that she was experiencing emotional upset—but the passion in her tone, the way she held herself, spine straight—it was bold and exciting. Intriguing and sexy as fuck.

"And now they're here on this date in this seriously wonderful little bistro. I apologize," she told him.

"You apologize too much for things you don't own."

"You brought me flowers again. Daffodils and larkspur. And pastry shaped like a heart. You're bringing your A game."

That pleased him. That she teased and opened up a little bit, sharing a private part of herself, though he hadn't failed to notice her changing the subject about always apologizing for things other people did.

"I don't do anything halfway," he said of his courtship game.

"So, today I dealt with that stuff with my parents. The attorney is going to handle all the response to this conservatorship stuff as well. Then I went back to work, but on my way stopped at that little clothing shop between my bus stop and Ink Sisters. There was a sale. Always a good thing. So I then went to work, where they'd just ordered lunch including a burrito for me. Also a good thing. Then it was super busy until I got off work and met you at the curb. And now I'm here with you."

He took her hand, turning it to kiss her wrist before letting it go. "And now you're here with me. Which is most definitely the best thing in *my* day."

"I've told you all about my day. Tell me about yours."

He watched the deliberate way she moved, the

choices she made, how she combined and tried new things as they arrived at the table.

"Work. Stayed after we closed to help with cookie baking for this group my mom and aunts are all into at the church. They bake and then take the stuff to all the older people who are on their own. Visit with them a little, you know? She sent me and Evie over here to the market to pick up some fruit. Then made me bake for them and drink tea. They were heading out when I left to come get you."

"Of course all those babushkas wanted you to cook for them and make tea. I mean, look at you. Anyway, it's nice. Your whole brood are just really nice people. Except Rada. She's a jackwagon."

Vic nearly choked at the mention of Alexsei's ex, who had been less than friendly to Maybe. "To be fair, she did give him a head's up about your sister looking like she might need help." Rada was complicated. As Evie's best friend, she'd been part of their family a long time. She'd been worried Maybe would push her out of the family for good since she and Alexsei had already been broken up for nearly a year.

"I didn't say she was an evil master villain. But she's not nice. I'm not nice either, it's how some of us are."

He thought about that for a bit. "I think you're nice."

"I do nice things sometimes. But I'm not nice. It's not an insult. It's just a personality type."

"Huh. Okay, I'm going to ruminate over that awhile because I'm not sure if I agree or disagree. Were you… Never mind."

"What? Was I nice before?" she asked the question he hadn't known if he had the right to.

"Yes."

"I think I did all the things I was expected to. I helped people in trouble in my job. I had a fiancé who had a very good job and very nice teeth."

"Always important," he said to make her snicker.

"Anyway, it was a good life. I don't want to make it seem like before I was taken I hated my situation. It was a life I was happy in. And then something happened and turned it all upside down. A lot of things weren't strong enough to survive the carnage. But some of those, like the fiancé, weren't quite what I believed they were from the start.

"And after I'd come through it all, after everything insubstantial had burned away, I started a different life. And I wasn't nice anymore."

He ate as he got himself back together. She unraveled him. Not something he was entirely comfortable with.

"Okay. I can see that." Though he thought she was pretty damned nice, he sure as hell wasn't going to tell her what she felt and who she was. "What are you doing this weekend? I've got both days off and I was thinking of a hike up at Tiger Mountain. It'll be cold, but clear. Have you hiked it?"

"No, but it's on my list."

"It's not super strenuous, but a good workout. I promise to take it easy on you."

She snorted. "How do you know you won't need it the other way around?"

"Who says I want you to take it easy? Maybe I like it hard."

He hadn't meant to say it. Or maybe he did but he hadn't meant it to sound so very suggestive.

But she wasn't offended. Not at all, unless he was misreading the way her eyelids went half-mast.

"Perhaps I like it hard too."

Holy shit. What the hell was he supposed to do with that image? Except think about how to make it reality.

"I think we need hot chocolate. And a fire," he said around a suddenly thick tongue. "I even have the supplies to make whipped cream for it. I'll walk you home afterward."

She should have said no but she didn't.

Instead, he tucked her up on his couch and made them both hot chocolate with fresh whipped cream while she basked in the heat of the fire and watched him.

His house was the same sort of tri-level ranch house their neighborhood was dotted with, but with a modern touch. Dark wood floors with burnished steel. The overstuffed couch she was on was plush and deep green with nail head accents.

It was a decidedly chic, adult space. Classic. Sophisticated. He was way more than she'd expected. Her mistake really, she should have paid better attention. But naturally she got caught up in that face of his.

She was only human, after all.

"So tell me about your favorite tattoo lately," he said as he joined her.

"That I've given?"

He nodded.

"I'm still giving it. A half sleeve. It's a cardinal. Full color." She indicated the way the bird lay around the curve and muscle of the upper arm. "Wings open. There's a lot of fine line work with the feathers."

"What about it makes you so proud of it?"

She thought awhile about the exact words to use. "It

takes a steady hand. It's scary at first when you're inking someone. This is a big piece. A mistake is forever. I was nervous but since I just jumped and did it, it's turning out really awesome."

"You're a risk taker."

"Not so much anymore."

"Making art is taking risk. You create something and throw it out there to rise or fall. That takes guts. And tattooing is forever. Well, there's cover-ups and removal but you know what I mean."

"I do." She hadn't thought of it like that but he was sort of right. "You've got the heart of a poet."

"Evie says the same. I can't see it."

Without thinking about it, she reached out and pulled his hair free to tumble down. "You even have the hair and the face of a fallen angel." It had been intended to tease but damn it if it wasn't true.

"I tell myself I'm going to keep it slow and easy and then you go and say things like that. So delicious, right here under my nose for three years. You'd think after three years I'd have more chill, but I don't."

She drew a shaky breath. "I really shouldn't be doing this. I shouldn't be here. I shouldn't be telling you all this stuff and thinking about how you kiss. There's something about you, Vic. I say things I don't intend to. I want things I shouldn't. It scares the hell out of me."

It was only the second date, but it was way deeper than that. They'd been developing a relationship for years and it seemed like now that they'd finally stepped into this new romantic thing between them, the intimacy had sharpened.

After years of living a very pared-down life, focused

on herself and surviving, it was tender, nearly raw to let someone as close to her as she found herself doing with Vic.

"I'm not that person. I make good choices. I'm responsible. I pay my bills on time and I turn the water off when I'm brushing my teeth," she told him.

He put his mug down, taking hers as well before turning back to her and enfolding her hands with his own.

"Are you suggesting I'm a bad choice?" he asked, teasing.

"Do these pants make my butt look big?"

He leaned closer, touching his lips to her cheek quickly. "You have an amazing butt and anything you wear makes it look great."

"You're not a bad choice." Especially when he said stuff like that. "I'm just being weird. I did warn you. Let's make out."

His smirk told her he knew she was changing the subject and also that he was down with a lot of kissing.

He pulled her closer and then into his arms, crosswise over his lap. She squirmed just enough to get a lay of the land, so to speak.

Well now. There was some big country going on.

With a growl, he cupped her jaw, turning her to angle her mouth just how he wanted it. Their first kisses the day before had been sweet and sexy. But this...*this* was an utter devastation.

He nipped and nibbled, licked and sucked every part of her mouth until she was a warm puddle of purring woman, arms around his neck to keep from drowning in him.

He branded himself all over her. The heat of his

hands—one splayed on her thigh, the other at her hip—seared. His taste burned itself into her memory so deep she knew she'd never forget.

A sexual fire within her burst into life, sending sparks of need through her as she urged him closer.

Yes. Fuck yes. More. More. More. She shifted her hold, fingers digging into his shoulders, holding him to her.

He hummed, as if she were delicious. "Gonna take a while to get down to the center of you," he said against her lips.

She might have come just hearing those words.

Against her ass, his cock was hard and ready and big. All the protestations that she wasn't a size queen flew out the window in the face of the very large penis that came along with this very hot Russian.

"I'm not going anywhere, so feel free to be thorough."

He laughed, setting her back on the couch beside him. "I plan to spend a great deal of time on you, Rachel Dolan, with your wary eyes and that mouth that makes me weep."

"I don't want to make you weep," she said, her lips quirking up into a smile. "Well, maybe I'd like to make you beg."

He leaned in and stole a kiss that left her mouth swollen and tingly. "I'll be sure to keep that in mind. I'm going to walk you home now."

"Wait. What?" She looked at the clock, noticing it was already after eleven thirty. He had to get up early and she'd gotten all caught up in her hormones. "Later than I thought."

He pushed his hair away from his face. "It's not that. The occasional night where I don't get at least six hours is fine. You're worth it and I can always nap after work. I just want to take some time. I want you to crave me the way I crave you. And when we finally end up in bed— and we both know we will—it's going to be mind-blowing. I like this stage. Full of anticipation. Discovery. I know your favorite color, but I didn't know you'd like heart shaped pastry."

"Who doesn't like pastry in any shape? What are they? Monsters?"

"I like to sip and savor." He stood and held a hand out. "You're complex and layered, I'm going to enjoy you."

She allowed him to pull her to her feet and then he helped her into her coat, again pausing on the porch to zip her up.

"I liked our second date," she told him as they walked up her front steps.

"I did too. I think the third will be awesome as well."

"I have high hopes," she told him, deadpan.

Once they'd gotten inside it was to find Maybe and Alexsei were sprawled on the couch, all snuggled up and looking adorable.

"You get points for walking her in," Maybe told Vic.

He bowed to her and then turned back to Rachel. "I'm sure I'll see you before Saturday."

"Chances are, yes."

He bent and kissed her right there in her house and even though they'd just kissed for like forty-five minutes, it got her all starry-eyed again.

He and Alexsei blabbered on about something or other before he headed out and she pretended not to watch his progress from her bedroom window. Which worked until he turned, looked right up at her bedroom window and waved.

CHAPTER FIVE

MAYBE SHOWED UP before Rachel had even finished taking off her makeup.

"No, we didn't have sex. Yes, we kissed. A lot. Like, he's a tasting menu of kissing and it's mind-blowing. I think I might combust when we finally fuck."

Maybe closed her mouth and just watched Rachel finish up before following her out to the bedroom.

Finally her sister broke with an excited little dance. "So this is really good and I'm trying hard not to show just how excited I am so as not to spook you but I need details."

After she got changed into warm pajamas, she and her sister got under the blankets. "It was a nice date. He took me to that little French bistro at Pike Place. He asked me questions about who I was as a person, as an artist." She fell silent for a bit. "Perhaps that's why I react to him so strongly."

"That or the fact that you've known him for a few years and over the last six months especially you two have been circling one another slowly. That's like foreplay."

"He just clicks all my buttons. It feels like a lot. And the old Rachel would have been suspicious of it and avoided him until it went away."

"As I happen to be feeling pretty intensely about

Alexsei right now I can relate. It's a loss of control to be that into someone. To be feeling all those chemicals bubbling around. The attraction, the sense that this person is unlike anyone else you've come across."

It did feel a little like the way she did just after riding a roller coaster.

"And," Maybe continued, "you're not that Rachel anymore. So there's a thing. An important thing. And it's not like you've been choosing one terrible dude after the next. You just haven't really been choosing at all. Past the scratching that itch stage."

"It's intense."

"Totally." Maybe rested her head on Rachel's shoulder a little while. "Tell me the rest."

"We had dinner. He's a door opener and a chair puller outer. You know? He's gentlemanly without being controlling. Bossy and used to getting his way probably through charm alone. And, Maybe, his face! How the hell can I resist? Which is rhetorical because I'm not resisting. I haven't made out with a dude in a long time. Probably since college. It's a simple pleasure. I could do it every day, much like eating bread and drinking coffee. Funny how he's related to two of those things. I just…when I'm with him I don't feel broken."

Or maybe that the way she was broken was okay. And beautiful.

"We're going on a hike this weekend."

Maybe turned to give Rachel a face. "Ew. Well, you two kids have fun while I won't be hiking. Or outside in the cold when I don't have to be. Weirdo."

"It's nice to be able to go on a hike. It's been a while." She loved hiking but after the kidnapping it had taken her two years before she'd drummed up the courage to go into the woods again.

"You do look super cute in your hiking gear. Wear those spandex pants that make you look like you're training to be in the next dystopian action movie I can't wait to watch."

Rachel laughed even as she knew the exact pair of pants her sister meant and put them into a contender spot. They were great in wet weather, kept her warm and made her butt look fantastic.

"I have heart-shaped *vatrushka* with strawberry. I was going to have a cup of tea. I'll share with you and your wild bearded Russian."

"Score. He brought gelato home and I think it should go with all that."

"He's a super useful new roommate. I'm just going to get that out there," Rachel said.

"I agree. He's even more useful to me. And I mean that in a totally sexual way," Maybe told her as they got out of her bed.

"I figured that out."

"Just wanted to be sure you understood."

Rachel flipped her off.

FRIDAY EVENING WHEN she and Maybe walked up the street from the bus stop, Irena came out to the front porch and called to them.

"Come have tea. I made *golubtsi*, you can have some too."

"We'll be over after we drop our things off," Rachel told her as they hurried up to their front door.

"Looks like a full house over there. I can't believe Alexsei didn't mention that." Maybe dumped her backpack into the closet. "I need to change. I'll meet you back here ASAP."

Naturally, she freshened up and brushed her teeth. If Vic was there, she might kiss him. But she did it quickly because neither Dolan sister wanted to make Irena wait.

"Come over for tea," Maybe muttered as they approached the front door. "There's a full-on family dinner situation going on in there."

Rachel really liked the big family events at the Orlovs'. Loved not just the volume of food, but the people, the easy back-and-forth between them as they teased, lectured and shared news.

Sometimes it got heated—well, often—but it wasn't mean. Lots of passion. Rachel hadn't known how to handle it at first. They'd grown up with quiet judgment from their mother and reprimand from one source only, their father.

Vic opened up, smiling at them both as he stepped back to admit them. "Come through. She's already making you plates."

He gave her a hug and brushed his lips over hers. A kiss that told everyone in the house they were together. A kiss Rachel knew the rest of the family was okay with as no one stopped what they were doing, though they *all* noticed.

Pavel shouted a hello before enveloping Maybe in a big hug and then, surprising Rachel, he gave her one too. Though not as ebullient as Maybe's, which made her choke up a little. He knew enough to want her to know he was happy to see her but also knew she needed to be approached gently.

And then Vic was there, drawing her away toward the big dining room table where, as he'd noted, his mother had set out overflowing plates she described as "a little bite."

Rachel wasted no time tucking in. She'd last eaten hours ago and the food smelled as good as it tasted. This was comfort food at its most perfect. Warm and hearty. The sauce on the *golubtsi* was spicy rather than sweet. Nestled up against that were the potatoes that padded the carbs until all her cells relaxed with a sigh.

She must have made the sigh audible because when she snapped from her food fugue, she noted Irena giving a satisfied nod. Vic draped an arm over the back of her chair, leaning back so he could continue flirting with his aunt Klara.

Klara gave his arm a blatant look and then tipped her chin. He grinned like he had a secret, unrepentant.

Before Rachel had kissed him that first time, she'd been able to appreciate his charms but keep a distance between them. Now it was like her attraction to him— her *awareness* of him—was at ten.

He was fucking adorable. Irresistible. God help her.

Irena sat across from them at the table with a tired sigh. "Get the girl some tea, *Vityunya*."

He kissed the top of her head as he stood and went off to do his mother's bidding.

"This is all so good," she told Irena as she made the superhuman effort not to stare at Vic's butt while he puttered around in the kitchen.

Vic's mother attempted a casual shrug but there was pleasure on her face at the compliment. Irena loved taking care of her family and friends. She baked you something if you were happy or sad. She made soup or dumplings if you were sick. A cluck or a tsk. A hug, a congratulations, a stern talking-to. A whole emotional language through food.

"Until we moved next door I'd never had cabbage rolls. I had no idea what I'd been missing," Rachel said. Their mother had been a good cook, but for her, food had been a means to an end. Fuel and nutrients.

One of the reasons Rachel had been active from an early age was her mother's constant focus on weight and clothing size. It had been Rachel's way to control food and her body.

Still, she liked food and while she knew she tended toward obsession when it came to exercising and physical strength, she felt like she had a better handle on it than she ever had, even before the kidnapping.

Irena frowned and then pushed some bread and butter her way. "I will teach you. It's easy."

Rachel somehow doubted it was what *she'd* consider easy, but she liked knowing things. Liked learning and mastering things. And she liked being in Irena's kitchen, in the heart of the house. Liked being part of what the Orlovs had built.

"I'd love that. I'm always happy to learn whatever you're willing to teach me."

"If she learns them then she can make them at our place," Maybe said.

"Or you could make them for the rest of us. I'll pay for groceries," Rachel said before she thanked Vic for the mug of much-needed tea he brought her.

"I know you like the kind without caffeine so I bought some," Irena told her.

"Better sleep at night without it so late in the day," Vic said, as if to remind her he hadn't forgotten about her sleep problems.

When Vic and his mother doted on her and did nice things, it made her extra blushy and a little shy. Sometimes she wondered what they saw in her that made them like her so much.

Evie joined them. "You're here. Let's talk about the tattoo I want."

Panicked, Rachel looked to Irena and then Pavel. Evie's parents frowned, but they didn't say anything.

Vic snorted. "She's a big girl. If she wants ink, they're not going to stop her."

"Not when *you* have it and they didn't stop you," Evie told him.

Irena chuckled as she waved a hand. "Don't worry, Rachel, we don't hold it against you."

"I do. But you're too sweet to stay mad at," Pavel said.

That cracked her up. Vic's dad was hilarious and nearly as adorable as his son. The noise level rose, but it was pleasant instead of annoying.

"Since your specialty is bird tattoos, I've been thinking about a firebird. The mythological kind. Which isn't real of course, but it's a bird," Evie said.

"Why a firebird?" The answer would guide the design.

"When I was little, my mom would read us fairy tales from this beautiful old book she brought with her from Russia."

"Color?"

Evie nodded.

Orange and yellow. Rachel could see the design in her head already. Placement would be key.

"Where?"

"I'll leave that up to you. I have another small tattoo on my calf already. But. I want it big and bold."

Irena said a long stream of something in Russian at that. Evie was an adult and if she wanted to get a head-to-toe tattoo it was her business. But that was between her and her parents, and as a child's girlfriend, Rachel had no place in the discussion.

Finally they stopped sniping and Irena rolled her eyes, sitting ramrod straight. She'd said her piece and it was over.

Evie looked back to Rachel with an expectant smile.

"Call the shop and tell them to set you up with the appointment. I'll work up a few sketches so you can look them over first."

Evie clapped her hands, clearly excited, and it was impossible not to get caught up in it.

Vic's sister wanted a tattoo from *her*. She mentioned other ink on her calf so she already had a tattoo artist she knew of. But the design she wanted meant something to her, which meant something to Rachel.

It also made it easier for Rachel to create an image meant for Evie and Evie alone. There would be other firebirds, but only one like what she'd put on Evie.

Every piece Rachel did was unique. Little details that no one else would have. It was just a little thing she did. And now she'd do one for Vic's sister.

Stuffed and feeling rather warm and loose, Rachel sat back and rubbed her stomach. "That was so good. Thank you for inviting us to dinner."

"A full house makes her happy," Vic said.

"It does until a quiet house makes me happy," Irena replied and Rachel could totally relate.

"Let me clean up," Rachel said, standing and beginning to gather plates.

Irena made a dismissive sound. "You can help."

Maybe joined them in the kitchen as they put away the food and then began the process of tackling the dishes. Vic came in to ferry whatever food that hadn't fit in the fridge to the one in the garage.

It didn't take very long and, in the meantime, the cards had come out, along with a chessboard, and Evie's best friend—and Alexsei's ex-fiancée—had shown up.

Maybe rolled her eyes, but only when no one could see her face except Rachel. Rada and Maybe had achieved a truce and were fine being civil with one another but Rachel knew her sister still thought the other woman was an asshole.

Vic grabbed her by the waist to waylay her, drawing her close. "It makes my mother happy to teach you things," he murmured in her ear.

"It makes me happy to learn things and eat what she cooks." She tried to get a little space, knowing they were being watched. "Really, I like your family."

"That's good. Since they're part of the package."

It was a pretty spectacular package, all teasing aside.

"Come play cards," his father called out from the dining room.

"Aren't you tired?" she asked Vic quietly.

"In a good way. If you want to go home, no one will be offended. But I'd like it if you stayed. They would too."

A warm wave flowed over her. She knew the look on her face was goofy but it couldn't be helped. She was happy.

"I'm a night owl. You're the one who gets up at four every day."

She'd be worth a tired day. "Not tomorrow though. I get to sleep in." He wasn't going to beg, but certainly a cajole would be fine.

Especially when it made her features soften and get a little more tender. He was a sucker for her soft side. Wanted to coax it out. And when she was kind to his family, laughing and playing with them, it was like nothing he'd ever experienced.

"All right. But don't expect me to take it easy on you tomorrow on our hike."

"I'd never expect anything less. Now go lose some money to my father and I'll get you some tea and me some vodka."

CHAPTER SIX

HE KEPT AN eye on her—and her ass—as she climbed the trail ahead of him. Her hair pulled into two short little pigtails, sleek gear clinging to her figure. A strong, fit figure.

Out here she tended to move with measured confidence. He found it sexy that she knew what she was doing. Her strength and skill made it possible to enjoy the hike the way he did when he was out with his buddies in his hiking crew.

She didn't need taking care of. Didn't want it certainly. Out here she was in her element as much as he was. Another sexy thing.

It was cold but mostly clear, though he got the feeling she'd have been okay in the rain too. And when they got to the top of the trail where they'd be turning to head back, she pulled out a thermos. "Want some coffee?"

He sat on a log and patted the space next to him. "I do. I propose to trade cookies in exchange."

"You're handy to have around, Orlov."

He pulled the cookies out while she poured them both a cup of coffee.

"Did you make these?" She indicated the cookie she nibbled on.

"Fresh yesterday morning. I set some by for this hike. I know your secret."

She turned, a question on her face.

"You have a sweet tooth. Just know I'll happily seduce you with whatever tools I have in my arsenal."

Laughing, she stole another cookie from the bag on his lap.

"Have you loved baking since forever? I imagine growing up in the family business it's easier that way. Were they bakers back in Russia?"

"My mother was a nursery school teacher. My dad worked in a factory. They came here in the early '80s and they started the bakery on little more than a hope and a prayer and a Russian community here in Seattle hungry for a taste of home. We grew up in the bakery, but I didn't always want to run the business."

Life sometimes just happened to you. She'd know that better than most.

"So, what happened, if you don't mind saying?" she asked.

"At one time I had planned to be a cop."

One of her brows went up. "And yet you make the best bread I've ever eaten in my life. You have a lot of talents, Vic."

He laughed. "That's how I know Seth. I've been volunteer search and rescue for the county. My team and I were helping some King County Sheriff's officers find a kid who'd run away from a campsite. There was some Seattle PD crossover and he was there to help when we brought the boy back. Cristian came by with Alexsei and they met."

"Aw, I love that story. What changed it? I mean from sheriff wannabe to baker? Family expectations?"

He took a deep breath. "You know we had an older brother who died. Danil. We don't often talk about the how. Anyway, he was supposed to take over for our parents. So I worked there part-time but mainly stepped out of his way. But he was troubled. Sick. Addicted. As he began to fray, it got more and more obvious I'd have to step in full-time."

The pain of the memories rolled through him. Held back a little by the distance of time.

She took his hand. "You don't have to say it if you don't want to."

It wasn't his shame. But it sure was his pain.

"He robbed a store. For drug money. And got caught. He went to jail. Which was good in that he got clean. But then he was released and he wasn't clean. Not really."

She put her head on his shoulder.

"He overdosed before trial. My parents…they fell apart. They were ashamed and felt guilty and responsible. My aunt did all she could. People worked overtime to shoulder the load, but it was necessary for me to commit to running the bakery full-time. Danil was supposed to do it. It was supposed to be his place. But I'm doing it."

"I'm sorry. What a tragic situation."

He sighed. "When we were kids he was my protector. Always the life of the party. I guess that should have been a clue. He just didn't know when to stop. And it killed him and nearly destroyed the family."

But in the end, it had given Vic a future he'd never imagined. And he'd been part of keeping the family together. He'd learned a lot about himself. About what family truly meant.

"Your parents aren't the only ones with survivor's guilt." A statement.

Vic looked at her carefully. It was cold enough that their breath misted around their faces. The scent of the coffee mixed with the pungent evergreens still lush even in winter.

"That sounds like you might know a thing or two about it," he said.

It wasn't that she never spoke of her experience. He knew the basics. But it never went very deep. He never pressed and she never offered. Until then.

"I know what it means to understand one thing and occasionally *feel* another. I know what it feels like to second-guess every choice. And what it feels like to know some of those choices were bad ones. Did you go to therapy at all?"

"The whole family did a few sessions. Evie had a lot of trouble in school for a while. It happened during her senior year of high school. My parents are very skeptical of therapy in general, but they did agree to attend a few sessions. I wish they'd done more, but they were so reluctant and after a while it turned into a fight every time. And you know, I'd had enough fighting with them. I just wanted them to be happy and be able to get past his death."

Rachel nodded. "I understand."

He got the feeling she really did. And something inside him that had been knotted loosened just a little.

"I'm glad, by the way, that I made the choices I did. I enjoy the bakery. I love that it's a family business and that despite the bickering, we're all working toward the same goal. I love to see my aunt and my cousins pretty much daily."

"And it means you bring bread to me. Which is always a plus as far as I'm concerned. And if I fall into a crevasse you can save me."

He laughed, standing to brush off his butt and begin to put away their impromptu snack. "I will always save you from a crevasse. Not that there are any close. But if we climb Rainier or something, I've got you covered."

She got her pack secured and gave him a face. "That was just talk. I don't go near crevasses. I love hiking and biking and kayaking and that sort of thing. I don't go ice camping or do any sort of extreme climbing."

"I'm sure you'd be really good at it, though."

"Maybe. But I've done enough time in hospitals so I try to avoid more."

He kissed the top of her head. "I'm on board with that."

"Thank you for trusting me enough to share that story. I'm sorry for all of you. But I'm glad you all had one another to get through," she said.

"I learned a lot about who I was and who I could be if I tried harder," he said as he took her hand.

They walked side by side for a while until the trail narrowed and they had to move single file.

"Valentine's Day is coming up."

She gave him a glance over her shoulder as she hiked in front of him. "I don't have any expectations. I mean. This is new and—"

He interrupted her. "This is *not* new. I've known you for years. Alexsei and I were thinking of making you and Maybe a dinner at your house. With chocolate cake for dessert. The recipe is a closely guarded secret and I only break it out for the people who matter most to me."

Now that she'd let him close he had no intention of

sliding back into anything less than true honesty between them. Skittish was fine. Aloof wasn't.

They made their way back to the parking lot, not talking. But he knew it wasn't that she was ignoring him, but thinking of a response.

He enjoyed the birdsong until she stopped, turning to face him. "I love chocolate cake. And I love it when people make me food. You have excellent forearms and I like to look at them and your butt when you're in a kitchen. I'm fairly sure I'd like to watch you bake."

Her words spilled out, tumbling one after the next and he caught each one.

"You should feel free to come by the bakery when I'm working and I'll set you up in the corner with a cup of tea and something sweet while you watch me knead dough."

"Don't joke. I think I just had an orgasm at that visual."

He paused at the revelation of another layer of this woman. Then he grinned. "It's not a joke. Especially after that comment. I'm there pretty much every day we're open. Otherwise, should you need an orgasm, I'm happy to deliver that as well as dinner."

She pinkened and he ducked to kiss her.

People came up the trail so they moved to the side as they started back down once more.

RACHEL WATCHED THE scenery whiz by as he drove. Ideas came often enough that she had her notepad out and began working on a new idea, not realizing how close they were to home until he stopped at a stop sign just three blocks away.

"Would you like to come over?" she asked him.

"Yes. I'll shower and come over after."

As her bathroom had a pretty small shower, one that would challenge the width of his shoulders she was sure, she didn't invite him to share hers.

He dropped her off and waited until she'd unlocked all three locks on the front door and went inside. Where she relocked everything, reset the alarm and toed off her shoes, tucking them into the hall closet before padding into the kitchen, where Alexsei stood at the sink.

Maybe was cleaning up what appeared to be an exploding blender.

"So I thought, how hard could it be to make smoothies? This is why I don't cook," Maybe said when she caught sight of Rachel.

"I suggested moderation in the total volume of fruit in the blender," Alexsei said, making Rachel laugh.

"Maybe thinks moderation is for suckers," she told him.

"Only when it's about food. And sex. And sleep," Maybe added.

"Atta girl. Vic is coming over in a bit so I'm going to clean up from our hike and be back down."

Of course, Maybe was sitting on her bed after her shower.

"You're in ambush mode all the time now," Rachel said as she got changed. "One would think you'd have less time to stalk me like a jungle cat when you have a hot dude in your bed to take to bone town."

"He sleeps with me. Believe me when I tell you I have a frequent flier card for trips to bone town. Speaking of bone town, I note the very sexy matching underwear you've got going on. I like to see you all giddy and sexy and stuff." Maybe picked up a candle on the nightstand, sniffed it and put it back.

"Did Alexsei tell you about Valentine's Day?" Rachel asked her.

"He did. It'll be my first Valentine's Day with like a for-real boyfriend. I know this is old hat for you but as such things go, it's pretty cool so far. Except I don't really know what to get him. What are you going to get Vic?"

"Jesus, Maybe! Now I'm going to be all nervous about it. I have no idea."

"Well fuck. You're the expert. What did you get Brad? You lived with him. He was all serious business until he put his penis in someone else while you were in a coma and all."

Rachel snickered. Leave it to her sister to know just what to say to make her laugh. "Well see, that's why you shouldn't ask me for my opinion."

"I highly doubt he cheated on you because you got him what? A watch or something?"

"I'm sure he'd say so." Her ex was a total dick. A cheating dick who'd stolen money from their joint account while she was in that coma Maybe had just mentioned. "As for presents, I got him a cashmere sweater once. A watch, but a really nice one he wanted and wasn't going to shut up about until he got it. And the last one I got him a Coach duffel. All very good gifts. All things he wanted. But I don't think I'll give Vic any of those things."

"Why? He'd look gorgeous in a cashmere sweater."

"He totally would. But I don't think those presents would be for Valentine's Day. I don't know. It just feels like he'd appreciate a gift that meant something to him."

He struck her that way. Sentimental but not in a negative sense. "I'm going to look around and when I see the right thing it'll jump out at me. I hope. It's not like I can bake him something."

Maybe nodded. "Not that you should complain because that means he will bake for you. And by extension, me. But you did give me good advice just now. I've been looking for the right present but I haven't found it yet. I should be patient."

"You got him that antique shaving set for Christmas and he loved that. You're doing fine."

"Look at us, panicking about Valentine's Day like adults." Maybe linked her arm with Rachel's before heading back downstairs where the commotion signaled Vic's arrival.

CHAPTER SEVEN

"So," SHE SAID quietly to Vic as the rest of the house played a round of *Guitar Hero*.

He turned and pulled her a little closer. "So?"

"You want a tour? Like to see my room?"

"Hell yes."

She waved discreetly at Maybe who waggled her brows, and then led the way to her side of the house, where her bedroom was.

Once inside, he took a deep breath and then smiled. "I've been wondering just what your bedroom would smell like. Jasmine. Like your perfume."

No other men had been up there. She did her fucking in other people's houses, or in hotels. This was *her* space. Her intimate place she made and kept safe. Here she could truly let down her guard and be open.

Vic wasn't anyone else, though, and she most certainly wanted him all to herself. Wanted him all over her sheets.

He waited for her to set the boundaries. Kept an eye on her and took his cues from that.

There was something comforting and yet sweet about how he was with her. Totally focused on her. Absolutely clear that he wanted more. But he didn't rush into her space. Not that he wasn't dominant and charming and didn't still manage to get his way with that roguish thing he had going on. But he just let her lead in these moments.

Which was perfect.

"You should fuck me," she said.

"Should I?" He closed the door at his back, leaning against it as he watched her with that smirk.

"Or, I can fuck you. Either way." She shrugged.

"Hmm. Why don't we take this step-by-step?"

She whipped off her sweater.

"Or, you could take your shirt off and show me just how fucking gorgeous you are without it. In fact, I'm thinking that's the better choice," he murmured.

"Now you," she said, turning out the overhead lights in favor of her bedside lamp.

She lit some candles while not taking her gaze from him. Not wanting to miss the reveal she was sure was going to be really fantastic.

And when he pulled his shirt up and off, she knew she'd been right. He was beautiful.

"Your body is amazing. I want to lick you," she murmured as she walked his way.

"I'm available for licking by you at any time. In fact it's been a recurring fantasy of mine for years."

He reached out, brushing his fingertips over the curve of her breast where it heaved from the bra she had on. And she was so glad she chose the sexy cute matching stuff instead of her comfy granny panties.

He told her in a voice rough like a caress, "For so long you were *right here*. So close. I saw you all the time and I had no ability to touch you this way. No ability to make all those fantasies of mine a reality." He circled her, looking his fill until he stopped behind her. "Oh, your back. Hold still, I want to pet and look."

He did exactly that. Slowly stroking his hands over her skin until she was all relaxed and tingly.

"This is beautiful."

"It's the first tattoo I got."

From shoulder to shoulder, across her back, a branch with a birdcage hanging from it in gray-and-black dot work. The door open. The bird was on the branch and not in the cage.

Never again with the cage.

"Tell me," he murmured before kissing the back of her neck.

Not only had it been her first tattoo, it had been her first tattoo design, one of her first drawings in therapy, and that theme had become a central concept in her life.

But she wanted to fuck him, not have that discussion.

"After. I'll tell you after," she said, turning to face him.

He gave her a raised brow but she popped open the button on her jeans and that stopped him.

"You fight dirty," he said.

"Not the only dirty thing I like to do."

"You're killing me. And you haven't even taken your pants off yet."

Rachel stepped from her jeans to remedy that.

He hissed and dropped to his knees, which only made *her* knees go rubbery.

"More birds." He traced over the spots of red on the breasts of the three red house finches inked across her lower stomach in various states of wing movement.

He licked over her hip bone and she was the one who hissed. And again when he found the lines of her various scars. She flinched away but he followed, dropping gentle kisses over places born of an experience that had burned her to ash.

He kissed her scars like they were the most beautiful thing he'd ever seen. To be seen like that by this man staggered her.

Humbled her.

Made her feel like a fucking goddess.

She held on to his shoulders, keeping her balance as he destroyed her with those sweet, gentle kisses as he murmured what she assumed were some panty droppers in Russian.

Rachel dug deep into the sensation of the scrape of his beard against her side, just below her breast, the lazy flick of his tongue tracing the curve underneath, stopping short of her nipple as she held her breath.

Waiting for that explosion of pleasure when he scraped the edge of his teeth over her nipple before licking away the pain.

Her head dropped back as he slid one arm up her torso, his hand so big and powerful as it reached her chest, the edge of his fingers brushing against the hollow of her throat, bringing a gasp from her lips.

Every part of her was super-sensitive. Cells alight with sensation and each time he kissed or touched, it set off little sparks of desire.

On his knees before her like a supplicant, he coaxed every part of her awake. Need rolled over him in relentless waves as he struggled to hold it back. Hold back his instinct to gorge on her.

But it would be over too soon that way. She was so beautiful, he wanted to worship her the way she deserved. Wanted to learn her from head to toe. Wanted to burn himself into her memory, his touch into her skin so that it was him she thought of and no one else.

He hadn't expected the matching lingerie, but it had been the ink, the owl on her thigh, the birds in flight from ankle to midcalf that had been so perfect. So sexy.

He had an idea about the story, but he wanted her to share it.

She grabbed at his shoulders then, attempting to get him to stand. He resisted a moment, pausing to breathe her in deep and press a kiss against the front of those pretty lacy panties.

"What is it I can do for you, then? Hmm, sweet?"

Amusement slid onto her features briefly. He stepped closer to steal a kiss while she got his pants unzipped.

He could have told her to slow down but he didn't want that. He fucking burned for her.

Given the flare of her pupils, the parted lips and the gorgeous flush she wore, she burned equally for him.

He shoved out of his jeans and shorts while she watched. Couldn't deny the pride when she caught sight of his cock and her smile went very satisfied.

She reached out to trace over the tattoo on his chest. "I admit I've wanted to see this for a while but there's never been a good opportunity to get your shirt off."

The full color, 1950s vintage-style death's head moth had been his tribute to Danil.

"You could have asked. I'd have complied immediately." He sucked in a breath as she tiptoed her fingers over to the piercing in his right nipple and flicked a fingernail over it.

"Noted for future reference."

She kissed up his neck as she rubbed herself against his body. Setting off all sorts of alarms but in a good way.

He'd wanted this for so very long it was sort of a trip that it was actually happening.

That she'd been trying to get his shirt off amused him. How long had they both been ready but neither moved for fear of spooking the other?

She was warm and sweet and he didn't stop himself from sliding his hands all over her skin, removing the last bits of clothes as he went. Acres of it and all for him.

He braced an arm around her waist and picked her up. She wrapped her legs around his hips as he walked her over to the bed and fell to it with her.

They fit. Perfectly.

She undid his hair, running her fingers through it as she pulled him closer. This kiss was different. This kiss wasn't a prelude to sex. *This kiss was sex*.

Her taste undid him as he licked into her mouth. The scrape of her teeth against his bottom lip sent a shiver through his body.

She'd landed with her legs still around him so he rested in the cradle she'd made for him. Again, fitting perfectly.

Rachel rolled her hips, grinding her pussy against him. Her wet heat sliding against his cock, rendering him nearly unconscious with pleasure. He wanted to be in her. Wanted that clench around his dick as he sank deep.

But first he had every single intention of making her come. And come hard.

He kissed down her neck, over the hollow of her throat, down her side and over each rib. She writhed slightly, so responsive to his touch. Her nails, short and neat, dug into the muscles at his shoulders, sending spikes of pleasure/pain through him.

Her nipple stood hard against his tongue as he swiped it over. Her whispered moan echoed in his head. Her muscles flexed against his as they moved against each other.

He was so hard his cock leaked. He pulled away from her a little to clear his head and keep her safe. Condoms. Yes, he needed to grab some from his pocket. But for the moment he needed to be about her.

Licking over velvety, sensitive skin, he kept heading toward her pussy, pausing again at her hip bones, nibbling around her belly button until he got to the other hip.

The sound she made when he paused, shoulders holding her thighs wide so he could look his fill at her—an entreaty, an order—tore at him as a pulse of exquisite pleasure fogged his senses and battered his control.

He spread her open and took a long slow lick. And then another, reveling in that silky sweetness. In the fine tremble in her muscles. He knew on some level that a loss of control wasn't something she allowed herself very often. And he understood why.

He pushed though. Right to that edge. He licked and kissed her pussy like a lover. Told her just how addictive and sexy he found her.

What drove him hardest was the unabashed way she sought pleasure. There was no shying away. She was all in. Rolling her hips against his mouth. His hair in her very tight grip as she pulled him where she wanted.

She wasn't exactly noisy, but she made the hottest moans, especially as she approached orgasm. He supposed she probably kept it up during her climax but she clamped her thighs over his ears so he couldn't hear anything.

IN ONE LONG BREATH, Rachel released all the tension in her body, falling limp to the bed.

She would have praised what had been a very fine blow job, but she wasn't sure if her lips—and the rest of her orgasm-stunned body—would be moving again for at least another minute or two.

He heaved himself up, resting his head on her belly, and she managed to get her muscles working well enough to reach out and caress some reachable part of that taut skin.

Rachel honestly couldn't wait to tell her sister what Vic looked like without his shirt.

Well, okay, she could definitely wait until after some more sex with Vic.

"My toes are still tingly," she told him as she reversed their positions so that she was on top of him, resting between his thighs. That first real look at his cock had made all the spit in her mouth dry up.

He laughed, easy and confident. Preening a little as he shifted his arms above his head, he lured her in for a kiss that tasted of her.

"You're a lot like a big cat at play. Most of the time you're sassy and charming, but when you want something you *move*." That he'd gone so suddenly from laid back to hyperintense and focused was dizzying.

And it made her wary. This close, this intimate she could see the predator in him. Like to like. He could hurt her.

She closed her eyes against the panic attempting to well up, instead redoubling her focus on him. On the way he felt skin to skin with her. On the taste of him as she licked over his nipple and the bar she'd suspected but hadn't seen until that night.

"This." Pulling back enough to look up into his face. "Quite the surprise under those shirts."

"Good surprise?" he teased as he slid his palms up her sides and around to cup her breasts. "As in, these were a very good surprise. Better than I'd imagined."

As if he'd sensed she needed to lighten up a little so he could charm her back from her panic.

He'd been right.

"Yes. A very good surprise." Like a fucking hot secret she hadn't known until she got to find out *this way*. So much better than seeing him working in the garden without a shirt or something. "Very sexy."

She kissed her way down his—ridiculously firm— belly, down that trail of hair leading to his—seriously impressive—cock.

"Now this?" She traced a fingertip from the root to the tip, slick with precome. "This is an *excellent* surprise." Gaze locked with his, she licked her fingertip before grabbing him in her fist, sliding her hand up and down a few times.

He groaned, a little growl at the end that had her bending to lick around the head to the crown. That growl went into a snarl.

Feeling very satisfied with all that power, she changed positions to better get at him, licking and sucking until he was little more than the writhing mass he'd reduced her to.

He was big enough that she couldn't get the whole thing in her mouth, but it didn't matter. Not really. She did the best she could with what she had and he seemed to be pretty happy with the result.

Happy enough that once she dipped her head to kiss down to his sac and back up, he picked her up and set her to the side while he rolled off the bed and began to pick through the pockets of his pants until he held up a square packet.

"Thank god," she said, getting caught in how he looked all naked, hard and ready to fuck.

He took a long, careful look at her. Intimate as a caress. She let him see just how ready to be fucked she was, needing him to understand she was good to go with whatever he had in mind.

"Ass up," he said, voice rough with sex.

She rolled and looked back at him over her shoulder. He grinned for a moment before rolling the condom on.

"Brace your hands on the headboard."

A shiver worked over her skin as she shimmied up the bed a little so she could grab the bottom of her headboard, which handily was a spindle big enough to hold comfortably.

His hum of satisfaction seemed to echo through her nipples. She hadn't been so exposed and vulnerable, not during sex, in at least six years.

So when he aligned his body behind hers, the backs of her thighs seemed extra sensitive where they brushed against the hair on his. Enough that she turned her face into her pillow when she moaned so the whole house didn't hear.

He was *so* big, the heat seemed to radiate from his skin over her like a blanket. The hands petting down her back and over the curve of her ass were powerful. But leashed. Creating nothing but pleasure. Showing nothing but delight.

His hands left her hips and shortly after that, the head of his cock nudged against her, pressing ever so slowly inside.

Sweet baby Jesus eating pizza, that was good. So good she began to push back as slowly as he pushed in. The edge of the burn at his invasion wisped away as she adjusted around him.

He lapsed into Russian at a few points, holding for a few breaths before continuing. It had taken all her control not to shove herself back as hard as she could.

He swiveled, sending sharp zings of pleasure through her and her breath shooting from her lips.

Still, she held on because when he finally bumped all the way home, he bent over her, kissing up her spine.

"You're so fucking sexy," he murmured right before sinking his teeth into her shoulder. Just shy of leaving a mark. All while continuing a slow controlled thrust in and out. The way he'd shifted, his body dominated hers, keeping her exactly where he wanted.

He controlled the speed and depth, the angle. It enabled her to let go and still have the ability to tell him what she needed. And left her with an absolute surety that he'd respect anything she said.

How it could be scary and comforting at the same time she didn't want to think about too much. Especially as he began to go harder and deeper. She allowed herself to drown in feeling.

The way he stretched her, coupled with the angle, began to build a new orgasm deep in her gut.

"Beautiful. Soft. Wet. So hot," he murmured as he reached around to pinch her left nipple. He left her speechless with the way he saw her. With the raw need she apparently evoked in him.

She let her head fall forward as she tightened herself around him. He slid a palm down her belly and found her clit, circling in time with his thrusts. Before long, climax slammed into her as she writhed around him, nearly overwhelmed with sensation.

He bent again, his face in her hair as she whimpered with the last of her orgasm when his came.

HE'D ROLLED OFF to the side and gone to rid himself of the condom before joining her in bed, this time under the blankets where she'd burrowed. It pleased him when she sighed happily and snuggled into his side because he'd been worried he'd been too hard with her during sex.

Given the way she slung her leg over him and looked up, smiling sleepily, they were both okay.

"I'm hungry."

"Want a sandwich? There's bread and corned beef."

Her smile went soft. "You're offering to make me a sandwich?"

"Yeah. You just made me come so hard my teeth ache. I'm totally good with making sandwiches."

"You're pretty handy to have around."

He kissed her slow, easing back into that soft, intimate place they'd newly carved out.

"Is your sister going to run in here when I show up in the kitchen?" he asked, pulling his jeans back on.

"Probably. Best to just get it over with and she'll scamper off when her prurient interest is satisfied. Hopefully by the time you return with sandwiches and grape soda."

He wrinkled his nose. "For you I'll bring grape."

He tried not to stare too long when she got out of bed to get dressed but failed, so she tossed a pillow at his head. "Go on!"

Laughing, he headed out to make his woman a sandwich.

Alexsei was in the kitchen as he came in. He gave Vic a long up and down and then smirked. "Go on, hummingbird," he called out to Maybe, who scampered off to interrogate her sister.

There was no need for Alexsei to question Vic. He was the quiet one in their relationship. It was Vic who loved to talk.

He assembled the food as his cousin did the same.

"The Dolan sisters need to be coaxed to eat more," Alexsei said at last. "So busy all the time."

Rachel was driven, as was Maybe. Vic liked that about them. They had dreams and aspirations and they worked for them. Both sisters were so smart and tough.

They were also vulnerable. Not so much physically, though certainly he was concerned for Rachel's safety. But emotionally. Their father had a great deal of power to hurt their hearts. He couldn't prevent that.

"Fortunately, I have a connection when it comes to food. My mother won't let them starve," Vic said.

"Your mother is one of my favorite people of all time." Alexsei held up one of the noxious grape sodas the Dolans seemed to love. "Strange."

Alexsei didn't ask if he was serious about Rachel. Didn't probe for details. He knew that Vic wouldn't be there if she'd just been a casual hookup. He wouldn't have let Rachel get close to his parents if he wasn't serious.

And Vic understood Rachel enough to know he wouldn't be in her kitchen after having sex when her sister was home if he'd been a casual hookup for her.

The words didn't need to be spoken. He and Alexsei

would be united in protecting Rachel and Maybe the best they could.

"They're very close," Alexsei said as he cracked two beers open before handing one Vic's way. "It's not about you. Or me."

"Understood and agreed." He'd never dream of coming between Rachel and Maybe.

Maybe came back into the room, gave Vic a thumbs-up as she reached between him and Alexsei to grab a beer. "You better get that sandwich up there. She's super bitchy when she's hungry."

"Wouldn't want that." With a quick goodbye, Vic grabbed the food and headed back to Rachel and her bed.

CHAPTER EIGHT

THE NEXT DAY at work, Cora tossed herself into a chair and watched as Rachel worked, finishing up a pretty little kingfisher on a client's calf.

"So."

Rachel gave her friend a look and then back to her client, who most definitely didn't need the details of her sexytimes with Vic.

"This is what you get when you come into work two hours late," Rachel muttered. "You have to wait for the juicy details now."

Her client snickered as she took photos and texted them to her boyfriend.

"I wasn't late. I was over at the venue dealing with some details for Walda's upcoming show."

Walda was Cora and Finley's mother and a Seattle-based composer and media artist who'd been prominent since the 1980s. She took being weird to a whole new level and Cora was her official handler.

Mainly because Walda was bananapants and no one else could manage to get her to do anything. Cora was sort of the handler for pretty much *everyone* in her family.

Once Rachel had cleaned and wrapped the new ink and her client had left, she turned back to Cora. "Yes.

It was awesome. His penis is massive and he is a master at oral."

"Wow. That answers several of my questions. But not all."

"Naturally. You should see him without a shirt, Cora. Like. I don't even have the words to describe it."

"I bet. I figured his equipment would be prodigious."

"Yeah, that's one way to put it. He gets the job done. Heh."

"Did he sleep over?" Cora asked.

"No. We stayed up, watched a movie. Had more sex and then he went home at like two. He has to be up so early and everything." She shrugged. And also she wasn't quite ready for that.

"Twice in one night?" Cora nodded her head, approving.

"Well, if you want to get technical, three times. Because he went down on me to start the whole thing off. He's an excellent date, lemme tell you."

"Says you. First he made you climb up a mountain. No sex is worth that."

"It was a hike." Rachel seriously dug that he enjoyed the outdoors and the sorts of recreation she did like hiking and biking, and he'd promised to take her kayaking in the spring.

"You say it like that makes a difference." Cora's expression said she considered most outdoor activity that wasn't reading in the backyard under a tree worth avoiding.

"There's a difference between mountain climbing and a moderately strenuous hike. And, I need to correct you that oh yes, sex with Vicktor would be worth climbing a mountain for. He's got stamina."

"And a big peen."

Rachel snorted a laugh. "That too."

She went to check the appointment log and realized the woman approaching the front door of the shop was her mother.

"Shit."

Cora, who'd been bent over a computer screen, snapped her head up at the alarm in Rachel's voice.

"Isn't she supposed to stay away from you?" Cora demanded.

"No. Only him." She quickly ran through her options.

"I'll handle it and tell her to go," Cora said. "You call and warn Maybe."

Though Rachel was touched by Cora's loyalty, she didn't want anyone else getting put in the line of fire from her parents. "Alexsei's got Maybe's back just now. I'll deal with my mother. It's long past time," Rachel told her. True enough. Her father had been the one to push this whole conservatorship so hard, but as far as she could tell, their mother hadn't done a damned thing to stop him. Worse, she was part of the legal action to take away Rachel's freedom and chain her to their decision making.

She squared her shoulders and went to the doorway, blocking her mother's access.

Rather than retreating back into the shop, Cora remained at Rachel's back. "Fine. But I'm staying right here with the phone in my hand and I will call the police on her without hesitation."

"Why are you here?" Rachel demanded.

Her mother narrowed her gaze. "Don't you speak to me in that tone."

Refusing to give an inch, Rachel repeated herself. "I said, what are you doing here?"

"Let's go somewhere private," her mother said, voice prim.

Rachel used to find some measure of comfort in her mother's calm demeanor—certainly as a counterpoint to her father's bluster—but now that she'd heard the whole story about how they'd blamed Maybe for the obsessive behavior of one of their adult friends who'd pretty much stalked her, Rachel found that tone irritating.

Mothers were supposed to *protect* their kids. They sure weren't supposed to show preference for one child over the other to the extent it caused lasting damage. Thank goodness she and Maybe were as close as they were so their parents couldn't bust them up.

But they'd broken something deep inside Maybe and now that Rachel knew exactly what happened, it had broken something inside her too.

"I don't want to speak to you at all, much less in private," Rachel said.

"You need to stop this legal business right now." Her mother's voice was just above a whisper. *Mustn't air our dirty laundry in public*, said the woman who allowed her daughter to be shamed for being sexually harassed by an adult man. "You're hurting your father very much."

"I wish you'd stop all this legal business right now too. I will if you will," Rachel said.

Her mother flinched slightly as a loud car passed on the street. "That's different."

"Why? Because you're doing it to me? I don't want any contact from him. I told him that. He didn't respect it. Then he showed up at my house and made such a mess he can *never* fix it. Back up and back off. Stay in Seattle or move back to LA. I don't care which as long as you both leave us out of it."

Her mother's mouth firmed up. "He's going to fight this protection order. It's just another example of just how sick you are. You don't know what's good for you right now."

Rachel *hated* it when her parents used that tone with her. As if she were so fragile she would shatter. If she didn't shatter after three weeks of torture in Price's basement of horrors she wouldn't let this break her.

"I am *not* sick. And he can fight it all he wants. But I want him out of my life. I won't tolerate his threats anymore and I'm strong enough to protect myself and Maybe. I'll do just that. You two started this but I'm going to finish it. And you have no one to blame but yourselves."

Cora put a hand on her arm, reassuring her, lending support. Telling Rachel she wasn't alone.

She wasn't alone and she wasn't powerless in a cage. She never would be again.

"You're turning your back on your parents. You were raised better. Think about it. Before your ordeal you were never defiant like this. You never surrounded yourself with these types of people." Her mother gave Cora a look before turning back to Rachel. "Your sister has let you get yourself all twisted up with a bad crowd but you have choices and we're going to be sure you have them."

They wanted to make everything in her life about those weeks. Only saw her as the sum of an *ordeal* she'd survived. She wasn't that moment in time. It changed her, yes, but she was more than one harrowing experience.

"You want to make my choices for me. Which is

pretty much the opposite of what you're saying. Don't talk about Maybe after what you did to her. It's a good thing she's got Aunt Robbie, who's a far better mother than you ever were."

It pleased Rachel to see her mother cringe as the strike landed, though there was a twinge of guilt too. She'd been raised to show deference and respect to her parents. It was difficult to let go of that, even when she had a good reason.

Part of her would always love her parents for what they were at one time. But the parents they were to Maybe and the way they sought to take over Rachel's life to force her to go back to the FBI and live a life she didn't want anymore had burned out most of what she'd felt for them.

"You weren't this way before the incident. Surely you can admit that."

"Before the incident I hadn't seen you for longer than three days in over five years. I haven't lived at home since I was eighteen. You don't know what I was like before that. I have a different job. My life is different in a lot of ways. But I'm still Rachel. And I never would have wanted you to put me in a cage."

"Before you were so traumatized you made good choices. Understandable choices. Now you're self-destructive. On a bad path. The Rachel I know wouldn't stop her parents from helping her get better."

That Rachel, that long-ago version of herself, had faded as she'd been manacled to a wall. As she'd listened to the other women weep and scream. That Rachel had handed off to who she was now. A survivor.

And yet, that Rachel still would have realized that her mother had a professional delivery. One that made

Rachel suspicious. She'd been coached by someone who was building a case against Rachel.

The flare of betrayal that soured her belly was enough to get her focused again. Her mother was attempting to manipulate her with words someone else wrote up for a desired result.

She was smarter than this.

She erected the armor of her mask once more. Cool. Calm.

Which is why she thought of Vic suddenly and realized his laid-back demeanor was a mask sometimes too.

Huh.

Before she could say anything else to her mother, Vic came around the corner and upon seeing them all standing in the doorway and who exactly she was speaking to, his expression hardened and he quickened his stride until he approached.

"You have an appointment in half an hour. Have a cup of tea and a snack in the meantime," Cora told Rachel as she stepped forward to admit Vic into the shop but keep Rachel's mother on the sidewalk out front.

"I made cookies," Vic said, all his focus appearing to be on her, but Rachel knew a predator when she saw one. And Vic was very aware of where her mother stood, Cora's protective stance and the tension in the air.

And then everything was all right. Because he was there. And Cora was there. And she was free and well.

She turned her back on her mother.

"Rachel! Don't you dare turn your back on your mother!"

She kept walking, attention on the details that made the entirety of Vicktor Orlov so damned irresistible as he poured tea and laid out the promised cookies on a little napkin.

In the background, she heard Cora speak to her mom. "You are banned from this shop. The next time you attempt to come inside we'll consider that trespassing and I'll call the police."

Her friend's voice was flat, but firm. They were giving her mother nothing to grab on to to use as a weapon. It warmed her that Cora was protecting her in tandem with Vic.

"Want to talk about it?" he asked her as he leaned against the wall near her station. He indicated a steaming mug. "My mother sent me over. I can see her timing was spookily perfect."

Irena had some witchy ways. "I don't want to talk about it," she said. "Not now, at any rate. I have a full schedule and I need to focus on that."

He nodded. "Later, I was headed over to Whiskey Sharp for a drink. How about we have one and unwind?"

She could think of some other ways he could help her unwind after that drink as well.

"Yes, that sounds good. I'll meet you over there at seven thirty?"

He shook his head. "I'll come by to get you at seven thirty and we'll walk over together."

"I don't need you to escort me."

He kept that charming smile in place. "Of course you don't. It might come as a surprise but I enjoy being with you."

She could have told him to fuck off and that she'd meet him there. Underline her earlier point. He'd respect it and give her the space she wanted.

But.

She liked being with him too. And it was nice that he wanted to walk with her the short distance to Whiskey Sharp.

"If we come in together, they'll all know we're *together*."

"Yes, that will be another benefit."

He made her laugh. Real laughter. Because he was so delightful and wonderful and apparently he was all good with the whole world knowing they were dating.

Cora cruised over. "That's handled. Don't give it another thought."

"Sure. That's going to happen."

Cora smirked. "I know, baby. But she came to deliver his message. Like a good little lap dog."

"He's going to fight the order," Rachel told Vic.

He nodded. "You figured he would. Doesn't mean you won't get one though. Just that he's going to say he isn't an asshole who terrorizes his children to get his own way."

Rachel sighed. He was right. Cora was right. It was all going to be a mess her father created and she had to accept that while keeping him at arm's length as long as she could.

"I need to let Maybe know about this. What if she goes over there?"

Vic's smile flattened. "Alexsei wouldn't allow it."

"And let's be honest, they don't care about Maybe in any way except that she's a way to get to you," Cora said.

And it was true and hurtful and Rachel hated it. But she supposed in this instance it was a good thing.

"I'll save it then. Tell her in person instead of calling

and ruining her day. She'd only worry about me," Rachel said before shoving a cookie into her face.

"She's your protector. It fills her with pride to do that."

It was super adorable that Vic understood what it meant to Maybe to keep Rachel safe instead of the other way around. No matter how uncomfortable Rachel was with it—she was the older sister after all, she should be protecting Maybe—she knew her sister loved her and took that role seriously. Especially in the aftermath of the kidnapping.

Not that it was fair that her little sister had to be her protector. Rachel hated it. But it was a complicated thing to express that and not insult Maybe. She stepped carefully because her sister meant the world to her, had been at her side through all the worst moments. Rachel never wanted to take that for granted, or to do anything that hurt Maybe if she could help it.

Then she realized Vic might have meant that as it applied to his life and the loss of his brother to substance abuse, which had been a foe no one could successfully protect Danil from.

He was always so smooth and charming that it was easy to forget the layers beneath that surface. And now that she'd seen more of those layers, they only drew her to him with more urgency.

"Hopefully it'll keep the focus on me and not her. She doesn't need another moment of pain from them."

"You can't keep her heart safe. It's also impossible to tell your sister what to do."

Rachel laughed at the truth of that.

"I have a client coming in a few minutes. Thanks for the tea and cookies. I'll see you at seven thirty."

If he stayed she'd find it harder to get anything done. He was a distraction. In a good way most of the time. But she had work to do and gawking at his butt and forearms wasn't part of it.

Unfortunately.

She needed him to go back to his day so she could do the same and focus on something less heartbreaking than this mess with her dad.

He let her guide him to the door, smiling and waving at the other tattoo artists watching them both with unhidden curiosity. They were a close-knit group and the moment they got the chance, they'd leap on her for details.

Then he stepped into her space, crowding her, but she didn't retreat. He dipped down to kiss her. A brief, affectionate and lovely kiss.

"See you later, sweet."

He protected her and laid a very public claim on her at her job and she was all goofy and love struck and it felt sort of awesome.

She watched him lope off down the sidewalk, surprisingly graceful for such a big guy, and also conveniently was able to check out his butt.

When she turned, half the shop had been staring out the window at him walking away.

"What? *You* of all people should realize how amazing he is to watch walk down the street," Finley told her.

"She's totally right," Cora said of her sister's comments. "I think you should call your lawyer. Let her know about this. Just to keep her updated." She pointed a stolen cookie Rachel's way to underline her point.

"It's a Sunday. I'll send her a quick email." But Rachel knew the score. Her mom hadn't made any threats and had left. Her father hadn't been there.

But her mother had delivered the message. Her father was going to fight to remain in Rachel's life even though she'd gone to a judge to keep him away. And her mother was, as ever, his errand girl.

So she tapped out the note, addressed it to her attorney and deliberately decided to focus on the work.

CHAPTER NINE

VIC WAS GLAD of the opportunity to take a brisk walk back to the bakery. It gave him the chance to work off some of his anger at the situation. How fucking dare that woman come to Rachel's workplace and upset her that way? These people, her parents, were garbage. They didn't deserve the kids they had.

They certainly didn't deserve to keep twisting the knife into the wounds they created with their shitty parenting.

He hated them. Hated that it ripped at her heart. The mother had the same holier-than-thou attitude her husband had. Self-righteous.

Vic changed course to Whiskey Sharp. If his mother saw him in this state, it would only upset her. But Alexsei would know what this felt like. He could vent to his cousin. On Sundays they opened late and did happy hour cuts and shaves. Sundays featured a gin-heavy specials menu so he had extra incentive.

While he waited for his gin and tonic, he sat in Alexsei's chair and found some relaxation in a shave and a trim before he and his cousin settled in with drinks to chat about what had driven Vic there.

After he gave the details—quietly because Maybe was just across the room—Vic sighed, sitting back and waiting for Alexsei's response.

"These fucking people," Alexsei snarled in a whisper. "Let Rachel tell her sister. Maybe is going to be agitated that I knew and didn't tell her first. But she and Rachel have a relationship that comes before anything else."

"You say that like a warning."

Alexsei's laugh was rueful. "You know as well as I do how close they are. And this garbage with their parents is something I'd love to squash. But you also know as well as I do that Rachel and Maybe see themselves as one. United as a front against their parents."

"Doesn't mean we can't be there to help." Vic sipped his drink.

"No. But it means we have to be smart about it. The Dolan sisters aren't going to tolerate anyone getting between them."

Vic watched Maybe finish up with a customer. "That one is clearly soft in the head to be in love with you."

Alexsei smirked and held his glass aloft. "If you think I won't use that to my advantage you don't know me well at all."

Vic clinked his tumbler against his cousin's. He too would use all the tricks in his book to make Rachel fall in love with him and keep her satisfied at his side.

"I'm no longer half in love with her. I'm head over heels in love with her," he said.

Alexsei's expression told Vic he'd known.

"I think I've been in love with her for about a year, but the last few months—even before we started dating—it's been pretty undeniable."

Alexsei said nothing, just listened.

"It wasn't the sex. Not that it wasn't astounding." Mind-blowing. Raw and intense and addictive. Espe-

cially the part afterward when she was loose and playful. "It's her heart. A warrior. A poet. She fells me,
Lyosha."

Maybe caught sight of them and smiled.

His cousin smiled back. "Such gifts come to us in
unexpected packages," he said in Russian.

So fucking true.

"I told her about Danil."

One of Alexsei's brows rose. "I'd been wondering if
and when you would."

"She feels guilt for this situation with her parents.
I wanted her to know she wasn't alone." Vic paused a
moment. "There's something about her. Like there's no
one else on earth who sees me the way she does. I just
wanted her to know I understood."

"For a while I was worried," Alexsei said. "It seemed
like she was deliberately not seeing just how destructive
their parents were being with Maybe. But I have seen
so much since. So much that has convinced me your
Rachel would move mountains for her sister."

Maybe scampered over and slid into the chair between Alexsei and Vic. "Hi!"

Vic smiled at his cousin's girlfriend. He liked her a
great deal. Had already considered her like family. By
that point, Vic saw the sisters as a positive influence
on one another. And on his family as well.

She was very cheerful, which amused Vic endlessly
as Alexsei was dour and liked quiet and he'd gone and
fallen for a chirpy little hummingbird, always making
noise, always moving.

"Hello, darling. How are you today?" Vic asked her.

"Not so bad. Good tips. Lots of handsome men to
ogle." She laughed as Alexsei rolled his eyes.

"Your sister will be joining us in a bit. Something happened today but I promised to let her give you all the details."

Her smile darkened. "I like that you told me. I was pretty sure you would. She texted that she had something to tell me. Cora is coming over here as well so whatever happened I'm guessing it happened at the shop and you saw it."

Naturally Maybe had already been piecing together whatever had happened. Though really the only drama in their lives appeared to be caused by their parents so it wasn't much of a mystery.

"You have a thing for my sister," Maybe said after staring at him for several moments.

Vic laughed at that. "You say that as if you're surprised."

"Not surprised you're hot for her. Duh. She's gorgeous and talented and totally mysterious. Who wouldn't be hot for her? And you've been around the house a lot lately and she's been sort of goofy and lets you kiss her in front of other people."

"It's nice she indulges me as I like to kiss her, and sometimes when the impulse arises we're around other people."

Maybe's delighted laugh made everyone around them smile at the sound.

Alexsei just heaved one of his oh-so-put-upon sighs at the back-and-forth between Vic and Maybe. He, like Rachel, was the quiet one in a relationship with a talker.

But Vic knew his cousin's game. He adored Maybe, including her constant chirping and playful nature. It evened him out. Gave him balance. The sighs and eye rolls were for show. Mainly.

"When she was with Brad there were very few PDA moments. Granted I didn't see them on a day-to-day basis as we lived on opposite coasts. But in the time they were together I don't think I saw her snuggle him. Or kiss him romantically in public. And I bet you would never be with a woman who didn't like that."

Vic gave Alexsei a look but his cousin shook his head. "It works out best for me when she's in other people's business."

Maybe sputtered, socking Alexsei's arm. "Just for that, next round is on you."

When he moved to comply and order them another round of drinks, Vic turned to Maybe. "I can't say whether I'd like it or not. It'd be an individual thing most likely. Your sister likes to be petted."

Maybe's brows flew up as she hooted her surprise. "My god. She is so sweet on you. *Petted.* I've known my sister all my life and no one has ever said that about her."

"No one knew she needed petting, apparently. It's a good thing I do." If anyone needed petting it was Rachel. She needed cosseting and spoiling, snuggling and adoring.

"You really get her, don't you?"

"No. Not yet and probably never all the way. She's got a complicated life full of complicated history. But I do get that she feels a lot of guilt for things she had no control over. And I get that instead of being lauded for what kind of shot she was, or how fast she rose up the ranks of her last job, she needs people who see her heart and don't flinch away."

Vic hadn't really meant to say all that, but it came out nonetheless. He wanted Maybe to approve of him not just as a fun companion to date her sister, but find him *worthy* of Rachel.

"Yep. You see her all right. That's nice. You have my permission to court her. Or whatever you want to call it."

Charmed, Vic leaned in to kiss her cheek. "Thank you, darling." It wasn't a joke, he understood that if she hadn't liked him, or worse, felt him unworthy of Rachel in any way, she'd have made it clear.

"My parents are going to continue messing with her. My dad doesn't…he's not used to being thwarted."

"It's not even about what's best for Rachel at this point." He hadn't meant to say it out loud, but now that he had, he needed to be careful. There was so much love and loyalty all tied up in the situation.

"No. I'm not sure it has been for a long time. They want to be in charge because that's what they want. Or, let's be totally honest, what he wants. My mother is just going to do whatever he tells her to do."

It made him want to punch her father in his fucking face. At least three times.

"She's so logical. It's hard to deal with something so illogical when you're that way. She can't understand why they'd want to hurt me to get to her. Or hurt her because she won't give in to what he wants. He will, Vic. He will destroy whatever he has to to get his way."

"He underestimates Rachel. And you."

"He's high on himself." She shrugged. "He used to ease back on it around Rachel. Gotta keep up appearances and all."

"But now she's seen the truth." Which would make him far more aggressive, anxious to get his way even if he had to force his way through.

"He won't be willing to believe he broke their relationship. Not even at this point after that scene in our living room. Not even after she had the court tell him to leave her alone."

Ice slid down Vic's spine. He worried for them both so much, protective of each sister for different reasons. Richie Dolan was unstable and that only made him more dangerous to those people Vic cared about.

He'd need to stay on the alert, but be sneaky about it because his Rachel wasn't one to be handled. Even when she needed it.

Strong, independent women were a lot of work. But good god above, they were worth it.

"He'll stay backed off if I have anything to say about it. I'll stand between him and the two of you. Understand that."

Maybe smiled prettily. "You and Alexsei are really very sweet. Also if you think my sister is going to let you do that, you're really missing the point of who she is."

"More now than ever, I believe. Finding out the extent of the abuses you were subjected to, things that happened and she didn't save you from. She kept trying to get them to accept you and be kinder and that whole time they were messing with you. And then they used you to hurt her." Vic wanted to say more but he didn't want Rachel to feel uncomfortable or like they'd been gossiping behind her back.

"My sister is a mama bear. He really has no idea what he unleashed with this whole thing. All this time Rachel has been focused inward. You know? Getting her head and heart in order as she also got physically better. She's like a shark, always moving, always thinking. What he's done is awaken that protective part of her and aimed it at himself. Like a wildfire. He's the enemy now. The target or suspect. He never really understood how good she was at her old job. He'll find out now."

"Perhaps that's for the best. The painful lessons are the ones that stick." Vic shrugged.

"I just hate that it'll hurt her too. But it would anyway I suppose. Now you get to be part of the conspiracy against them. My dad is going to see your relationship with her as something I put you up to. Just more of me interfering in her life to manipulate her. Bend her to my villainous will."

"I'm sorry this is happening. I'll help however I can." He'd shield them as best he could.

For the time being, he needed to head to Ink Sisters to pick Rachel and Cora up. He wanted to be sure her father wasn't lurking around. Though, to be honest, Rachel could probably handle a physical threat better than he could.

He'd hold her bag while she kicked ass, he supposed with a smirk.

CHAPTER TEN

Vic waited outside the courtroom, trying not to pace and failing.

"You'll wear a hole in the floor," Alexsei said mildly from his chair, his attention on the double doors of the courtroom just beyond.

They'd both written statements of what they'd seen occur between Richie Dolan and his daughters at the behest of her attorney, but they'd come to the courthouse with Maybe and Rachel to testify in person as well if needed at their hearing.

And to keep as close an eye on the sisters as possible.

"I don't like being out here when they're in the room with him," Vic said. "What if they need us?"

"There are armed guards in there. And in case you hadn't noticed, your Rachel is a former FBI agent more than capable of handling herself. And the moment we hear anything we go inside. Those are the choices we have right now," Alexsei replied. "You're usually a lot calmer than this, *Vityunya*. The voice of reason. Don't let her see you upset and make her take that on too."

Vic straightened his tie but kept pacing. "I'm not an idiot."

Alexsei just gave him a raised eyebrow.

He'd managed to get himself halfway under control once again when Richie Dolan and his dumbass wife strolled out and gave both Vic and Alexsei a sneer as they walked past.

Vic clamped his lips shut to keep from saying anything that could hurt Rachel's case but holy shit did he want to brawl with this loser.

Alexsei came to his feet with a whispered curse, striding over to stand next to Vic as they waited for Rachel and Maybe, who came out about five minutes later. Rachel was buttoned up tight. Her ice queen mask firmly in place.

"They didn't extend the order," was all she said as she allowed his help into her coat before they headed outside.

As requested by Alexsei and Vic, Rachel told them what had gone on.

Dolan had argued that he did not physically threaten anyone. That he was simply trying to get his daughter help and that nothing he'd done warranted a protection order. He brought up his position in the community and his reputation and how that would be seriously damaged if he had an order like that against him.

And the judge had believed the story, cautioning him to stay away from his daughters outside necessary interactions. The judge also asked Rachel and Maybe not to harden their hearts against their parents who might be wrong but loved them.

This was all related in a tone with only the slightest emotional inflection and Vic was pretty sure if he didn't know her well he wouldn't have seen it at all.

He wanted to put an arm around her shoulder, pull her close and tell her everything was going to be all right. But the sight of her said she needed the space so she could hold it together.

Alexsei gave him a look that had him in agreement. The sisters needed to go home and be spoiled. It was impossible to be strong all the time and they both needed the privacy and pampering to fall apart a little bit.

Even in the car everyone kept to small talk. Vic knew she'd tell him when she was ready and Vic was very glad his parents were still at the bakery so his mother wouldn't be calling or texting, demanding to be updated. When he told them they'd be upset too and he wanted to spare Rachel the additional anxiety at having to shoulder anyone else's emotions just then.

"We'll have whiskey in our tea while we eat," Vic said as he took Rachel's coat to put it away in the coat closet. "I'll even watch reality television with you."

Her sideways glance made him feel a little better about her mood.

She tiptoed up to kiss him quickly. "I'm going to change and be right back."

He narrowed his eyes at her enough that she sighed.

"I'll be right back, eat your food and give you some more details, okay?"

He hugged her, leaning down to whisper, "What can I do?"

Her arms tightened a moment. "You're doing it."

RACHEL GOT TO her bedroom and within a minute Maybe had arrived and pulled her into a hug.

"I can't believe it played out this way," Maybe told her.

Rachel began to change from her dressy court clothes into yoga pants and a long-sleeved shirt.

"She warned us it might," Rachel said of their attorney. "He used all the excuses we figured he would. It worked on the judge."

Maybe watched her carefully. "Don't think I can't see you're upset. You can try to lock it all down and pretend this ain't a thing, but you and I both know you're shaken up."

Rachel took a deep breath. "They decided our potential safety wasn't as important as Dad's reputation possibly being impacted by his own fucking behavior. It sucks. Of course I'm shaken up. Who wouldn't be? But it changes nothing, Maybe. Nothing. We will keep him out of our lives. Period."

"How?"

She took Maybe's hands to stop her from going any further down the panic rabbit hole.

"A protection order would have been a way to have the court underline that he needed to stay away. Let's be real, he's going to feel like he's gotten a pass to keep on acting up. So, we'll just use all the other tools at our disposal. We have the law on our side. He comes over here, we call the cops for trespassing. He's banned from Ink Sisters and Whiskey Sharp. Once we squash all this conservatorship bullshit we'll make a deep moat around our lives to keep them on the other side of it."

"Filled with hungry crocodiles," Maybe added.

If he wanted war, she'd give it to him. No one was ever going to cage her again. He was a bully, leading with how he felt versus how things truly were in the big picture. He could have been their advocate and instead had made himself into an obstacle. An engine of chaos that she would absolutely eliminate. She'd just have to be very clever and a lot ruthless to find her solution.

"He's not going to hurt you anymore." Not as long as Rachel had anything to say about it.

"Same goes, Rach. This is all on you now. I've only ever been an impediment and now that things are finally all out on the table, his focus will be all about you."

Though she'd apologized for being so damned ignorant to the true depth of what had happened between Maybe and their parents, it still hurt that Maybe had dealt with so much after Rachel had moved out to go to college.

It hurt that she hadn't done her job as a big sister and protected Maybe. And while she hated that Maybe had been driven to run away from home at sixteen, she was grateful her sister had ended up with their aunt and uncle in Spokane. They'd given her the home, the love and family she'd so desperately needed.

By the time the sisters had come together again it was Maybe who'd been the protector in the months and years following Rachel's kidnapping and all the physical and emotional aftermath.

Maybe had been a fierce advocate and it had given Rachel the chance to get better. To heal and find her balance again. Find her strength again.

"Thank you," Rachel told her as she hugged her sister. "I love you. You've done so much for me. We'll get through this."

"We will definitely get through this. And on the other side we'll be stronger. We're stronger together and that's what we are. Now I'm going to nap and then have postnap sexytimes with my wild bearded Russian. I think you should do the same. I mean, with your own wild bearded Russian because I'd hate to have to hurt you for touching mine." Laughing, Maybe headed out to her side of the house and Alexsei.

Which meant she'd have the living room and Vic all to herself. A treat for surviving a pretty craptastic day.

AFTER HE GOT her tucked up on the couch with a blanket, a cup of tea and a grilled cheese sandwich served with tomato soup, he joined her, settling her legs over his lap.

"I'm sorry about today," he said.

Lot of that going around. "This happens all the time in far worse cases than mine," Rachel told him—and herself—before taking a big gulp of tea and nearly choking at how much liquor was in it. "Holy shit."

"Why do things halfway? You had a terrible day, get drunk, eat comfort food and let your boyfriend take care of you while he sneaks a feel here and there."

"*Boyfriend* seems a very pale word for what you are," she said, her tone slightly accusatory.

"What can I say? I'm an overachiever. As for surprise? It's one thing to know something in a professional capacity and another entirely to live it."

Rachel nodded. "Good way to put it. Yes. I had a good attorney. Witnesses to the blowup. But it's hard not to feel like in the end that judge weighed my dad's reputation higher than my potential harm. Or even just the ability to say, 'Don't speak to me again.'"

"You think he'll be emboldened now." Vic shifted a little closer.

"I think this isn't about my health, mental or otherwise. Now it's about winning. That's his mindset and look, that's what makes me successful in a lot of ways.

He raised me with a finely honed sense of competition. I achieved because that's what I was trained to do."

He tucked her hair back because he wanted to see her features, wanted her to look into his eyes and know he was telling her the truth.

He said, "We're all, in some part, who we are because of who raised us and how. Your achievements are yours. You worked for them. You were a great FBI agent and now you're a great tattoo artist. Same Rachel. Different paths. Not because your dad is a controlling asshole, but because you took the reins in your life and have been doing your very best since you've been born."

She looked like she was going to argue, but finally shook her head before speaking again. "This is the best lunch I've had in a while. Thanks. The judge did tell my dad to stay away from the house and to just leave me alone except communication through official channels."

"At least there's that." Not that Vic thought Richie had any intention of taking that advice.

"He knows just exactly how far he can go and he's going to ride that line. Just because he can. To prove a point about who's in charge."

"He thinks you're weak but he's so wrong," Vic told her, taking her hand briefly to kiss her fingertips. "You're amazing. And brilliant. And strong."

"I was taken by Price because I made a mistake. That's not my very best. It was a stupid mistake and I made it because I thought I was better than I actually was. I wasn't a great FBI agent or I wouldn't have gone in alone. I would have waited for backup like I was supposed to."

He didn't move. Not wanting to startle her into shutting up. He braced himself and knew it probably wouldn't be enough. But he had to react right or risk her not sharing with him again.

"I'm not brilliant. Oh sure, I can shoot well enough. I'm good with hand-to-hand. I was an excellent investigator. I did love that part. It was like putting together a puzzle every time. Obviously with far higher stakes, so mistakes had grave consequences. I thrived on that though. Pushed myself but in the end, I thought I knew better. And because of that, because of my ego I got taken. And in the time after he took me, he kidnapped two more women and killed a West Virginia state trooper."

He had no idea how she lived with the weight of guilt she carried around. But he knew the basics of the story.

"You saw Price at a local store in a small town outside Lynchburg, Virginia. Why did you move when you did?" he asked.

"He'd taken a woman from her backyard just seven hours before. I didn't know if he had her in a vehicle or if she was stowed away somewhere and he'd come into the town for supplies. Or even if he'd killed her, but I had to wait to see what car he was in. If I'd waited and he'd gotten away, or if something had happened and we hadn't found her or the other missing women by that point, they could have died still in whatever captivity he had them in. He went to the register to check out and I got myself into a place I could easily track him to the car and take him down there. But he got the jump on me. As I started to approach, he spun and shot me. Then he knocked me out after tossing me into the car. When I came to I was there. In the basement. Manacled to a wall. Because I made a risky move." She rubbed at her wrist. At the scars there. An unconscious thing he was sure.

"Because you had to make a choice. You weighed all the risks and you acted. I saw the news reports. Your boss said he'd have made the same choice in your place. Your investigative work is what led them to finding you and the other survivors. Not because of a bad choice. Because you had limited choices at that time and took the one you thought had the best chance of success. You're human."

She sighed. "So. The judge sort of pooh-poohed the whole situation. Told my dad to give me and Maybe some space. He urged *me* to find a way to work things out with him. Like this is about him not liking my college major, or me crashing the car at seventeen. And now he's going to be worse and I'm fucking tired. I just want him to leave me alone. I want him to leave Maybe alone. He won't and I'm going to have to resurrect parts of the old Rachel to make sure he doesn't win. Not this time."

He touched her chin so he could kiss her. "I want you to understand I know you're avoiding the subject of bad choices and limited choices, all bad. But I'll let you for now and thank you for sharing this. I know it can't be easy to talk about."

"I don't actually mean to tell you as much as I do most of the time. The words just come out and I find myself sharing. It's got to be the dick and those forearms. Aside from that, you give good pep talks."

He laughed. Only this woman.

"Thank you, I think." He paused. "I'm here. Anytime you want—or need—to share. I'm not unbiased when it comes to you, but I'm always on your side."

She nodded, keeping his gaze for long moments before turning to finish her lunch and tea. Within an hour she was asleep so he fired off some texts to update his parents and then spooned her from behind and napped with her.

CHAPTER ELEVEN

RACHEL KEPT HER breathing even as she ran. The pound of her shoes hitting the track beat like a heart. That rhythm relaxed her, sent all the right feel-good chemicals into her system and she could allow it.

Here at the track at her club she knew the exit and she knew the entrance. Even though she tended to zone out as she ran, she was able to stay aware of everyone and everything else around her.

It was safe.

Vic was a street runner. Safe enough at four in the morning, she supposed. Not a lot of traffic. But it was too exposed. She'd tried when they'd first moved to Seattle, but it had been too much. She hadn't been able to zone out enough and instead had felt claustrophobic and paranoid.

For a time, back in that basement, the fear had edged her right to the breaking point. The wilderness of disconnection from reality was a breath away more than once. Even still, the memory of it could break her into a cold sweat.

She'd had to rebuild the foundations of her life and part of that was controlling as much as she could. If she allowed fear into her life, or it came in ways that were unexpected, it sent her spiraling.

At some point, he'd need to hear the story. Under-

stand why it was she ran how and where she did. The
need to explain herself to him confused her. Scared her.
But she couldn't seem to stop herself. She liked sharing herself with him. Liked that it brought them closer
together each time.

Liked the feeling of overcoming the fear each time
she was able to do normal human things.

This romance between them was refreshingly awesome. Free of any negativity—and God knew she had
enough of that just then anyway. He was, as he and
Maybe called it, courting her. With flowers and bread
and very good wine.

And awesome sex.

They had a date for dinner at her house later that
night after she got off work. Cora was coming, as were
Gregori and Wren. It'd be casual. Sandwiches, chips,
pasta salad, soda and beer.

Most likely a game of cards would break out because
Vic and his cousins were bananas about card games
with very complicated rules. She got the feeling they
cheated like a motherfucker but as she hadn't quite figured out all the rules she couldn't be totally sure. She
did know the cousins learned to cheat at cards from
their fathers, so chances were high.

She'd stopped worrying so much about him getting
enough sleep if he hung out with her. He napped during
the day after he got off and generally she made sure he
was done with anything with her by nine or so. Plus, as
he reminded her, he was a grown-up and fully capable
of managing his own sleep schedule.

It was still sort of fun to poke at him over it, so she
did. And he seemed to like it.

He hadn't spent the night yet. But she felt like if anyone was going to stay over, it would be him. He wanted to take care of her, but he gave her some room. Like she was a skittish cat he wanted to tame.

Which made her snicker because she was *totally* a bitchy cat but damn, she wanted to rub all over him all the time.

And without a doubt, she was in love with his family. They were what she'd always wanted and never knew until she experienced all that overwhelming noise and busyness of the Orlovs.

They'd simply enfolded her into their lives and it was glorious. And safe.

She still felt awkward and weird, but they were all seemingly okay with her awkward weirdness. It took a weight from her heart.

ACROSS TOWN, VIC pulled a tray of dinner rolls from the oven, leaving it on the rack to cool.

His little sister bounced into the room like a cartoon.

"Good morning!"

He gave her a look. "Why are you so cheerful? What have you been up to?"

"Some people are happy in the mornings, you know." She winked and then began to make the pastry cream. "I'm going to look at condos later today," she added.

She'd been saving for several years for a sizable down payment for a house. In that time the market had begun to rebound and prices began to nudge upward so she'd decided to move or get priced out altogether.

"That's worth being cheerful over."

"I like to think so. Not that living with a roommate forever in a craptastic apartment where the halls smell like cat pee isn't super attractive and all."

He'd offered to let her live in one of his spare rooms but she'd balked at the reality of living that close to their parents so she and Rada had rented a place in a fun neighborhood with no parking and sky-high rent.

His frugal parents were mortified but to Vic's mind, she was just being a young person. Learning lessons was part of being an adult and the harder they frowned at her and disapproved, the more she wanted to do it.

But he wasn't going to tell his parents that, even if they had been able to hear it. Nor was he going to tell Evie that their mother and father only wanted the best for her and living with them rent-free would have given her an even bigger down payment.

He planned to stay the hell out of that altogether to support her and be her big brother. A safe space to vent, because she didn't need another father.

"How are things with Rachel? *Mamka* said she helped unload after a trip to the warehouse store."

Vic snorted at the memory. "As you can imagine, it was several trips to and from the garage and pantry to store everything. She was in fine form, snapping her fingers and ordering everyone around. Rachel just let it roll off her back. And then? She rearranged the shelves."

Evie's brows flew up. "No way! What did Mom say?"

"I was worried I'd have to tackle her, but she thought it was awesome. Started adding her own twist."

"*Mamka* really likes her. Which is nice because I like her too. You're more serious with her."

"I'm a very serious person," he said, defensive.

"Many layers down, yes. When it's necessary, yes. But you're also lazy. You're cute and well groomed and you've had yourself quite a nice little romantic life for many years with a variety of pretty women who made you happy enough but you never had to work for a single one of them. You never bothered to. None of them made you more serious. More thoughtful of them and whatever they needed."

All the women in his life were far too insightful and free with their opinions. Vic frowned until he had to leap away from the snap of the towel she'd had in her hands.

"It's too bad they don't have a brother, or a close male cousin, eh? Just make the whole lot of us a matching set."

Vic snorted a laugh. "No more siblings or male cousins that I know of, sorry." The world could only handle so much Dolan and he figured Rachel and Maybe took it all up and then some. "There's dinner at their house tonight. You should come."

Evie was an important part of his life. He saw her every day at work, but also as part of his extended social circle, which he loved. He'd never had a girlfriend included in that in more than a surface way.

Rachel was different on so many levels. He already knew his parents approved of her, he wanted his sister and his woman to get to know one another better.

"Can I bring Rada?" At his frown she forged ahead quickly. "She's part of us. One of our family. It's hard for her with Maybe. Not that she wants Alexsei back, but she's afraid to lose us."

He sighed. "Ask Alexsei, but I'm a yes as long as Rachel and Maybe are okay." And he figured they would be because the Dolan sisters understood the importance of your chosen family.

As long as Rada kept her distance from Alexsei and got to know Maybe a little, things would be all right.

When his cousin's ex-girlfriend wasn't being a protective bitch, she was pretty likeable.

Evie grinned. "He's fine with it. Said to ask you. I guess Maybe is cool with it and as long as she is, you know Rachel will be."

He groaned. "Sometimes you can all be mercurial. I'll just keep out of kicking range and agree with everything my woman says."

"You're very smart. Which is why Rachel is so into you." She kept working for a bit before speaking again. "She didn't get the protection order extended for her dad? How's she doing?"

He finished up the first knead on a batch of dough, turning it into a bowl where it would rise again.

"She likes to put on a tough face. But it's no fun to have the court not take your side in any situation, much less when you're asking them to help protect you."

He was grateful she had Maybe and Cora to lean on, grateful too that she let him take some of the weight as well.

That nap on her couch had felt like they'd moved forward a year in their relationship when it came to intimacy level. She'd trusted him enough to sleep in his arms. That was huge. He wanted to make sure she knew he understood and that it meant so much to him. But he didn't want to spook her by making a big deal of it.

"She has you now. You're a good hugger. And you listen. It's not a thing most people do very well. You're pretty enough and you have a good job. You do also have a bananapants family. But we come with bread." Evie shrugged while filling a piping bag with the cream.

"Rachel places great emphasis on that too. I may

get some sort of complex that she only wants me for the bread."

"I highly doubt it. You're too confident for that."

And his Rachel liked the way *he* delivered her carbs.

"For dinner tonight it's sandwiches and chips. So you can bring dip. Maybe likes dip. We'll eat at seven."

SHE LET HIM back her against the sink in the hall bathroom. "We've got a houseful of people, you rogue."

The smile he gave her was rather roguish indeed. "I just needed a small taste." He dropped his mouth to hers until she was all jelly and goose pimples.

She gasped his name and he nipped her bottom lip just shy of pain.

"Much better. For now." He looked at his phone for the time. "I'll meet you in your bedroom in forty-five minutes. That gives us both enough time to wrap things up with everyone." He kissed down the side of her neck.

They'd already been done eating for a while by then. Watched *Jeopardy* while shouting out answers, followed by a double episode of their favorite cooking competition show, so plenty of time had elapsed. She could sneak away and not be considered rude.

Even though they'd all know she and Vic were running off to have sex.

"You've got a deal," she promised.

"Hey." He took her arm before they left the room. "Thank you for being so cool with Rada."

Rachel had understood that Rada came along with the rest of the Orlov family as Evie's best friend. Rada and Maybe had started off on the wrong foot, but each time they all hung out and no one acted up, Rachel had liked Rada a little more.

The other woman had a sharp wit that fit in just fine. A dry sense of humor and a sweet affection with the Orlovs Rachel found touching.

A totally *platonic* sweet affection toward Maybe's boyfriend.

"She's actually pretty cool."

He slung an arm around her as they headed back to the living room, where *Mario Kart* was loading up and people were getting ready to play.

They'd be around for hours more.

Whatever. Everyone else was free to play whatever they wanted. Rachel had a game she'd far rather play with Vic so she quietly told Maybe she was going off to bed and would see her the following morning.

She tried to take her time and be casual about saying good-night, but she rushed it, wanting to be alone with him.

He must have as well, because when she got to her room, he was naked and stretched across her bed. He'd turned off the lights and lit her candles so the right kind of sexy shadows danced around the space.

"Damn. How lucky can I be?" she asked.

"Let's test that, shall we? Get rid of those clothes and come over here." He crooked a finger her way.

As he moved, his muscles did all sorts of visually arresting things so she nearly tripped over her pants as she stepped out of them like a toddler and left them there on her floor as she hurried his way to take him up on that very fine offer.

He'd gotten to his knees on her bed as she'd been stripping and when she nearly hit the ground he swooped in and pulled her to the mattress, laughing as he rolled atop her body.

Her laughter wisped away as his weight settled in, warm and solid.

Yet her heart remained light. Strange to feel anchored and free all at once.

"Hi," she said, stretching up a little to kiss him.

"Mmm, hello. You locked the door, right?"

"She knocks!" Rachel dissolved into laughter at the memory of the day before when Maybe burst in to tell her something as Vic was getting dressed.

"It doesn't count if she won't wait to be told to come in first," he groused.

"I locked the door. And the squeal you gave when she came in and saw your ass probably ensured she won't ever burst in like that again."

"She must be sad Alexsei isn't as good-looking as me," Vic told her as he kissed her throat.

"If I were her I would be. But I have you so I don't need to feel sad. My life works out pretty well."

"Give me a few minutes to make it even better." He nuzzled her just below her left ear and made her slightly dizzy as the blood rushed to her nipples and clit.

This sent her into a fit of giggles.

"There you go again, trying to give me a complex," he said, a smile in his voice.

"Do you need me to kiss it and make it better?"

"The opposite. I want to kiss you, make you better and then I'll feel better."

"You're full of it," she said, but it was all breathy and sex-drunk so it wasn't entirely convincing.

He traced the tip of his tongue around her nipple and a full body shiver broke over her skin. It was like he knew every single one of her buttons and he pushed them. Every touch set her aflame.

He wanted her with such raw greed, there'd never been anything hotter. It made her feel like a queen.

"Your tits are fucking magnificent. Perfect," he said, lips against her skin as he moved to the other nipple to scrape the edge of his teeth against the sensitive flesh.

She arched into him on a cry.

With slow, thorough attention, he paid homage to each breast and nipple until she was flushed and tingly all over.

He kissed over her belly, around her belly button and down again. Down to the heart of her as he paused to breathe in deep, his mouth hovering just above the skin of her pussy.

A long hum of satisfaction before he danced his tongue around her clit. The way he held her open for his mouth, his strong, wide palms nearly scalding the inside of her thighs.

More nuzzling, brushing his mouth over her as he continued to lick and suck at her pussy like he was starving. He built her up until she splintered apart, back bowed, two handfuls of the comforter in her hands as orgasm sucked her under.

Moments later he was back, pushing into her body.

She opened her eyes to stare up at him, to watch the muscles in his neck and shoulders, the sheen of the sweat on his skin.

Her body, ready from the climax, still stretched nearly to painful and then it was all pleasure. All heat and fire but in the right kind of way.

There was a sense of abandon with him. That she could let go and fly.

If she fell, he'd catch her. Like he did just minutes before.

Restless, needing more, knowing he'd give it to her but when he wanted to, she writhed, arching against him to take him deeper.

He hitched her knees up and out, changing her angle, sliding home with one last push.

She gasped, nails digging into his sides as she held on. Panic rose a moment and she fought it. He was big, his body resting against hers, pressing her to the bed. Held down. Captured. Her system wasn't sure whether to break free or wallow in it.

If it had been anyone else, she'd have been across the room, pulling her clothes on, but it wasn't anyone else. *It was Vic.*

He pulled back a little, concern on his features.

"Don't stop," she gasped. Normally she'd have rolled her hips or pushed against him harder, but she was pretty immobile so her words had to do.

"Are you sure?"

Swallowing back the panic, she nodded.

Taking care to not put any more of his weight on her, he continued those slow, deep thrusts. She focused on the way his skin smelled, how he felt against her in all the amazing ways. Pushing the fear aside for the slow build to another orgasm.

VIC WAITED FOR the unbunching of her muscles before he dared move again. Need beat at him with closed fists, but he wasn't going to harm her and he'd maim himself before he'd ever take her anywhere she wasn't totally on board with going.

He'd looked into her eyes, making sure she'd meant what she'd said and then, gathering his control, pulled back out and slid back into all that velvet heat.

Her trust that he'd never hurt her was humbling.
And sexy as hell.

Her body hugged his so tightly the ghost of it echoed up his spine. He wanted to bury himself in her, forget everything but the moment, wrapped up in *this*.

This warrior wearing the skin of his favorite woman on the planet. This siren beneath him, open to him, trusting him with her flaws.

She held his heart and while it should have terrified him, it filled him with pride. She chose him. Of all the people she came across, it was him she gave herself to. Him she trusted with this part of herself.

Not only had she chosen him, she *wanted* him.

Over and over, he slid deep, the relentless beat of climax pounding in his ears. He had to have her. Needed to wring every bit of pleasure out of her. Nothing felt like making her come while he was inside her.

Her inner muscles spasmed and grasped his cock, nearly blinding him with a burst of white-hot sensation.

He cursed, teetering right on the edge. "You first," he snarled.

"I already did," she gasped. But her body didn't mind.

"You're hot and wet and so ready to come again," he told her. "You were made to come for me."

She moaned low and frustrated, not getting enough contact in their current position. He shifted his weight so he could reach down and give it to her. The moment his fingers brushed her clit she gasped.

Sweat broke out over his brow as he held on with the barest of control. She felt so fucking good around him it took everything in him not to wallow in it. Wallow in her.

She grunted, still pinned by his weight, but not afraid. Her gaze held his, passion-blurred, but clear. She was with him all the way.

Before he had to say anything else, she splintered around him, coming in a heated rush and dragging him right behind her with claws dug deep.

He managed to stumble into the bathroom to get rid of the condom before joining her in bed once more with a happy sigh.

CHAPTER TWELVE

ON THE EDGE of a strangled scream, Rachel came out of a nightmare, hands out, fingers curled into claws. She was there, again, in that tiny little cell Price had made just for her in his basement. The stench of fear and pain didn't go away even with copious amounts of the perfume he sprayed on all his captives every day.

Bile rushed up as the sensory memory hit and she fought through the panic. Needed all her wits when he was around.

In the midst of that state, it was the sound of Vic's voice that led her back. She grabbed on to it.

"Rachel. You're safe. *Rachel*, I'm here with you. It's Vicktor. You're in your bedroom. Everything is all right. I've got you."

He said it over and over, staying close but not restraining her. His hands running over her back, petting her as the rhythm of his voice lured her back, enabling her to put the memories away.

"I'm awake," she croaked, licking her lips.

He helped her sit up, propping pillows at her back before handing her a glass of water.

He didn't ask her what had happened. That seemed pretty obvious. And the expression he wore told her he was worried but would put her well-being first. Instead he waited for her to tell him if she chose to.

It'd be a lot easier to hold him back if he wasn't such a great listener. That and the shoulders. And the forearms.

The scent of him in her bed and on her skin helped her rebuild her armor against the memories.

They were just memories. Dreams. Things that happened in the past and she was not there. Not helpless.

She made her choices.

Thomas Price would never harm her again. *She* had made sure of it when she killed him.

Feeling a little better, she put her glass aside and snuggled back under the blankets. After a moment, he settled in beside her so she could curve into him. When his arms came around her, she felt a thousand times better.

"How often do these nightmares plague you, *tigryonak*?" The rumble of his voice vibrated against her back.

"Not nearly as often now." For a year they'd been relentless. They came and went, usually triggered by something she'd encountered during the day. "And what did you just call me?"

"Little tiger, because you are. Now, do you want to talk about it?"

Little tiger? Gah, why the fuck was he so perfect? "I'm sorry I fell asleep on you," she said. Jeez. He'd fucked her into a sound sleep. Probably in midsentence as they'd been talking in that lazy, after sex way.

"That's a stupid apology. I do not accept it." He broke off in Russian for a few sentences, the angriest she'd ever seen him be with her.

It wasn't scary at all. Just the opposite, it fascinated her. And flattered her that he'd come to believe she was strong enough to take his being mad at her.

"It's not stupid," she said, more to poke at him than because she truly agreed.

He snarled as he shifted to face her better, arranging her body the way he wanted, which always amused her.

"It's stupid to say you're sorry for falling asleep. You have an adorable little snuffle snore. It's stupid—and offensive—to assume I'd be upset with you for sleeping. Am I such a monster?"

Snuffle snore? She found herself softening, smiling at his silliness. She nuzzled into his side and took a deep breath. "You smell really good."

The tension in his muscles eased. "You think you can get around me on this by being adorable?"

"Only if it works."

He snorted, bending to kiss the top of her head and making her feel so damned safe she decided to share a little.

"You asked me the other day why I like bird tattoos. But then you unleashed your penis and I forgot everything else."

He squeezed her, laughing. "So good for my ego."

"Inside, where I was being kept, *none* of the sounds were good. But just outside, when things were quiet enough, I could hear birds. At first it was a way for me to figure out where we were being held. Whip-poor-wills and nighthawks, and every morning I'd hear a yellow-bellied sapsucker. That gave me a general idea of where we were." Her mind had grabbed on to the first birdsong she'd heard, beginning to catalog and analyze to stave off panic. The song she'd heard told her he hadn't gone very far from where she'd been taken.

"And then it became a way to mark time. A reminder that there was a world just outside the walls of the house."

She tried to hold back tears, but wasn't entirely successful. He knew, he had to have known because he was so damned in tune with her. But he didn't say anything about it, merely held her and let her tell the story in the way she could get it out.

"It was birdsong that kept me from losing my mind to the fear. Birdsong that reminded me I could still *find a way out*."

When he spoke, emotion choked his voice. "Birds are freedom and you, my *tigryonak*, are like them now. Free and full of life and art. And your parents are trying to cage you. Again."

She managed to burrow even closer into him, her body overruling her impulse to run the other way because this man could hurt her like no one before. This man and his open heart and endless patience and understanding eased right in to her innermost self.

And that self felt so fucking fragile sometimes. It made her mad and guilty and ashamed that she was weak and scared. That for three years not a single person other than her sister had slept next to her. Nightmares and insomnia had sent her into survival mode when it came to bedtime.

She should run but she didn't want to. She didn't want to hurt Vic, but that was a ruse anyway. She didn't want to walk away from this growing thing between them.

Being known was the most miraculous thing in the world. So few people came into your life who could *truly* know you. She had Maybe and Cora who saw her heart and loved her not despite it, but because of it.

Feeling like this with Vic, coupled with their chemistry, filled her with happiness. Made things in her life more vivid. He smelled good, brought her bread, had a giant penis and loved giving her oral sex. It was like her birthday every day.

She'd have to be a lot more unbalanced than she currently was to turn away from all that.

And she might be weak and fragile but she wasn't a coward.

VIC HATED THAT she would have normally been alone when whatever memory had been served up as nightmare fuel hit. Hated the expression on her face. Terror. Hated most of all that Price decided to focus on her, kidnapping and holding her for three weeks while he tortured and killed his other captives.

He'd known the details mainly from newspaper accounts and the like. She'd said things here and there over the years that had added to his understanding. But nothing had driven it home like the sound of that strangled scream and the hopeless fear on her features.

That she tried to make him mad by apologizing for sleep had been aggravating, but he simply stepped around it. He wasn't in this thing to play those sorts of games.

And now, the story about the birds.

He'd had an idea, of course. But the telling had frayed the rest of his nerves. He wanted to gather her close and protect her from anything that could hurt her again.

Right at that moment he had to settle for holding her close. She'd cozied up to him, wriggling to get as close as she could. At first he figured it was a way to keep him from pushing where she didn't want to go. To change the subject and get him all addled with the way she felt against him.

But then, as she'd sighed and relaxed, her nose against his neck, arms around his body, he'd realized she'd needed comfort and had taken what he so freely offered.

Humbling.

"I'm here for you to lean on now," he said quietly. "Go back to sleep."

"I don't have men sleep over," she said, groggy.

"Of course you don't. But I'm not someone you picked up to satisfy your carnal urges. I'm not going anywhere."

"You work pretty well on my carnal urges. You also happen to get up very early though." She said this still pressed against him with no indication she planned to move.

"Somehow I think you'll sleep through it when I leave. I'll be extra quiet." He paused. "Let me be here to chase the dreams away. You need sleep. I like to be around you and just now I feel very lazy and warm and don't want to go back out into the cold night all alone."

"You're so full of it." Her voice was lazy, as if she tumbled toward sleep again. "Okay. Stay over and save me money on my gas bill by being so warm I don't have to keep the heat up so high."

So brave and she didn't even see it.

Not one to look an opportunity cross-eyed, he tucked the blankets around them after quickly turning out the bedside lamp.

"How's Rachel?" Gregori asked him a few days later. His cousin lounged, drinking a cup of tea while watching Vic work.

"The first few days after they found out the order wasn't going to be extended were hard. But she's...Rachel." Vic shrugged. "She's titanium."

Gregori raised a shoulder in agreement. His broody artist cousin had taken a liking to Rachel. He'd joked that it was the fact that Rachel was broody and artistic too.

"At least she's letting me be there. I can't protect her from everything." God knew he wanted to storm over to Richie Dolan's house and beat the shit out of the man for treating his daughters the way he did.

"She doesn't need you. She wants you."

Gregori's girlfriend, Wren, was a pretty amazing match for his cousin. Strong, bold, artistic. Apparently the kind of woman who didn't need, but wanted him in her life.

Seems the men in their family turned out to be blessed in that department.

"I hate to push but I want to know how she's feeling." He hoped it looked effortless to Rachel, but it was difficult not to be a lot more up in her business.

"Sometimes it's fucking alarming how much I care about Wren's well-being." Gregori frowned.

Vic got that so clearly it was nearly painful.

He huffed a breath as he tipped several more loaves of fresh bread into a basket before he hung it on a rung at the bottom of the stairs with the others. Someone would collect them and replace them with empties for him to fill up again.

Gregori finally sighed. "You like to fix things. You

can't fix this, *Vitya*. You can't fix *her*. She's messed
up. Who wouldn't be in her place? She has darkness
you will never breach. That's the price with a woman
like Rachel. She's not easy. She's messy. And comes
with baggage."

Vic didn't argue. Mainly because it was true. Gregori's delivery didn't indicate derision or judgment, he
wasted little time on small talk, especially with those
he trusted.

Gregori continued, "I've found in my life though,
that messy is better. Difficult women are sexy. *Not* dra-
matic women." He made a face. His ex-wife was one of
those. "Some people are worth the work, yes?"

As he turned dough out onto the worktable and began
to knead, he thought about that.

"I know that there's never been anything in my life
that approaches how this feels. I want to make her tea
and tuck her in. I also want to go to war to protect her.
The sex too." He looked up at his cousin with a smirk
that was impossible to repress.

It was beyond anything he could begin to put into
words. He was so connected to her, especially during
sex. It made the entire experience so much more intense. She fit him. So perfectly it left him a little raw.

Exciting and terrifying and bone-deep satisfying.

"Sometimes it feels like I can't ever get enough of
her. As if there will never be a moment in my life when
I don't always carry this burn for her in my belly."

Gregori smiled a little as he nodded in agreement.

"Have you told her this?"

Vic scoffed. "She's skittish. She needs a slow seduc-
tion and then after she's in love with me, I can tell her."

"Having been the skittish one in the relationship,"

Gregori said of his own life, "there will come a time when she retreats and you have to storm her gates."

That made him laugh. "Is that what Wren did?"

"She flew to New York and got in my face and was so delicious and delightful I lost all the will to stop running. She wouldn't let me." His smile returned a moment. "She demanded I love her. How could I resist that?"

As his cousin had changed only for the better in the years since he and Wren had gotten together, it was easy to only like her more. Respect her more for the work it must take to be in a relationship with his cousin.

Like Rachel, Gregori had his own kind of darkness. His own pattern of jagged edges. Clearly Vic needed to pay attention to how Wren dealt with it. He could undoubtedly learn a few things.

And she was an artist like Rachel. Wren had branched out from comics and manga to a short animated film that had made the indie film festival circuit. He'd need to make it a point to invite the two of them to more social things with them.

His aunt Klara, Gregori's mother, popped down to grab the basket of fresh bread. She paused to leave a plate of pastries for them, kissing Gregori on the forehead as she left.

"She's happier being here full-time," Gregori said. He'd wanted his parents to retire and let him take care of them but his father was a proud man and he liked working. And after Danil had died, she'd filled in a lot until she'd come back full-time. Klara had been at Vic's side, bringing his parents back from the brink, keeping the bakery successful.

"I couldn't have kept this place going without her.

And she and my mom are a mini mafia running this place. It's good. They still travel. But once you and Wren marry they're going to start in on you about kids," Vic told him.

"*Start?* She's past the hinting point. She asked me if I was going to freeze my sperm because they were getting old and while I was at it, to tell Wren to get a move on before her eggs went bad. I keep telling Wren if she just marries me at least part of that will stop. Of course then she'd be on us about the wedding details and the like."

"I could totally see my mom doing that to Rachel." He wondered if he should warn her and decided to let it roll. It wasn't like he could tell his mother what to do—or that anyone could. She saw Rachel and Maybe as her family already so of course she'd meddle and love as well as defend.

And if anyone ever needed family in that sense, it was the Dolan sisters.

"Rachel can handle it."

Vic was pretty sure she could too.

And the truth was, he couldn't change what he came with. A big, nosy family with lots of opinions and no hesitance about sharing them. He wouldn't even if he could.

"I wish you luck, *Vitya.* I need to get moving. I'm working on a new piece and I should get back to it. Just thinking about Wren and I'm feeling creative again. I'm taking all this pastry to present to my woman as tribute," Gregori told him as he stood and stretched.

"I'll see you later this week. Tell Wren I said hello."

Vic grabbed a few of the baskets he'd refilled with

bread and headed upstairs to switch them out and charm his mother a little.

And to his surprise and delight, Rachel walked in right as he got upstairs. He gave his mother a look and then grabbed Rachel's hand, tugging her close and around the counter.

She smelled like salt water and a little bit of wood smoke and always, of jasmine. He pulled the knitted cap from her head to expose the raven's-wing black of her hair. Tenderness crashed over him at the sight of the mittens she wore. He'd left them on her bed a few days earlier, wanting her to be warm.

"This is a nice thing. I wasn't expecting you," he told her before he brushed a kiss over her mouth.

"I had some time so I thought perhaps—" She broke off on a blush.

She'd come to him. Triumph made him kiss her once more before drawing her into a hug.

"Before they try to steal you away, come with me and I'll feed you fresh bread and pour you a cup of tea," he said into her ear.

"That's an offer I'd be a fool to refuse."

Her blush made him feel protective but naturally, his mother wanted a hug from Rachel so she bustled him aside and got one.

"You look pretty today. I like you in this color. You need more color. Eat something." Irena swatted Rachel's butt with her towel, startling Rachel into a laugh he'd never heard from her before.

He'd heard it from his sister plenty, though. A totally carefree moment with her mom.

His mother flicked her gaze to his quickly and he saw the emotion there, knew that she'd understood how casual maternal affection had become a scarce thing for Rachel.

"I have bread waiting for me to pull from the ovens," he told Rachel as he grasped her hand once more and brought her through the prep kitchen and then around and down the back stairs.

"I came to watch you bake so that works out," she said.

"Well," he said, taking care to slowly roll his sleeves up, "I think I can accommodate your dirty fantasies."

"Awesome."

Because he could, he got close enough to steal a kiss. "Sit. There's tea in the pot already." He pointed at the stool his cousin had just been sitting on before he turned to pull several trays of dinner rolls from the ovens and slide them into racks.

"I've never been down here." Rachel hopped up onto the stool and poured them each a mug of tea. "I think I gained three pounds just from how it smells."

Rachel was pretty sure it was a sin to be all hot and bothered at the sight of him, forearms all muscly as he moved around his domain. He was just so self-assured, graceful in his way.

It occurred to her with a flash of heat that he often got that same look when they were having sex. Focused, enjoying what he was doing, confident that he was kicking ass at it.

"In that fridge to your left there's some milk and preserves left over from the *vatrushkas* Evie made earlier," he told her before grabbing three wire baskets full of pretty sandwich rolls and dashing them upstairs.

He wasn't gone long and when he returned he joined her at the little counter where she'd placed his tea.

"I'm pleased to see you," he said, pushing some brioche toward her. "Evie also made that this morning."

"Your sister's got some skills." Rachel smeared some of the preserves on the fresh bread. She was quiet a moment before continuing. "I'm pleased too. I mean, I'm happy to see you. I was thinking about you and then I found myself in downtown before I needed to be at the shop and then I found my way here."

She snorted, shaking her head. "I'm a liar. I mean, I was thinking of you and I'm happy to see you. But I came here on purpose."

He grinned her way. "Good."

A buzz sounded and his aunt called down a thank-you. At Rachel's questioning look, he said, "She thanked me for the bread." In a quieter voice he said, "She and my mom are getting older. I was starting to worry about one of them falling when they came down to get the bread so I added hooks at the entrance to the upstairs kitchen. I just cart the baskets up, hang them on the hooks and it's one less thing to be concerned over."

So his mother wouldn't feel like she was a burden or that she couldn't do as much as she used to.

"You're a very good son."

"Mom's had some dizzy spells but you can't tell her anything. She comes up with one kooky health fad after the next. Usually it's harmless. Once I did have to go down to some shop where this dude was selling bullshit cures. It's bad enough that he was taking advantage of older people. But then he took advantage of *my* mother. We had a word. She pouted for a while, but she came around in the end. Just like with the baskets. Anyway, I can always use the exercise. It's not a big deal." He tried to look stern but she saw through him. Remembered the man who brought her mittens because he wanted her to stay warm.

That it wasn't a big deal to him was what drew her closer every time. Each time she thought about not giving in to her desire to see or talk to him she would remember what made him so irresistible to start with.

He was a nosy, bossy control freak but he took care of the people he loved. He zipped up jackets and made sure his mom didn't have to go up and down stairs too often.

He was a good man. A kind man who volunteered and flattered old ladies and babies. Worth more than all the carbs in the world. "I'm so turned on right now if your parents weren't upstairs I'd do some seriously filthy stuff with you."

His grin, damn, that expression of his, sent a shiver through her. "Later. Save it all for me. I'll collect. I promise."

CHAPTER THIRTEEN

"WE'RE GOING OUT for a drink. Come along?" Cora asked, approaching Rachel as she was finishing up for the day.

"Yes, please. And tacos." Now that she'd finished up her last tattoo, she realized how hungry she was. If she was going to drink, she definitely needed food.

Cora's eyes widened and then she beamed. "Oh my god, yes, yes! Maybe is on her way over from Whiskey Sharp. I know she'll be up for tacos. Are you single tonight?"

"Vic is off doing something churchy with his mother. I probably won't see him at all, but if I do, it won't be until nine or after. Most likely he'll just go home and I'll see him tomorrow."

He never seemed annoyed that she liked plenty of time to herself. Even though she liked being with him and with her friends, she needed solitude. Needed to draw and think and lose herself to the process.

She sprayed things down, put her tools away and locked up right as Maybe glided in. Her hair was currently what Cora liked to call peacock feathers. All shades of brilliant blue and teals with small glimpses of yellow.

And her sister made it work. On her it was sassy and sexy and fun. If Rachel had tried such a thing it would have made her look like she was playacting. Maybe had worn a crisp white button-down shirt with suspenders holding up gray pin-striped trousers.

By contrast, Rachel wore jeans, Vans high-tops and a black sweater. She had allowed Maybe, who was amazing with hair color, to add some blue at the tips of her dark brown hair.

At first glance they didn't even look like they could be related but once you saw the way they smiled, the shape of the eyes and all the shared mannerisms, it was obvious.

"Tacos," was all Cora said as she linked arms with both Dolans and they headed to the tiny hole-in-the-wall Mexican place right around the corner that had happy hour tacos and well drinks. It sounded perfect after the day she'd had.

Once they'd secured a rickety table and ordered a round of margaritas and some food, they turned to gossip and basic catch-up.

"I was thinking of texting Wren to see if she wanted to join us," Rachel said. "I spoke to her earlier about some ink she wants and mentioned that we should hang out."

Maybe and Cora gave her a thumbs-up so she dashed off a quick invite and within a few minutes, Wren showed up.

"Hey, kids! What's up?" she asked as she joined them. "Thanks for the invite. I've been working all day and just realized how hungry I am."

A platter of tacos arrived and they all dived in, going quiet as they ate awhile.

"I was thinking you might be interested in a project I'm working on," Wren said to Rachel.

"Oh yeah?"

"It's a multiartist thing I'm doing with the art collective I'm part of. I've seen your drawings. Have you ever considered doing more than tattoos?"

"You mean like pen and ink drawings? Painting?"

"Definitely pen and ink drawings. I'm looking for someone interested in doing art for a calendar. There's a wall calendar and a desk design. It can be whatever you want. Whatever floats your boat. Submit a few pieces, see where it takes you. What do you think?"

Maybe watched her with careful—but hopeful—eyes while Cora nodded.

"I don't know. I mean, how much time would you need? What's the deadline?" With a full-time job could she do something like that? It sounded exciting and interesting and something she might want to do. The thought of failing though…

"You've got right about a month until the March 15 deadline. I can show you what the other groups are doing if you want. Our collective has meetings every few weeks to talk about the project so if you're free it'd be a fun way for you to see what we're doing and for you to get to know the others. I hope you will. Because I like you and I think you're talented and what we need."

"You can't have her. But you can borrow her," Cora said with a grin.

Wren laughed, reaching out to squeeze Cora's arm. "Okay."

Of course, Cora already knew Wren and Gregori and a lot of high-profile people in the art world because she'd been handling her mother's career for some time.

Rachel truly liked her job and had no plans to stop tattooing anytime soon. But stretching her artistic wings in other directions would be fun. And part of continuing to put down roots in Seattle.

"I'd like that. Thanks." She looked up the website Wren directed her to and would check out all the information when she got home.

IN HER BED, as she listened to music and worked, her phone buzzed with an incoming text. She was smiling before she even noted that it was Vic.

Just delivered my mother back home and now I'm headed straight to bed but I wanted to ask you to go skiing.

Skiing? She hadn't been in ages, but she bet he was good at it and looked super sexy too.

Did you have a good time with your mom? And when for skiing?

Eight babushkas in my business, poking at my ribs while telling me I was scrawny and asking when I'd be marrying you so I could start having babies.

Scrawny? He was over six feet tall with big wide shoulders. Not her definition of scrawny by any means. Though the image of a bunch of little old Russian women backing him into a corner and demanding to know when he was going to have babies made her laugh.

I had tacos with my friends and no one called me scrawny or asked when I was going to drop a baby. I win.

She could imagine his scoff of amusement.

As for skiing-we can go whenever your next day off is. We'll head up the day before and stay over. One of my friends has a cabin up at Mt. Baker so we've got a nice place to sleep and it has a hot tub.

A quick check of her upcoming work schedule gave her a few options so she texted back and they settled on a Thursday and Friday two weeks from then.

She wanted to tell him she missed him but didn't because it made her vulnerable and she didn't want him to think she was clingy or weak or needy. Even if she'd slept the best she had in months when he'd stayed over a few nights before.

We're still on for dinner tomorrow. I'm meeting Alexsei in your kitchen at three.

He and Alexsei were cooking Valentine's Day dinner for Rachel and Maybe. The thought of it still made her a little shivery. He'd also made her bed. Even if they were going to get in it shortly for sex. She liked it that way. A freshly made bed comforted her for some reason and he'd noticed. He never mentioned it. Never made a deal of it. He just did it. Because it made her feel better.

Warm with affection, she nearly wrote back that he should plan to stay over. Thumb paused above the keypad.

Three? Dude, what sort of fancy dinner are you two making?

The kind of fancy dinner it takes to keep women like you and Maybe.

So charming.

Boy, the stuff you say is so going to get you laid. I'll see you tomorrow. Get some rest so you can court me extra hard.

Good night, tigryonak. Sweet dreams.

She did something ridiculous then, placing her phone on the pillow on the side of the bed he'd slept on and didn't curse herself a fool, even if she was still a little embarrassed.

THE FOLLOWING NIGHT, Maybe and Rachel walked up the street from the bus stop when Irena came out to her front porch and beckoned them over.

"Friday after work you come over and I will teach you how to make *golubtsi*."

After a moment where she had to place the word for cabbage rolls, Rachel pulled out her phone and said she'd stop by after six.

Maybe had a gig that night so she'd have to get her lesson another time, but Irena seemed pleased the two wanted her to teach them things.

As they headed up their own front walk, Irena called out to say hello to her boys.

"I want to keep her in my pocket," Rachel said. Irena had become a fairly important female figure in her life since they'd moved in next door. And most certainly more maternal as she'd been over there more often once

Maybe and Alexsei started a relationship and Rachel had begun dating Vic.

"She's scary but I really do love her."

They paused once they got inside and the smell hit them. Instantly Rachel's stomach growled.

Two gorgeous men in her kitchen, making by what all indications thus far was a delicious dinner for them. Her life was pretty damned good right then. And that was before Vic turned with a freshly poured glass of champagne for her.

"Happy Valentine's Day," he said, bending to kiss her before handing over the glass.

"If I'm dreaming I'm going to punch anyone who wakes me up," she told him after taking a sip.

He filled her with a foolish sort of happiness. Something she wasn't really used to dealing with. It was novel, a little scary and she liked it a lot.

"Go change. We have appetizers ready for you both when you're ready."

She took his hand. "You could come too." She added a brow waggle to underline the offer.

He grinned. "Don't tempt me. I have things to watch on the stove."

"Fine, fine. You can collect later," she murmured.

"Naturally. I'm very good at making you come," he said quietly.

Truer words and all that.

"Stop being so perfect."

"I can't. It's part of the package."

"You're trouble," she said, still pressed against him, holding the glass of champagne.

"So I've been told."

He kissed her once more and let go so she reluctantly

peeled herself away and headed to drop off all her things and change into something pretty.

And when she got to her room she noted the prettily wrapped packages on the bed with a note that said, OPEN ME.

So while she was wearing little more than her underwear, she tore into the first package to find a pair of gloves with a flannel lining.

Now you have gloves to alternate with your mittens to keep your hands warm, the card inside said.

The next box had a bluebird pendant inside on a silver chain. It looked vintage, possibly Victorian and she loved it, putting it on quickly. It'd go perfectly with the red sweater she had to put on with her skirt.

The last box had two books of poetry in them. A Neruda collection and some Mary Oliver. She smiled because he knew her so well.

After she brushed her hair and reapplied lipstick, she grabbed her gift for Vic, an old black-and-white photograph of historic Seattle back in the days when the block the bakery sat on had first been built. You could see the storefront at the far corner.

She hoped he liked it. It seemed a celebration of all the things he liked: Seattle, baking and the bakery itself.

"Where did you find this?" he asked after he'd opened it some time later, clearly touched and pleased by her gift.

"Used bookstore up on Capitol Hill had a bunch of stuff like this in a bin at the back. I was trying not to sneeze as I sifted through all the postcards and pictures and I found this and thought you might like to have it hanging either at the bakery or your place. Just a happy coincidence."

"It's fantastic. I'm going to hang it at my house. My dad will steal it if I put it up at the bakery and I'd have to visit their house to see it." He kissed her cheek and then over to her ear. "Thank you. I love it."

"I love the necklace, gloves and the poetry too." Both editions had been signed, which only made them more special.

"And the chocolate cake, which I am going to eat off your breasts in your bed in about twenty minutes," he murmured.

She excused herself and hoped no one noticed how quickly she finished cleaning up and scampering off to her room.

CHAPTER FOURTEEN

"Vic, come upstairs right now," his aunt called down in Russian.

The urgency in her voice had him moving quickly only to find Richie Dolan standing in the bakery, speaking to his mother.

"I'm simply trying to make sure my child is taken care of. Surely you can understand that," he said.

"Rachel is a grown woman, capable of taking care of herself. Which is what she has told you," his mother replied.

"It's not your business. Why are you interfering? What's in it for you?" Dolan demanded, losing some of his softer delivery to reveal the scumbag beneath.

"Whose business it is is up to Rachel. Why are *you* here?" Vic stepped forward, putting an arm around his mother's shoulders.

"Why are you interfering? This is not for you to be involved in. You foreigners need to back off."

"Foreigners?" his mother asked, clearly astonished at the gall of the statement.

"You're not Americans, that's for sure. So what's in it for you? You and your brother who has not so coincidentally moved in on my other daughter right around the time things got so bad. You think you can get your green

card that way? That what's going on here? You need
your ticket to stay here so you bamboozle my children?"

"You have some nerve coming in here," his mother
said, low and sort of mean. "You made a mess of your
family and you think you can blame that on everything
else. Never taking responsibility for what you do. Typi-
cal. *Foreigners?*"

Vic attempted to keep his voice level, "You have no
ability to see why both of your exceptional children
would be prized by others? How could you miss that?
In any case, they want nothing to do with you. So much
so they asked a court to keep you away. And yet here
you are. Because this isn't about them. It's about you.
If you cared about your daughters you'd have protected
them, not become someone they need protection from."
Vic was glad this was happening there in the bakery
in the middle of the day or he'd be far more tempted to
show Richie Dolan just how little he cared for the way
he treated his children. With his fists.

Nothing in his life had ever made him feel like wanting to do violence more than this man and the damage
he did to Rachel.

"Maybe ICE would like to know about you people."

"Are you threatening to turn us in to immigration?"
His mother's voice had stayed mean and gotten even
more quiet.

"To protect my daughters from your plans? Yes."

Vic snorted. "Go on then." He was born in a hospital on Seattle's Capitol Hill. As was Evie. His parents
were naturalized citizens. This bullshit was meant to
cow them the way he tried to cow Rachel. It wouldn't
work any better.

This asshole needed to understand what he was taking on. It was more than just Rachel and Maybe. His entire family would protect them. Vic would call Seth after Dolan left just to be sure the police knew what was happening as well. His cousin's soon-to-be hus-band would also have good advice.

"You assume that everyone who isn't like you is some sort of foreigner out to steal from you? That ex-plains so much," his mother said and Vic had to fight not to laugh.

"I don't need to take any shit from you people. Maybe might be a stupid whore, but Rachel is meant for better things than hanging out with losers in a tattoo shop."

"You shut your mouth about Maybe. You're a horri-ble father who has done some major damage to both his children. Speaking of that, why are you so invested in whatever Rachel does? What she *wants* to do? Why not be grateful she's really good at something that makes her happy and provides her with a living?" Vic urged. Maybe if Richie Dolan answered on video there'd be some sort of peace for Rachel. "This will only end in them resenting you more. You'll end any chance at all to ever be in their lives again."

"I don't need parenting advice from the likes of you," Richie sneered.

Irena squared her shoulders and leaned in closer, speaking before Vic could. "Then why are you here in my bakery speaking to me and my son? Eh?" Irena dismissed Richie before turning to Vic and saying in Russian, "Bullies. All the same, no matter where. Don't let him goad you into anything. Rachel needs you to be levelheaded."

"What kind of foreigner gibberish are you spouting about Rachel? You're probably terrorists too." Dolan stepped back, stabbing a finger in their direction. "I'm here to warn you and your family to stay out of this. This is *private* family business."

Vic tipped his chin and stood every last bit of his height as he stepped between his mother and Dolan. Though he kept the counter between them. The other man lowered his hand, which was good for him as Vic had been about to break his pointer finger.

But no way was he going to let Richie think he could come into their bakery and threaten his family or his woman. "I don't like threats to my family."

"Stay away from my daughter and there's no need for threats. Otherwise, I'll be calling the authorities to report you."

"I already told you to go ahead and do it. But stop claiming this is about your care for your children. This is about you. You're a fucking bully. A selfish asshole who thinks he can roll up anywhere he likes, to crap all over people and order them around. This is *my* bakery. *I'm* in charge here and I'm telling *you* to get the hell out and don't come back. If you do, I will call the police and have you arrested for trespassing."

Dolan's face darkened and the bully he'd been trying to hide behind all that faux parental concern leaked out.

"You'll be sorry. You messed with the wrong people, son. You have no idea who I am."

Vic scoffed. "It's you who don't know who *I* am. Sure as hell not your son." Vic pointed at the door. "I said, get out."

With some half-under-the-breath garbage about foreigners and drug-dealing tattooists and the criminal element, Richie Dolan made his windy escape.

"Did you notice he said 'daughter'? Not 'daughters,'

just one. How can he be so terrible not to see the glory of Maybe and the beauty of Rachel's independence? I do not like this man one bit." His mother sighed and he hugged her. "Call Seth. See what we need to do so we can do everything right," she said as she stepped back. "Thank god no customers were here."

Richie Dolan's level of aggression took nothing and no one else into account. The man was utterly about himself and how he felt about any given situation. It simply never occurred to him that the damage his behavior caused his victims was anything but his due. His righteous win.

And that's what it was. This guy was in some sort of competition he'd do a lot of damage to win. He wanted to impose his will on an adult child he barely knew. Because he wanted Rachel to submit to their authority and let him make her choices.

Her independence was what Richie thought was her illness. He wanted to crush that and have her fall in line. Could his ego be that tied up in Rachel working for the FBI? Was it something else? If he could get at whatever underlying thing was driving their father, Vic might be able to figure out how to deal with him.

In the meantime, one of Richie's recent targets was Vic's mother. "Are you all right?" he asked her. Yes, she was a strong woman, but it had to have been a little upsetting to have a raging guy twice her size up in her space that way.

"I grew up in Soviet Russia, *Vityunya*. I know how to deal with bullies. This will have been caught on our camera system? For the security?"

"Yes. Let me go switch out the data card so we can

show it to Rachel. I imagine her lawyer might want it as more proof of what her dad is up to."

He went into the small office where Evie did their books and handled the switch to a new card, labeling the one he put in a pocket to give to Rachel when he saw her later that evening.

His mom met him in the doorway. "Your father will not be pleased to hear of this so let me tell him. No use getting him worked up over something already handled."

His dad was one of those people who had what appeared to be a bottomless well of patience. He was a good man. A solid man who would usually seek the peaceful solution.

But, as many found out, once he was pushed too far, he would burn things down in defense of those he deemed under his protection. He was a badass and truly scary when he got to that point so Vic was just fine letting his mom handle that.

Agreeing, Vic headed back downstairs to finish work and to call his cousin's fiancé.

Seth cursed, pissed off on Rachel and Maybe's behalf. "This fucking guy. What the hell? Everything you told me you're doing is exactly right. Make sure they're documenting all the times the parents have been showing up too."

"He threatened to call immigration on us," Vic said, tone dry.

"What did he say when you informed him you were all citizens? What a fucking asshole this guy is. Of *course* he's a bigot on top of everything else."

"I didn't tell him. I don't owe him any help or information. And sure, he can't actually get us deported because we're all citizens, but he still threatened to try to ruin a family. And why? Because I'm dating his daughter? The one he wants to control like her independence means nothing to him? He's a piece of shit."

"I completely agree. Keep an eye out. Rachel is former law enforcement, trust that she's going to know what to look for to build a case. And to keep herself secure or if she had to, she could handle this guy. She's in excellent shape."

Perhaps. But her heart wasn't as well defended as her body and mind. Rachel hurt for her sister. Felt guilt for all the years Maybe had to live with their parents after she went off to college. For better or worse, they'd been her parents and she wanted things to work out.

And now she'd begun to accept they weren't going to. At least not the way she'd hoped at one time. There was no going back from the damage Richie Dolan had wrought.

Richie wasn't going to win. Not this time and Vic wasn't sure how he'd handle it, except he knew it would be negative.

"I wish I could do more. He's skirting the line, but staying on the side of it that keeps him out of trouble," Seth said.

"She's coming over to the house later today so I can teach her to make you *golubtsi*," his mother said some minutes later as she came down to get a basket of black bread he'd only recently put out.

"Let her have her lesson with you first. I'll come over after my workout so I can talk with her. All right?"

"And also then you can eat some food?" she asked, amusement on her face.

"Of course. I'm economical that way." He hugged

her. "If he comes around again and I'm not here, call the police immediately. Seth said you can call him directly." His mother wasn't going to treat Seth like her own personal police officer, but both would like the interaction with the other, each liking to feel useful and protective of family.

"Will you tell her before you see her tonight?" his mom asked.

"I sent her a text saying I wanted to talk with her later about some stuff regarding her dad. She's working on Evie's tattoo today, so she'll be too busy to take a phone call until she's done with work and by that point, I'll just come to your place. Which is a long way to answer that you can tell her some if you like."

He'd go straight to his parents' house once he finished his workout with his climbing and backcountry volunteer rescue buddies. There'd be food and Rachel and he'd be able to tell her face-to-face. Gauge her reaction far better than he would have on the phone.

In the meantime, as he punched dough and did his work, he considered how to approach her that night with everything that had happened.

No one was going to take away Rachel's freedom again.

THAT AFTERNOON BEFORE Rachel could even get to the top step, Irena opened the door and ushered her inside. "Come in, Rachel. Are you ready to cook?"

She figured she'd get an idea of whatever Vic had to tell her if it involved Irena. Otherwise she'd have to wait at least another two hours until he finished his workout.

She kissed Irena's cheek after hanging her coat in the front entry closet. She also left her shoes under the bench and that's when she noticed there was a labeled slot for her things now. And in it sat a pair of slippers.

"You needed slippers for the house. Those are warm. Put them on and come into the kitchen with me," Irena called over her shoulder as she left the room.

Her own slippers.

Funny how such a seemingly normal thing felt so freaking wonderful. Like she was one of them now.

In the kitchen before she could even thank Irena, she was handed an apron. "You don't want to get food on your nice clothes."

The jaunty white apron was emblazoned with a demand to kiss the cook. Pavel wore it when he was at the grill and it always made her smile.

"Thank you. For the slippers too."

A wave of a hand was the reply to that.

The double ovens were already preheating so the room was warm enough that Rachel shoved her sleeves up and then washed her hands before joining Irena at the big island where all the ingredients and tools she'd need were already waiting.

Irena made no secret of examining Rachel's wrists and up the forearm where the worst of the scarring was covered by one of her tattoos.

"*Liberté?* As in the French for *freedom*?"

Rachel nodded. *Liberté* scrolled up her inner right forearm. It had been her first tattoo.

"To you this means?" Irena asked.

Being with Irena was comforting and one of the reasons was she never played around. She said what she felt and she didn't play any games. There were never moments where she had to obsess about what Vic's mother felt that she might not be sharing.

"I broke free of several things. Not just being held captive. But moving from one sort of life to another. Leaving the anchor of what I knew to come out here and be the master of my own fate. To do this on my own."

Gently, Irena cupped Rachel's hand and ran a thumb over the scars. "This is where he hurt you?"

Swallowing hard, Rachel nodded, holding her arm up a little by way of example. "I was in a sort of manacle. It cut into my skin and got infected. It damaged the muscles." She shrugged. It hurt less and less that she wouldn't have the same range of mobility anymore.

Irena's mouth flattened and her eyes went very hard. "I am sorry."

Rachel sucked in a breath at how much it meant to see that sort of reaction on her behalf. "Thank you."

"You broke your hand to get free, Vicktor says."

They began to lay out the cabbage leaves as they talked. It was easy to talk about the details when she could focus on something else. Learning how to cook a dish Vic loved was something she wanted to do. Just a little thing. Hell, he cooked for her all the time. It'd be a nice change of pace to be able to cook for him.

"I had one chance." Her last chance. "And it required me to dislocate my thumb and two of my fingers to break free of the cuff."

"You are unlike anyone else I've ever met. Strong. Like a warrior."

A smile bloomed on Rachel's face as the compliment filled her with pleasure.

Subject closed, Irena began to order Rachel through the rest of the steps of the recipe.

It took her a while to get it to roll without tearing the

cabbage or leaving it too loose so the meat spilled, but eventually she got the hang of it.

Irena was all business, but she wasn't harsh or scary about it. That steady confidence was something she recognized in Vic.

"Vicktor always requests these on his birthday. Now you know how to make them for him," Irena said.

"I have no doubt he will always like yours best."

Irena laughed. "I am his mother, that is how it should be. Come, sit while they cook and have tea with me."

In the dining room, they sat at the table and drank tea. Outside a winter wren sang into the fading day.

"Your father came to the bakery today."

Which obviously had to be what Vic wanted to talk to her about. She fisted and unfisted her hands a few times. Humiliation slinked through her at the thought of what he may have done or said. What these people she had come to care for so much might think of her because of it. Sometimes it felt as if she wore her father around her neck like deadweight. He was always there in the background. Menacing her through his lawyer and harassing the people in her life to get to her.

"Oh my god. I'm so sorry. What did he do?"

"He is all words and aggression." Irena made a face. "Tell me about him."

Rachel wanted to get back to the subject and get more details about what had happened but Irena wasn't one to be rushed to a point. She said what she said on purpose.

"He thinks I need him and my mom to run my life. That I'm too sick to be in control so they have to. They want to wall Maybe out as well. Make me move in with them or into a private mental health facility for months."

Irena sighed. "And before, with your sister?"

Though she was sure Alexsei and Vic had given them the basic overview, Rachel ran her through what had happened with their father's coworker who'd been obsessed with Maybe and how their parents had made it Maybe's fault and had resented her closeness with Rachel as some sort of impediment to them.

"They want to push her away from you so they can control your life. Choosing one child over the other. Bah. Who does this? Children are a gift. They should be grateful for both of you."

People did it all the time. It wasn't that rare, though it was certainly sad.

"What did he say?" Rachel fought humiliation.

"Vicktor will tell you all the details. But I will say it's not important. What is important is that I let you know he came and that it didn't matter. He wants to sow the seeds of trouble. Don't give it to him. We know who you are."

If she'd been granted the protection order she might have been able to add the bakery because that's where her...*boyfriend* worked. But she didn't have one so she'd need to work with what was possible right then.

"I don't want him to hurt you anymore." Irena took Rachel's hand and gave it a brief squeeze. "He does not intimidate me or my son. He doesn't know you. That is his flaw. He doesn't like it that Vicktor is in your life. Especially when he found out Alexsei and Vicktor were related and close."

Rachel had no idea why. It wasn't as if their father cared about Maybe unless it was to harass Rachel.

"Did he threaten you?"

"Not physically and he has no power otherwise. He knows not to come back or we will call the police. I will *not* allow it. I will not have that man come into my bakery and threaten my son or you, for that matter. I wanted you to know he showed up and I wanted you to know we're on your side. You're one of mine now."

Rachel breathed out long, centering herself. "It means more to me than I can say that you would consider me one of your family. I'm so sorry he came to the bakery. And I'm terribly embarrassed and hope it won't influence how you feel about me."

"I'd be an awful person if it did. You had nothing at all to do with it." Irena hesitated, as though she had more to say but wasn't sure if she wanted to say it.

"Please. I'd like you to share your opinion with me. I'd like to hear your perspective. It's nearly impossible to offend me, if that was your worry and it probably wasn't. I mean." Rachel clamped her lips shut. Her hands up in entreaty.

Irena cackled and rapped the table three times in quick succession. It was a thing Rachel noticed she did from time to time to underline a point.

"Your father is a type. I knew them growing up. He's a bully. Throws his weight around. Always tells you how much he's done, how hard he works. Everyone else steals but *he* is special and deserving."

"Yes, that's him all right."

"He confuses control with love. He can't control your sister so he's got no room for her." She broke off in a long stream of Russian that Rachel got the feeling was all pretty derogatory. Irena huffed as that ground to a halt and then she began again. "As I said, it wasn't about you. It's about his inability to control you and the way you're thriving now in this chapter of your life. He doesn't know how to accept it even though he doesn't agree with your choices. Your father can't bully me. I'm immune to men like him." She narrowed her gaze for a moment. "Any decent parent would be proud of you and Maybe. Any decent parent would see how wonderful and strong you are. He does not know what a gift you are. But I have seen you nearly every day for over three years now. *I* know what you are. I'm proud of you."

Fighting back tears, Rachel lost the battle when Irena got up, circled the table and pulled her into her arms. Irena swayed slightly, rubbing small circles on her back until she got herself back together.

Irena handed her some tissues and tugged her into the kitchen where she imperiously pointed to the sink so Rachel could wash her hands before they checked the *golubtsi*.

Irena, standing at the oven, said, "He made several mistakes, including the fact that we have a camera in the bakery at the storefront where he came in. So the entire tirade is on video. Vic saved it for you immediately. I don't think you should watch it alone. Or at all. But you'll want to because that's who you are so Vicktor will bring it for you to watch."

"Do I smell *golubtsi*?" Vic called out as he strolled into the kitchen. "And watch what? Look at that. Two of my favorite women." He kissed his mother's cheek and then hugged Rachel before giving her a smooch smack on the mouth. "Oh, is this the inaugural batch from your lesson?" he asked Rachel.

"It is. We were just about to try it. You must have radar," Rachel said.

"When it comes to food, my children know when to just happen to pop by. Get plates for us, *Vityunya*."

"I'm starving and who knows how long it'll be before

Alexsei smells these on the wind and shows up?" He dished up three for each of them and spooned the sauce and dolloped a little bit of the crème fraîche on top.

Nervously Rachel cut into hers and forked up a steaming hot bite of what turned out to be pretty delicious. And now she had another comfort food meal for the winter menu. Especially since Vic liked them so much.

"Home run," he told her, holding his fork aloft a moment more.

"I had a good teacher and I get the feeling I could make these a hundred more times and they'd still not be half as good as the ones your mother makes."

"That's true. Don't take it personally, she's the best cook in the world." Vic winked at his mother and she waved a hand at him as she tried not to smile and failed. "What should she not watch?"

"The video from the incident with her father earlier today."

Rachel shouldn't have been so wildly flattered at the anger on his face. She should have been ashamed of the butterflies it gave her that he was that mad on her behalf.

He made her giddy that she inspired those things in him. That it riled up such an easygoing personality. That he found her—and their connection—worthy.

"I don't think you should look. I will tell you all he said. It's not healthy for you to see," he told her in a growl.

Though she was still touched, Rachel wanted to laugh. He had no idea the sort of video and pictures she used to have to look at as part of her job.

She'd want to see the video to gauge her father's

body language, hear his tone. She'd better be able to figure out what he was really up to once she was able to do that.

"I can see you're going to demand to look. But I'll be with you. To annotate so to speak. I don't know how a person like him could have had two awesome children like you and Maybe. It must be some sort of trait that skipped a few generations or something,"

That made her snicker. Her aunt Robbie often joked that she and the Dolan sisters were from the black sheep line of the family as most of them were unfortunately more like her dad.

After they cleaned the kitchen up and had been dismissed to take the leftovers home, he produced the data card the scene with her father was on and they headed to her room to watch. She didn't want to talk to Maybe about it until she'd seen it for herself.

He put a hand on her arm as they settled in with her laptop to look. "I'm telling you before we start that you are not responsible for anything he says or does."

Lovely. This was going to be bad.

Something borne out as they watched and she finally closed her laptop at the end.

It was impossible not to feel responsible for what he'd said and done. She felt sick that her dad had brought all that negativity and hate into the bakery.

"I can see you're about to apologize and I have to tell you up front if you do I'm going to get pissed off. He's a piece of shit and that is *not* your fault," Vic told her.

He totally fascinated her. Even when he was mad.

"I'm horrified. I'm sorry, even if you don't want me to feel guilty how can I not? He was so hateful. He brought that to you. To your family. Because of me."

"4 for 4" MINI-SURVEY

We are prepared to **REWARD** you with 2 FREE books and 2 FREE gifts for completing our MINI SURVEY!

FREE Value Over **$20!**

You'll get...
TWO FREE BOOKS & TWO FREE GIFTS
just for participating in our Mini Survey!

Dear Reader,

IT'S A FACT: if you answer 4 quick questions, we'll send you 4 FREE REWARDS!

I'm not kidding you. As a leading publisher of women's fiction, we value your opinions... and your time. That's why we are prepared to **reward** you handsomely for completing our mini-survey. In fact, we have 4 Free Rewards for you, including 2 free books and 2 free gifts.

As you may have guessed, that's why our mini-survey is called **"4 for 4".** Answer 4 questions and get 4 Free Rewards. It's that simple!

Thank you for participating in our survey,

Pam Powers

To get your 4 FREE REWARDS:
Complete the survey below and return the insert today to receive 2 FREE BOOKS and 2 FREE GIFTS guaranteed!

"4 for 4" MINI-SURVEY

1 Is reading one of your favorite hobbies?

☐ YES ☐ NO

2 Do you prefer to read instead of watch TV?

☐ YES ☐ NO

3 Do you read newspapers and magazines?

☐ YES ☐ NO

4 Do you enjoy trying new book series with FREE BOOKS?

☐ YES ☐ NO

YES! I have completed the above Mini-Survey. Please send me my 4 FREE REWARDS (worth over $20 retail). I understand that I am under no obligation to buy anything, as explained on the back of this card.

194/394 MDL GMYP

FIRST NAME	LAST NAME

ADDRESS

APT.#	CITY

STATE/PROV.	ZIP/POSTAL CODE

READER SERVICE—Here's how it works:

Accepting your 2 free Romance books and 2 free gifts (gifts valued at approximately $10.00 retail) places you under no obligation to buy anything. You may keep the books and gifts and return the shipping statement marked "cancel." If you do not cancel, about a month later we'll send you 4 additional books and bill you just $6.74 each in the U.S. or $7.24 each in Canada. That is a savings of at least 16% off the cover price. It's quite a bargain! Shipping and handling is just 50¢ per book in the U.S. and 75¢ per book in Canada*. You may cancel at any time, but if you choose to continue, every month we'll send you 4 more books, which you may either purchase at the discount price plus shipping and handling or return to us and cancel your subscription. *Terms and prices subject to change without notice. Prices do not include applicable taxes. Sales tax applicable in N.Y. Canadian residents will be charged applicable taxes. Offer not valid in Quebec. Books received may not be as shown. All orders subject to approval. Credit or debit balances in a customer's account(s) may be offset by any other outstanding balance owed by or to the customer. Please allow 4 to 6 weeks for delivery. Offer available while quantities last.

▼ If offer card is missing write to: Reader Service, P.O. Box 1341, Buffalo, NY 14240-8531 or visit www.ReaderService.com ▼

BUSINESS REPLY MAIL
FIRST-CLASS MAIL   PERMIT NO. 717   BUFFALO, NY

POSTAGE WILL BE PAID BY ADDRESSEE

READER SERVICE
PO BOX 1341
BUFFALO NY 14240-8571

NO POSTAGE
NECESSARY
IF MAILED
IN THE
UNITED STATES

Embarrassment rode her hard. She cared so much about Irena and Pavel; that her father came into their bakery and said the things he had—*threatened* the things he had—made her wish the ground could swallow her up.

She also couldn't deny how it made her feel to see both Irena and Vic defend her, to watch the anger on Vic's face as her father had said all the ugly things he had. It was an odd feeling to have someone care about her like that. Be so willing to go to the wall for her. For her heart. And her freedom.

Yeah, Irena had been right. They knew her.

"I'll have to call our lawyer in the morning. Let her know what's going on." She would have anyway as she had an evaluation with her therapist for the conservatorship case first thing. "I can't believe you didn't tell him you were all citizens. He's going to research you. Dig into your lives to make trouble."

She stood so she could pace a little.

"I didn't tell him because it's none of his fucking business. And let him dig. He's got nothing to find." His voice stayed so rational and calm. It should have annoyed her but it really actually was comforting.

"I'm glad you're so calm when someone like him is out to hurt you. Because of me."

"We're not doing this, Rachel. I know you. You're thinking maybe you should back off so we're out of the line of fire. Which is bullshit and I'm not going to allow it." Vic had his adorably stubborn face on.

"He's trouble, Vic." It wasn't as if she wanted him to walk away. But it was for the best. At least until all the court stuff with her parents was dealt with.

He waved a hand, just like his mother. Totally unconcerned. "He's a bully. You can't give in to a bully or they get worse. I'm not giving him a single bit of space on this. He's out of line. No one is going to threaten me and mine like that. Especially a paper tiger like him."

"Do you know how I'd feel if he managed to hurt you all in some way? In any way?" she asked, trying—and failing—to hide the emotion in the words.

He shot to his feet so fast it surprised her. That he'd grabbed her upper arms and it hadn't set off any of her internal alarms also surprised her. But she supposed her heart knew he'd never harm her.

"You think I would just walk away? Let you handle all the bad stuff and then waltz back when things cool off? Is that the quality of man you think you have in me?" His voice held a thread of anger but also she'd offended him and that's what caught her up.

She didn't want to hurt him like that. Even to push him away. She knew it was weak, but she couldn't help it.

"You should," she muttered. "Find a nice Russian gal who can cook and doesn't come with a crazy family."

"There is no such thing as a Russian who doesn't come with a crazy family. Even if I wanted such a thing. Which I do most assuredly not. I like the spunky American who spent hours with my mother learning how to make one of my favorite meals."

She tried very hard to retain her stoic expression but it was nearly impossible because he was sweet. And so bossy he wasn't going anywhere. Even when he should.

"I'm not a good choice," she said at last.

"Fuck off with you trying to tell me what my good choices are."

That made her laugh even though he frowned her way. He hadn't ever been like this with her before. Pushy.

Annoyed enough with her to actually show it without fear she would reject him or run the other way. Which she should. But she hadn't yet, despite knowing it was best.

Maybe it wasn't best. She'd gotten attached and clearly he was and not afraid to show it. Which pleased her and freaked her out too. She'd gotten used to him and everyone who came with him.

"I'm going to have to speak with Maybe about this," she said at last.

He harrumphed to let her know he was changing the subject but knew her game. "I told Alexsei some. Let's both go. That way she knows we're all in this together. Then we need to run by my house for a few minutes."

He seemed to underline the word *together* with his tone and some tense thing deep inside her gut seemed to unfurl a little.

"All right, let's go do this already." Rachel took his hand as they went to go speak to Maybe.

THREE STEPS PAST his front door after they'd run to his place to pick up something and she found herself backed against the low table behind his sofa. A knickknack of some sort toppled onto the floor with a clatter but it didn't slow him down.

He murmured against her skin as he pulled her sweater up and off, kissing over the hollow of her throat and over her breastbone. She sucked at learning new languages, but it sounded sexy as hell, even if he was just ordering pizza or something.

His hands were urgent and a little rough. He so rarely was that with her. Nearly always controlled. His skin was hot, wrenching a gasp from her at the sensation when he got rid of his shirt and slid, skin to skin against her.

She raked her nails down his back, a dark thrill tripping through her at his snarl in response.

When he dropped to his knees as he pulled her jeans, socks and panties off, she tried not to gasp. Or beg. Or cry.

In the quiet dim of the house, a shaft of light from the porch shone off his back, gleaming off his skin. Avarice at the sight. She wanted to mark his skin. Not just with her nails and teeth, but with ink.

Everything about him made her greedy.

"Widen your stance and lean back on the table," he urged, his voice rough with need.

Weak-kneed, she willingly obliged and he rewarded her with slow kisses and drags of his tongue from her ankle up her calf, pausing at the back of her knee and finding that place that never failed to send a shiver through her.

She'd dug her fingers into his hair, freeing it as she held on. He spread her open and licked. Thank god she had something to lean on or she'd have fallen over at how good it felt.

And that was before he slid first one and then another finger into her, easing her open. Readying her for his cock. She spasmed around him as he stretched, twisting his wrist until his fingertips brushed that sweet spot inside that sent a bolt of intense sensation through her.

An involuntary sound, a deep groan of desire, erupted from her chest.

He hummed his satisfaction over that. "So wet. Someone likes that, hmm?"

Uh yeah. What woman wouldn't like that?

He licked and kissed her into a state of bonelessness. Stroking his fingertip over that spot inside her in time with his tongue as she was pinned to the table supporting her weight.

Orgasm unfurled and spiraled through her as she cried his name.

One hand at her hip to keep her steady, he got to his feet and then turned her, bracing her hands. The *click-click-click* of his zipper sliding down seemed to climb up her spine.

The crinkle of a condom wrapper being opened sounded and there was a momentary loss of his heat as he stepped back to roll it on. She bit her lip to keep from begging him to hurry.

He petted down her back a moment, murmuring that she was beautiful. She *felt* beautiful.

Supremely sexy. Feminine.

The breath whooshed from her as he began to push his way in, the fat head of his cock sliding against her slick flesh.

Rachel closed her eyes and gave over to all he made her feel.

So full. Body and heart. He filled her up and saw her without any guise. Saw all of her, darkness and all and he not only tolerated it, he seemed to celebrate it. Accept it as just as beautiful as her face.

She thrust back against him to meet his inward progress and grinned at the sound he made. Her debonair, suave gentleman baker's normally impressive ease slipped a little.

Rachel made him do that. Power flared, thrilling her to her toes. Sure it was hot that he desired her, found her sexually attractive. Beautiful. But it was another thing entirely that she could draw something from him she was certain he didn't give often or easy.

He kissed her shoulder and then bit, making her writhe.

"So strong," he said in her ear before he licked it. "Beautiful. *Tight*," he said, voice strained.

It was his own fault. He did something to her when he bit her like that. Grabbed her with claws and dragged her toward another climax.

He palmed her nipples before tugging slightly. Freeing one hand, he slid it down to her clit where she nearly came at that first touch.

"Again," he said before brushing his fingertips over her clit in slow circles. Restless, she gripped the table's edge tighter, pushing back again harder, demanding more.

He gave it to her. Like she'd known he would. Sent her hard and fast over the edge, reducing her to nearly weeping at how fucking good it felt with him deep within her body.

He muttered a curse and followed, his fingertips digging into the muscle at her hip.

While the sweat on her skin was cooling, he pulled out, stepped away to deal with the condom and was back by the time she got her panties and jeans back on.

But she'd always feel naked with him.

CHAPTER FIFTEEN

"MY FRIEND SAID we could use all his backcountry ski-ing stuff," Vic told her as he unlocked the front door to the borrowed condo. "There are trails for hiking just be-yond." He pointed. He loved a good backcountry hike, especially in the snow.

She didn't respond, but he figured it was that their hands were full as they unloaded their things.

So he brought it up again several minutes later once they'd finished up.

Not quite looking him in the eyes—a huge red flag when it came to her—she said, "I love a good back-country hike but only when there's no snow. And I don't cross-country ski anymore. But I'm perfectly capable of hitting the slopes while you go out. I won't be of-fended or anything."

It was her tone that had him paying close attention. He took her hand and pulled her close, down into his lap on the big overstuffed couch.

"Tell me," he urged gently.

Rachel paused for a time and then finally spoke. "That's how I got… Where I was when Price held me. I can downhill ski. I can snowboard. But I can't seem to find the pleasure in being deep in a forest when there's so much snow. It slows you down. You can be tracked by someone else. It makes you slow." She shivered and he fought the urge to bundle her up and take her away from there and anything that made her feel that way.

"Will you tell me these things up front from now on?" He hated the idea that she might have felt pressured to do something that took her back to that terrible time.

She winced. "I'm sorry."

Seeing her flinch pissed him off. Not at her, but at the situation. He wanted her to know without even asking that he wasn't mad at her. Nor did he see those things she did to keep her peace of mind as silly or outrageous in any way.

It was the opposite. Seeing how she'd rebuilt herself in the wake of such a terrible tragedy only made him respect her more.

He took a breath and cupped her cheek. "I'm going to do my best not to ever hurt you. I know these are words and eventually I'll show you in deeds. I like going places and doing things with you so if I know some of the big things I'll feel more comfortable. I don't want to plan a trip and have it be really uncomfortable for either of us. And. I want to remind you that I don't want your apologies for this sort of stuff. There's nothing to be sorry about."

She nodded. "It took me a year or so after getting out of the hospital before I could get out in nature any more than a big park. Slowly I was able to hike short trails at popular times of the day so there'd be other people around. I don't hike alone anymore and I hate that. I've tried to do it, you know, make myself so I can just get over it."

"How'd that work out for you?" He made sure she heard the sarcasm in his voice.

She blushed. "Sometimes it does work. With some stuff."

"That's a lot of words for nothing specific."

"This is what I get for not dating only dumb guys," she mumbled, startling him into a laugh.

"You don't have to tell me. It just sounded like you had a story there." And he wanted it. Craved these confidences because he knew they were built on a foundation of trust. Intimacy of the deepest sort.

She took a deep breath and said, "I considered living in a high-rise, high-security building with a doorman and all that stuff when we moved out here. Maybe was okay with that as a choice but asked if we could look at houses as well. She likes to work in the yard, you know? We looked at both houses and condos. All nice. And then we looked at our house now. And I had this sense, standing on the front porch, that I had this choice to make about how I'd go about my day-to-day life. I knew Maybe would be happier in a house. I knew we'd be better roommates with more space to share. I also knew that if I chose the apartment, I'd be accepting a level of security that would hinder the future I wanted."

She was quiet awhile and he let her be.

"So we chose the house. I had to talk myself down from bars on the windows. But I have a state-of-the-art security system. It took me about six months before I felt truly relaxed here. I still have trouble sleeping, especially if anything sets off the motion lights in the side and backyard. So what I originally meant was sometimes I push past the fear and make a choice—one that might even freak me out—and it's the right choice."

He kissed her.

"And sometimes, like with backcountry skiing, I just

can't do it. It's too much. It takes me back in such a way that I can't do anything. I can't think clearly."

"You have limits and you respect them. There's not a damned thing wrong with that. I want to respect them too. So just mention something up front if you know, or if you don't and it just comes up. There are things I can't do since Danil died either."

"I hate being weak."

He snorted. "Only a strong person ever says that."

It was her turn to snort.

"Let's hit the slopes," she suggested. "We're here and it's still daylight. I haven't skied here yet."

He heaved them both to their feet, still holding her tight so he could kiss her in earnest. Slow and careful because he loved every part of her.

She put her forehead to his chest, tucking just under his chin for long moments afterward.

"First mulled wine is on me," Rachel told him softly.

"Deal."

She tensed slightly and then relaxed before speaking again. "Before we go I need to do a walk of the outside of the condo. Just to get a basic feel for it."

He should have thought of that up front. Given the security of her house and the story she'd just told him about choosing the house instead of the high-rise condo, of course she'd want to be sure this place was safe.

"Sure." He fought to remain nonchalant. He knew that's what she needed so he shoved his own desire to protect and cosset and gave her space. "Need my help?"

"No. Oh, and since I'm being honest and all. I was wondering. At your house there are a few little things. A window lock, a back door, some other stuff."

"Things I can fix to make my house safer? Induce

you to come over more often?" he asked, keeping his tone light.

"Yes."

"Show me what, or give me a good description and it's done. Not a hard thing to handle. Especially if it means you're there more often. I like it when I don't always have to share you with other people."

"Okay," she said, scrambling from his lap to grab one of the bags she'd brought along before heading outside.

He changed into ski clothes but would wait to choose which boots until she said which she wanted to do. Vic's father and his uncle would often take them out on hikes when they were growing up. He'd always loved being outside. That she loved it as much as he did was pretty awesome.

He looked forward to having many more days with her on the slopes.

RACHEL PUT UP her external alarms and then braced a window with the wooden dowel she found in a nearby closet. Each step she took gave her control, settled her sense of order and safety. She'd sleep well that night next to Vic.

When she returned to the living room after changing it was to find him standing at the big windows looking out over the snow covered trees like a spread in *Hot Russian Dude Monthly* magazine.

"I'm pretty sure you're why lumbersexual is an actual thing."

Delight stole over his face and she resolved to compliment him more.

"Is that so, *tigryonak*?"

She nodded, indicating the width of his shoulders,

only accentuated by the sleek and form-fitting shirt he wore beneath a for-real red plaid flannel shirt. "The clothes. Your beard is particularly strokable just now." Rachel allowed herself the sensory delight of a few pets. "A super hot Paul Bunyan. Yeah."

He took her hands and kissed each one. "I'm on board with whatever works for you. Are we skiing or snowboarding today?"

"I haven't been here before, so I'm all up for suggestions from you," she told him. "I'd say my skill level is intermediate at both. I love both so if we do one today let's do the other tomorrow."

"INTERMEDIATE MY ASS," he told her as they snuggled up on the couch several hours later. A fire crackled beyond the hearth and the stars wheeled overhead, brilliant against the deep evening darkness.

Her muscles hurt from hard physical activity but it was a good kind of ache. The kind the whiskey in her hand and the man at her side would make better.

"You totally overstate my skill. It's why I find you so adorable," she said. "And yet, compared to you I'm barely adequate."

He'd been a badass on a snowboard. That surprising grace of his meant he powered over the snow, ate up the slopes, glee on his handsome face as they fed off one another's energy.

In him she had someone who enjoyed being out there as much as she did. They had a competitive vibe, one that had them each zooming ahead of the other, only to watch as the other shot into first place.

It was unexpectedly hot that they could share a love of the outdoors. She bet he looked super sexy in the summertime, all slick with water as he walked out of the surf.

Yum.

"You're really quite good, so stop that," he said, pressing a kiss to her temple. "It's probably out for this season, but we should do Whistler next winter."

"I've been wanting to go, so I'm in. Cora's family has a house there and she's always talking about how we should use it. Naturally that means there's a chance she'd be there and if she's there, chances are Maybe will want to be included."

Vic's laugh rumbled through his chest, the wave of it vibrating through her bones. "And naturally where there is Maybe, there will be Alexsei. I think Gregori has a mansion of some type up there. They both ski."

"It's a handy thing that we share pretty much the same group of friends because they seem to follow us everywhere."

"Maybe is your protector. I am your protector. Where you go, we go," Vic said with such confident ease she believed it.

The *why* of it she didn't understand. So she found herself asking him.

"Why am I your protector?" he attempted to clarify.

"Why do you see it that way," Rachel attempted to box it in a safer way.

He just looked at her, his expression blank but for one slightly arched brow. Her silent treatment game was excellent. But his was world class.

Finally she exhaled and said, "Fine. Fine. You know what I'm asking."

"I do. But I want you to say it. I want you to ask it

yourself. It matters to me that you say it, Rachel," he added.

"The question isn't why you, Vic. The question is why me?"

Confusion washed over his face.

She moved so she could face him, tucking up onto the easy chair opposite. Then she pointed at him. "Look at you. I mean, take a good long look. Go on. You should because have you looked at yourself lately? You're like art. How on Earth did you get so fucking gorgeous? You're funny and sensitive and you're smart. Oh, and super fit and your body is like, well it's ridiculous and I should hate you because come on. But as you quite often put all those things to my service, I give you my blessing to keep on being a superior physical and mental specimen." She rolled her wrist, urging him forward.

His smile told her he was not unaware of his appeal. "Thank you. But if I'm so wonderful, how can you be confused?"

Rachel wasn't sure if he knew what she meant or not, but she was going to have to suck it up, be brave and be specific.

"Dude. Your family. Look at you all. You and Evie are first-generation American success stories. You have a business. You pull together when things get rough. Even the worst sort of rough imaginable. And you're spending your time with a chick who is so messed up she has to put her own alarms on the outside of a condo in a gated community with a fairly decent security presence. Your father left so much behind when he fled Russia with your mother at his side. They came halfway across the world to build a life from nothing and they did! I just look at you and them and wonder what the hell you're doing with a fuckup like me."

He sucked in a breath but instead of getting in her physical space, he remained where he was. And yet, the enormity of him began to seep her way.

"I've told you what happened to my brother. It didn't just show up one day out of the blue. His troubles were long-term. Fraught. Full of recriminations. Fights. Saying of things that couldn't be unsaid. My parents—maybe even to this day—wanted to downplay just how bad things had gotten. Who my brother really was. And maybe I'm a selfish fucking asshole, but between you and me, Rachel, by the time he turned sixteen or so Danil was a piece of shit. They see how he was at six or seven, but they don't remember how he was even at that early age. How selfish and petty he was."

Vic was lost in something that had happened long ago but had left a very deep mark.

Rachel wanted to fix the rift she'd stirred to life between them. What a dick she'd been to say what she had the way she had. Of course he knew what it meant to deal with tragedy.

"The last year of his life wasn't that bad. Not for me," he told her. "I was beginning the process to work for the county sheriff's office. To continue search and rescue and focus on more rural areas of King County. I knew he wasn't clean, Rachel. I knew it. I told my parents. More than once and they didn't want to believe it and I just got tired. So. Tired. And it was just… I pushed him away because I knew he was going to do something else terrible and then he assaulted his girlfriend. Nearly killed her because he found out she'd bought drugs without him. He was a criminal and he spoiled every fucking holiday. We all waited around for him to show up and if he did at all he was late and he still complained and my mom just wanted him to be glad. To see how much they loved him and I just wanted to be *away* from it. Nothing I said mattered to my parents because they saw my brother in a way I'd stopped trying to see."

"I'm an asshole. I'm sorry," she told him.

He snorted. "You're not an asshole. Your question though, the original one about why you? It's laden with a bunch of bullshit assumptions."

"I know. It's beyond entitled of me to imagine I'm the only one struggling with darkness and pain. Especially when you'd already shared the story of your brother," she said.

"Oh fuck that. I don't want it. Don't need it. However." His dark brows winged down as he frowned at her. "Do you not... Surely you can't miss the fact that you're exceptionally successful at pretty much everything. You're beautiful, a talented tattoo artist, intuitive about people—even if you are being surprisingly stubborn about not seeing all your positive traits. You asked why you? Because there's nothing and no one else for me but you."

He wanted to tell her that he loved her. Wanted to let the words free. But he knew it wasn't time. Knew she'd fight it and run the other way. So, he had to keep being smart. Patient. Easy. Stay cool and calm. Charm and woo. When it was too late for her to do anything else but know she loved him too. Then he'd tell her.

"Oh," she said. She blushed slightly.

"Yes, *oh*. I told you those things about Danil to illustrate my point. Not your silly attempt at a point." He frowned and it made her snicker. "We are both fucked up and broken. We both carry baggage. Where you are worn thin, let me be strong. This is what it means to be with someone and fit, isn't it?"

She stretched a hand out to take his. "I don't want to weigh you down. Do you understand what I'm saying?"

"I hear the words you use. I acknowledge you have arranged them into sentences you think make sense. And they do not. Because you're coming at this like you're some blight-faced old hag covered in boils."

She snorted and then started to laugh, which went on until she got the hiccups.

"Okay fine. I'm amazing," she gasped at last. "Of course you want to be around me all the time," she said as she launched herself into his lap.

"I'm glad we could finally come to an understanding," he told her as he snuggled her close. "This won't always be easy and full of delicious sexy chemistry. But I'm patient and steadfast, my mother says so. I will help you through the hard times and you will do the same for me."

She just hugged him tight without a word. Agreeing.

CHAPTER SIXTEEN

MAYBE PLOPPED INTO her seat across the small, rickety table from where Rachel had settled with her sketchbooks.

Cora wouldn't be at their weekly lunch date because she was visiting her boyfriend down in Portland so that day it was just the two sisters.

"Are you going to let me look yet?" Maybe asked as she cracked open her orange soda.

Rachel had been working on the pieces for her calendar project proposal for the last three weeks. Maybe had been trying to sneak a peek pretty much that entire time because that's how she was.

Of course Vic was equally bad. Especially as he was so used to women falling over themselves to give him whatever he asked for. Normally she was on board with that too, as he had a fantastically dirty mind and asked for all sorts of filthy sex stuff.

But her art was different. No one saw her first draft.

"Probably. I think I'm done with the twelve pages for the project."

She slapped Maybe's grabby hands away.

"These aren't the originals. They're just sketches and you can't see them. Also? We're in a restaurant where there's food and drinks all over the place. Sheesh. And you want to know why I'm so touchy."

Maybe rolled her eyes as she forked up some of the potato salad that came with the sandwiches.

Cora rushed in with a flurry of scarves, coat sleeves and several layers of clothing she got rid of before sitting with a sigh.

"Uh, hi," Rachel said. "I thought you were in Portland."

"I was. I broke up with Stephen so now I'm here in Seattle."

"Wait. What?" Rachel spun on her friend. Cora's boyfriend was doing his medical residency in Portland and over the last year their relationship had been long-distance.

As far as Rachel was concerned, it was always doomed for failure because he was all about Stephen. The way he spoke about art—which was an integral part of Cora's life both professional and personal—had been a long-term sore spot. He had naturally assumed Cora would move to Portland when he'd begun his residency because her job was *just art*.

Though he worked incredibly long hours and even when he wasn't working he was either sleeping or doing something with the other residents. Cora, by contrast, had a life in Seattle. Not just one job, but several. A big family who loved her and who she was connected to.

He always made it seem like his life was more important and Cora should fit into it.

But Rachel and Maybe, while disliking him, certainly wanted Cora to be happy and in love.

"You never liked him anyway."

"That's not the point," Maybe said. "We like *you*. And you seemed to like him. So that's what counted. What happened?"

"He told me I should institutionalize my mother. Oh, and he has a girlfriend now. I mean, other than me."

"How the hell does he get the time? I thought residents were supposed to be working all the time? How does he have the place in his schedule to cheat on you?" Rachel threw her hands up a moment. "Also, fuck all the stuff he says about your mother."

Walda was kooky and unpredictable in many ways, but she was Cora's mother. And Cora loved her family. Eccentric artist instability wasn't the same as put-her-in-an-institution instability.

"Is it weird I'm more offended that he'd tell Cora to put her mom in a mental institution?" Maybe asked. "I mean, look, I'm not surprised he cheated. But I did think he cared about you in his way. And he has to know how you feel about that sort of stuff about your mom."

Rachel sighed and leaned back in her chair. "What a gross, awful creep. How did he tell you both things?"

"Well, you both know I drove all the way down there because he had two days in a row off and we had plans. But I get there and he's not even there and he makes me wait another half an hour before he shows up and then he picked a fight. I guess cheating was fraying his precious nerves. Anyway, we're sitting in his apartment and talking about his life and he's saying I should move and I'm like dude we've had this talk, you still have years left and you may not even end up in Portland. I remind him I've got a job here and all the same stuff and suddenly he's saying my mother is crazy and dangerous and how she should be in a home and how she manipulates us all and I was like, no dick is worth this bullshit and then he's trying to say let's have sex and make up and dude there were a pair of panties in his bed. Not mine."

"For fuck's sake. He didn't even change the sheets between girlfriends? Ew. Not sanitary," Maybe said with an offended sniff.

It was the right thing to say because Cora started to laugh.

"Anyway. I'm single again and I'll be spending way less money on gas and way less time on I-5. Don't tell Finley about the stuff with my mom. My family doesn't like him either and there's enough tension between everyone without bringing more to the table."

"That's all on him. Your sister knows that. But I'll keep it to myself," Rachel said.

VIC WAS TIRED. So tired he should have turned left to walk up his own front steps. Instead he turned and at the sight of her light on in her room, he asked and was invited over.

"Hi." She opened the door to admit him, her hair held back from a face clean of makeup that only emphasized the size and beauty of her eyes.

He was so fucking glad he'd chosen this over his own bed. "Good evening, *tigryonak*. I would very much like to share a cup of tea with you and to take you up on the offer of looking at your pieces for the project."

"I just finished making a pot of tea. Come up to my room and after you look at the drawings, you can have a cup. Your mother sent over salmon if you want some."

As he found out when he poked in the fridge, his mother had also sent over cucumber salad and pickled veggies as well.

"I need to talk with her about not giving you all this

food without me. I like to be useful to you in procuring all the delightful things she makes."

She laughed, a hip propped against the counter as she watched him make plates for them both.

"How is everyone?" she asked.

He'd been at the pub with his buddies, thinking about her the whole time. They were all curious about her so he ended up talking about her the whole time too.

They wanted to meet her and he realized she was someone he could bring into that crew pretty easily. They were all about the outdoors and often hiked, biked, camped, boated, kayaked and the like together. She had the strength and stamina to fit right in with even the most extreme of their group.

"All still full of shit," he told her, following her to her room, she with the tea and him with food. "Trying to talk me into doing the STP next year."

"The bicycle ride from Seattle to Portland?" she asked, toeing her door open for their entry.

"Yes. I want to see your art first. Then we'll have tea and food."

The smile she gave him made him glad he'd shown his impatience to see her work.

But the work. Jesus.

It wasn't just that she liked birds. That much was apparent from the way it was featured in so much of her life. Not just on her body, but in the art she created. On her coffee mugs and soap dishes, on sheets and the pillows on her couch.

There was such a sense of intimacy in the way she saw them. And the way she drew them. Movement of wings, a flash of gold and black as a goldfinch left a branch and burst into flight. He wasn't sure how, but she'd been able to give real sass to its eyes.

The Northern flicker's flash of red at the back of its head against the white snow and evergreen bark. The fat little Western bluebird sitting on a branch next to a black-capped chickadee looked like a grumpy old man.

A few lines about each bird helped give a sense of why they were chosen for whatever month she'd assigned them.

Beautiful.

The entirety of the project was stunning. Life breathed into every line she'd put on the paper. There was so much of Rachel's heart and soul in it he found himself—yet again—humbled that she shared it.

He turned to her, touched that she tried to react as if she hadn't been nervously watching him. "This is fantastic. If they don't choose you there's clearly something wrong with them."

"I don't even know if this is what they really want or if I'm off base and missed the point. But it was what I was compelled to do. I'm proud of how it all turned out," she said.

"You should be proud. You're amazing and I'm so impressed. Beauty and brains. I'm lucky." He gave her a grin and she blushed again.

"Thank you. I'm taking my submission down before I go in to work tomorrow. I'm nervous. Drink your tea." She pointed at his mug.

He wasn't sure if she was nervous about him or the process. He guessed the latter, but oftentimes when she revealed some deep personal thing—as he'd realized her art usually was—she'd get a little shy.

It got to him in a way that was nearly painful.

He ate with her, listening to music, just being together, but at ten thirty she gave him a look. "Go home and get to bed. You look tired. I've been keeping you awake with all my relentless sexual demands. Recharge or you're useless to me. Especially since I can get food from your mother without you."

Though he'd slept over once since the first night when she'd had that nightmare, he usually went back home or she left his place.

It wasn't an issue. He understood why. Was willing to put in the time so she would be comfortable with it.

Still, mornings were way better waking up next to her.

He snorted. "Keeping you sexually satisfied is draining," he said, tone dry.

She walked him downstairs and they paused near the front door where he then backed her to the closet door. "Are we still on for that hike tomorrow afternoon?"

Wordless, she nodded, her gaze locked with his.

Even though he was tired, just being there with him seemed to ease the edges of the weariness. The scent of her, jasmine and spice, floated between them, settling into him.

She went to her tiptoes and he bent his knees, their mouths meeting in between. It was the way she sighed into him, her body melting against his, arms wound around his neck as she slid her tongue along his, that dug in with claws. Her taste, still like a miracle, was also something he was getting used to, though he craved her as much as he had before they'd ever touched.

Outside on the street he could hear someone out walking a dog. Probably the Swede with the husky. He worked a late shift at a senior center and often was out late with the sweet, blue-eyed dog.

But what seemed to thunder through his head was his own pulse, the one that pounded along with hers against the palm he held against her throat. She stole his breath as well as his heart and when the kiss broke, he leaned his forehead to hers a moment.

"I'll call you tomorrow," he murmured.

"Okay."

"If I don't walk out the door right this moment I'm going to stay to fuck you for at least an hour. Maybe two. I'll be super tired tomorrow morning, but it'll be worth it."

She snickered as she pushed him back, a hand at his chest. "I'm torn over which thing I should argue for. My pink parts are cheering for fucking me and being tired. But my heart and brain say go home and rest so we can have enthusiastic sex after the hike. I mean, let's be real, we could do both but you'd be more tired. So. Go home. I'll take a fuck-me rain check."

"I think I should be offended by half of what you say. Instead it turns me on. What can I say? I'm messed up." He dipped to steal one last very quick kiss and then managed to get out onto the porch where the bracing wind helped rein in his cock. "Sweet dreams, Rachel."

He left, her scent still clinging to his skin as he hurried through the cold, wet weather back to his bed. His cold, lonely bed where he passed out about five minutes after he flopped into it, pulling the blankets up high.

CHAPTER SEVENTEEN

RACHEL PARKED OUTSIDE the building where Wren told her to meet her and the others from the project committee. Her heart skittered in her chest, nervousness she hadn't felt in some time.

This was important. And all she could do was hope like hell they liked her stuff.

Wren buzzed her inside and waited at the open door at the top of the first open flight of stairs, along with two other women.

Butterflies in her belly, she pretended to be confident and strode up to meet them.

The collective turned out to be a group of seriously amazing artists of all types. Painters, sculptors, photographers, musicians all. And they all told her they loved her project application and they wanted her and her little birds.

They described what they were doing, what the timeline was and then she was lucky enough to see some of the other projects that had been chosen as well and hoped she could make something half as good.

She never could have imagined this moment five years ago. Even two years ago it was beyond her. And there she was, her future as an artist just really starting to open up and turn into something with real possibility.

An hour later, grinning like a loon, she headed out,

clutching the envelope containing her contract to her chest. Elation soared through her. This new stage in her life, despite some bad points, was really good.

She'd made this life. Built it along with help from her friends and small circle of intentional family.

Shooting off a quick text telling Maybe they were going to be celebrating later that night, she stepped out front to find her father leaning against the front fender of her car.

As she continued to walk, the old Rachel clicked into place as she took note of his stance and stopped where she was. He was old now, and had always carried more weight than he should. He'd be slow, even if he tried anything she'd be faster. She was stronger.

Naturally he didn't move, but stood to his full height, effectively blocking her way to her car door.

"I have a client coming shortly and I need to be at work, so let's get this over with. What do you want?" she demanded.

"Your mother and I want you to come over for dinner. Just us three so we can set this all right."

Wow, they had some nerve, she had to give them that. "The only way for you to set this right is for you to drop this legal harassment. That's it. Now, get away from my car door."

"So this is how you talk to your parents now?"

"I'm not interested in speaking to you at all. I've said this before. I tried to get a judge to say it to you since you didn't seem interested in listening to me say it. Stop showing up where I am. Stop showing up at my friend's family business. Stop showing up at my job and at Maybe's job. We don't want you in our lives."

"You don't know what you're saying."

"Stop telling me what I know."

"Why are you so intent on starting a fight? I'm your father and you're hurting your mother so much."

"I'm done with both of you. She's your errand boy and you're a bully."

"We care about you and want you to be well. You're not yourself."

This fucking asshole! *Not herself?* How would he know? He hadn't bothered to know her in at least a decade. Not really since she'd gone to college at eighteen. As far as he was concerned, she'd reached perfection the day they'd issued her a badge and a sidearm at the FBI and for him, anything deviating from that meant failure. Meant there was something wrong with her as far as he was concerned.

For him, it wasn't the weeks held in Price's basement that was the tragic moment in Rachel's life, it was the fact that she wasn't an FBI agent anymore. Jesus. The realization hit her so hard it nearly stole her control altogether.

"Stop," she said shortly, reining in her temper. She knew how to do this, damn it. She stepped closer, using the fob to unlock her door.

"I guess we'll see you in court, then. Since that's what you seem to want. We're not going to go away, Rachel. We're your mother and father and we're not going to let Maybe ruin your life any further."

That control she'd fought for slipped as she narrowed her eyes at him. "*Maybe's* ruining my life? Are you kidding me? *Fuck you.* You've done enough damage to her as it is so leave her name out of your mouth. *You're* doing all the damage here. You. For nothing. *Because I am not sick.* And I don't need you or anyone else to make my decisions for me. You don't know me. You don't know anything about my health when it's not about you. And as for court? You need to direct all inquiries to our attorney because all you are to me is my harasser and you're using the courts to do it."

Think of him as a suspect. One who believes he's smarter than he is. You can do this.

She grabbed her car door handle and pulled, displacing him enough to get the door open.

He turned, reaching out to grab her upper arm. Her training had clicked into place and with a slight adjustment, she moved from the way so he'd miss her and stumbled into the car as he left the curb.

"You don't touch me, old man," she said in a voice she hadn't used in many years.

He righted himself but stepped back to the curb a few feet away, keeping his distance.

"I have the legal right to defend myself and I will. Do you understand me?"

His face darkened at the not-so-subtle threat.

Wren came hurtling from the building's doors and skidded to a stop in front of them. "You, get your hands off her! I've called the police so you need to beat it."

It was so unexpected, so sweet and also funny that Rachel was able to take a breath and get herself back together.

Her father made another run at it, trying to modulate his voice to sound sympathetic. Just a good cop trying to help her out of a bind. "These people are bloodsuckers out to take advantage of your situation. Your so-called boyfriend and his whole family are trying to separate you from your family. It's an old tactic."

"But why? Are you saying they're a cult? Handsome

Russian Americans who own successful businesses? Oh no. Out to do what?"

"You have money from your settlement. Money Maybe knows about and why she's stuck so close to you all this time," he spat out.

It wasn't even that much and most of it was in investments and tied up in the house. Moreover, Maybe would sell her plasma to help Rachel, there was no way she'd ever consider taking a loan from her, much less steal her money.

"It's criminal how little you understand your children," she said at last. "You lack even the most basic compassion. Is it so hard to believe the people in my life are there because of me?"

"There are good white American men for you to be with and you land with these foreigners? You were raised better."

She physically recoiled from him at that. "Who are you?" she demanded, sickened at this hatred. "Never mind. Just piss off and get away from me. The cops will be here soon."

Her father muttered something about green cards and hustled his bulk toward his car, parked across the street.

"What an asshole. Are you all right?" Wren asked her, a hand on Rachel's arm.

Rachel scanned up and down the block, watching his exit. How the hell did he know she'd be there? Was he following her? That was paranoid of her. Right?

"Come back inside. I'll get you a cup of tea. I didn't actually call the police yet because I wasn't sure what you wanted. We can do that inside too," Wren said as she pulled Rachel gently toward the doors.

"No. No, I'm fine. I have to get to work." The last

thing she wanted was to be fussed over. It'd only make her edgy and she did truly have a client coming to the shop shortly so she needed to go. "I'm sorry for that entire scene." She focused on Wren, continued to pretend she wasn't utterly humiliated. "Thanks for coming to the rescue and I promise this…this won't be an issue on the project."

Wren frowned, cocking her head. "I'd never imagined it would be. Are you sure you don't want to come in? At least for a few minutes. I'd be shaken up if I were you. I can contact Vic if you like."

Good god no. Rachel shook her head and pasted on a smile. "I'm all right. Thank you for rushing out to my defense. I'm sorry he brought this here."

"That's his problem, not yours. Okay?"

Easy to say but if Rachel hadn't been there, he wouldn't have shown up and caused that scene. It was hard to be confident with new friendships when that sort of thing colored how they felt about her.

Rachel gave a noncommittal nod just to be done. Embarrassment roiled in her belly.

"Well." Wren took a step back, concern still on her face. "Congratulations again. I'm so excited to be working with you. If you need anything you know where I am."

She smiled, knowing it was wooden, and got into her car and hoped it didn't look too much like a panicked escape.

She had to tell Maybe about this but she wasn't entirely sure how to do it. She didn't want her sister to feel any more pain because of their parents. No more guilt. No more negative weight. If she could get away with it, she wouldn't have told anyone. But Wren would eventually tell Gregori and once the Russians knew it would get back to Maybe via any one of them, most likely Alexsei.

Damn it.

When she parked at the pay lot a few blocks from the shop she called a familiar number she hadn't had to use in a while.

"I was just about to walk out the door for the day but I see your name on my screen so you know I'm all about answering," Bee said as she picked up. "Tell me what's going on in Seattle."

Bee—short for Beatriz—was Rachel's previous therapist. And also big sister to Cora and Finley. She still lived in Virginia and Rachel had a replacement therapist in Seattle she still saw on a regular basis, but at times like this, she reached for old friends who'd known her at her weakest.

Rachel got Bee up to speed on what had happened. "I know I need to tell Maybe. Any advice on the best way?"

Bee sighed. "There you go, putting other people first. How do *you* feel about it?"

"How do you think I feel? Helpless to make this shit stop. Agitated that I have to face it over and over when I just want to live my fucking life. He's out there doing God knows what, always trying to mess with my life. I hate it. And then I feel selfish and petty for thinking that when there are real problems in the world."

"So everything is your fault again. Makes sense. Look, sweetcakes, just be open and blunt with your sister. That's what she needs. And what she needs is what you need. I get that. You can't make it hurt less when it's about him. But I have every confidence you'll say it the way you need to. She loves you and she trusts you. He doesn't know what to do with that. Because he doesn't inspire that love and trust. Your love and trust sustained him for a long time."

"I only loved and trusted him from afar. And because I didn't know about what he'd done to Maybe."

"Whatever. The point is, he's not being sustained the way he was before. When you did the job he saw as a way of validating him as a father and a man."

A job she'd walked away from.

A job whose echoes still rattled around in her head at least three times a week.

"What can I do to make him go away?" Rachel heard the pleading tone in her voice but there was no sense pretending. Not with Bee who'd heard her at her very worst.

Bee sighed. "Oh, honey. I wish I had the power to do that for you. I can't believe the court didn't give you that order. Assholes."

"Well there was a good chance they wouldn't. You and I both know that. He never threatened to harm me. Not like that. And he's one of them. He knows how to talk to a judge. Knows how to make himself look like a dad trying to make things right with his kid. He has no record."

"Still. What could it have hurt to just give you the order?"

An old complaint. One she herself had made more than once. She understood the legal whys in the abstract. But it wasn't abstract. It was her life and she had to live it.

"Even today he was careful. He tried to grab my upper arm but I evaded him easily. That's what he'd say to a judge. Maybe he'll claim I was going to stumble or whatever. And I look like a complainer and he gets to be the concerned father. And in the end, nothing will change except he's used the system to force me to react. Again."

"Seems to me you have the basis of what to say to Maybe then. She trusts you but she also knows you're not superhuman. You can't stop this from happening to her. It already did. She's strong and smart and she's got a wonderful support system. Right now you're the one he's focused on. You're his target."

Rachel pinched the bridge of her nose.

"I wish there were easy answers, sweetcakes. But one thing remains. It always remains. You survived. You are a survivor and if you can survive Price, you can survive a petty asshole like your father."

It would be so nice to have someone come in and make all this go away. But she *was* a survivor, damn it and she wasn't going to let her father steal that. She'd have to handle this. She *would* handle this.

"Thanks for answering when I called," Rachel told her. "And for the pep talk. I mean it. I have a client so I need to run."

"I'll always pick up or call you right back. You got this, Rach. I believe in you. I've seen your strength over and over."

When she got out of the car, it was to see the swoop of black wings as crows flew past. "Smart, wee beasties." Grinning, she tossed them some sunflower seeds she kept in her bag just for that occasion. These birds were a murder that often hung out near Ink Sisters and whenever she saw them she liked to feed them.

They cawed at her, knowing her, thanking her for

her gift. Or so she liked to think. Whatever it was, it pleased her to feed them. Crows were clever and badass and slightly scary.

Qualities Rachel needed to embody if for no other reason than not letting her father win. He would *not* steal her freedom.

The phone call had been good. What she'd needed. Certainly enough for the time being. Enough to get her through the next few hours of her appointments. Enough that she was able to pull herself together and figure out what to say to Maybe when she got home.

CHAPTER EIGHTEEN

VIC POPPED INTO Whiskey Sharp to get a quick trim and shave before he went over to Rachel's. It'd give him a chance to check in with Maybe to see if she'd heard any news about the art project yet.

He preferred Maybe's shaves to Alexsei's. His cousin could be dictatorial and Maybe smelled a lot better and did what he told her to do.

She gave him a bright smile when he came in, adding a kiss to his cheek when he put a cup of coffee down for her.

"Good day to you, Vicktor. Thank you for the caffeine."

He sat in her chair and waited for her to put the drape over his clothes before asking, "Any news?"

"She didn't text you?" Maybe asked, clearly surprised.

"We did have plans to hang out tonight so perhaps she was going to tell me then. Since you obviously know, tell me."

"It was a quick text hours ago. Just that we were definitely going to celebrate tonight. She was running off to the shop to meet a client and would tell me more when she saw me. She's probably been slammed all day since."

He met Maybe's eyes in the mirror as she used the

clippers, happiness and relief settling into his system. This was an amazing opportunity for her. A blooming of her life.

"I love how happy you look right now." Maybe brushed the loose hairs from the nape of his neck with a brush before moving on to using the scissors.

"It's not hard to be happy when a beautiful woman is cutting my hair and we're discussing her gorgeous sister with the wary eyes and exceptional artistic talent," he said before sobering a little. "Those pages were freaking incredible. This will help her believe in herself."

Maybe finished with his hair and then moved to the shave. He let himself relax as he thought about ways to celebrate once they were alone.

"She needed this I think," Maybe continued. "My dad is always looking for ways to chip at this new life she's making. Undermining her, making her feel like all she could excel at is law enforcement."

He frowned. "I am not a fan of that guy."

She snorted. "Join the club and get in line."

Vic withheld—barely—a snarl of annoyance. "He can't have her life. He has one of his own."

"No kidding. I've got no argument with you on that. He's going to see you as a threat. It's why he came to the bakery."

"I *am* a threat. He'd be wise to understand that. I'll do everything I can to stop him from messing with Rachel and her future. One she deserves."

"Sometimes she might see you as a threat too," Maybe said, voice a lot quieter. "She's one of those people who puts others ahead of herself so often she doesn't even see it. And here you are telling her she deserves to make her own choices for herself."

Oh he knew that.

"I got it."

"He's going to make it hard on you if he can," she said.

The thing was, people like Richie Dolan had no real idea what "making it hard on you" really meant. They'd never endured truly harrowing times so they thought they understood how to fuck with others. But he'd been in some really dark places and survived. Dolan had nothing to hurt him with other than Rachel. And he'd protect Rachel with all his might.

When Maybe had finished, he was cleaned up, hair looking great and he was ready to see the woman who'd made everything else so clear to him.

He stopped by the market to grab some champagne and added flowers as well. He chose the brightest bouquet he could find, knowing she'd like the color against the relentless gray of March.

Every time he brought her a little gift she brightened in such a way he began to bring her things just to coax that expression into life yet again.

When he arrived at her place, it was Alexsei who let him in. "Rachel and Maybe are off in her room speaking in private. Their father tracked her down outside the building Wren's friend lives in."

"As Maybe would say, this fucking guy. What the hell, *Lyosha*?" Vic put the flowers on the counter for her and popped the champagne into the fridge.

"I don't know the whole story. I happened to overhear part of it." Alexsei shrugged one shoulder as if he wasn't just admitting to eavesdropping.

"You know it's nearly a certainty Rachel heard you

listening in," Vic said as he threw in to help his cousin with the big charcuterie tray he was putting together.

"I'm under no illusions that I can fool that one. She misses very little."

"I DEBATED EVEN telling you at all," Rachel told her sister as she poked through the closet to see if there were any new shoes she wanted to borrow.

"You need to stop trying to shield me," Maybe said. "*And*. Stop telling yourself you should have shielded me from all that stuff that happened when you weren't even living at home."

Rachel looked back over her shoulder at her smarty-pants sister. "I'm the big sister. It's my job to shield you." She added a stuck-out tongue to underline just how mature she was.

"Joking aside, Rach, you gotta share this stuff. Together we're way stronger. And so much ugliness hides in secrets. Even when you do it to protect me."

"Fine. I told the attorney. She said the reports from my doctors had been filed in this stupid conservatorship. Thinks it will probably put an end to this once and for all."

That had been a relief.

And though she was still nervous, their lawyer had been reasonably confident that their parents really didn't have a case. Rachel's health progress had been well documented and there was a very good chance a judge would bounce it once the response answering all the mental health challenges was filed.

It hung over her nonetheless. That anyone who claimed to love her while working to take away her freedom was sickeningly familiar. Something she had

begun to see parallels in lately with how Price would
speak to her while he held her captive.

She sank to the floor, purloined shoes in her hand,
back to the wall. "Jesus, hummingbird. I'm tired."

Maybe sat across from her, leaning on the chest at
the foot of her bed. "I know. He's trying to wear you
down. Break your spirit."

"Is that what he was doing to you? Before you ran
away?" Rachel asked.

"Yeah. Partly I think. With me it was something else.
Like a picture frame that just didn't match the rest of
the furniture. I offended him because I was different
from everyone else," Maybe said. "But with you? Yes
he wants to wear you down and break you, but because
he's all wrapped up in who you are."

"So when I'm rutting with hot Russians and working
in a gross tattoo shop he's degraded?" Rachel nodded.
"You're the second person to say something similar
today. I've been circling it awhile myself."

"It's sort of creepy. I'm sorry."

Rachel found herself snorting. Leave it to Maybe to
sum it all up so concisely. "I want to have a good night
tonight. I want to celebrate something wonderful." She
stood, reaching out to give her sister a hand up. "We
can talk more about this stuff later, okay?"

Maybe hugged her. "Yeah. Let's go celebrate with
liquor and dudes. If I'm leading you down the path to
hell, we may as well grab our guys on the way, eh?"

When they got back to the kitchen, Alexsei had finished making a yummy-looking tray of food and Vic
had brought champagne and flowers.

"I take it you already heard?" she asked as she took
the glass from him.

"Nothing specific. Tell me everything," he said, dropping a kiss to the curve of her cheek.

She gave them all the details she had. The timelines and release dates. Her nervousness was weirdly excited, but she didn't care. It was wonderful that she had this win, this thumbs-up for her talent. At a time when she'd really needed it.

A few hours later they'd all finished cleaning up and Alexsei headed off to bed with Maybe.

"Hey, wait a minute, nosy parker," Rachel called out to Alexsei.

Vic laughed at her back. "I told you she knew you were out there."

"Well, come on!" Alexsei said. "I could see it was something serious. You looked worried and naturally, I was concerned for Maybe."

"Sometimes it's not your business yet, you know what I'm saying?"

"I worry for *you* too. You're family now." At Rachel's continued silence, Alexsei went on. "I don't apologize for my worry, but I do apologize for making you feel like I was sneaking around or that I didn't trust you."

Rachel nodded, accepting the apology.

Up in her room once she got into her pajamas and brushed her teeth, she sat on the bed with Vic. "You've been really patient. It's beginning to worry me," she said. "You want the details too?" she asked him, meaning about the situation with her father.

"Yes, please. If you feel up to it."

She told him, trying to keep to the basic story and avoiding details that were unnecessarily upsetting.

"Anyway. That happened. But it happened right *after*

I got the good news about my submission so it wasn't as bad as it could have been on a different day." She paused.

As selfish as it felt, she was tired. Like she'd told Maybe earlier. And sharing that with him had lightened her considerably. Like he'd taken part of it from her.

He brushed the hair from her face. "What is it? You can tell me anything, you know that."

His voice was so gentle, she did. "Would you stay here with me tonight?"

He pulled her close, whispering sweet nothings in Russian. Then he got out of his clothes and under the blankets with her in his arms, her ear pressed over his heart, listening to the steady beat.

"You make me feel less alone," she said, her eyes closed as she soaked in his warmth.

His embrace tightened a moment. "I can say the same."

Him? He always seemed surrounded by people. He certainly had an active social life. Saw friends regularly. His mother doted on him.

"Everyone loves you. They actually perk up when you enter a room," she said.

His laugh rumbled through his chest and made her smile.

"Well, naturally because I'm amazing. But you look at me and you know me, *tigryonak*. I don't have to be anything but who and what I am with you. You don't need to be entertained. You don't need to be charmed—though I do love charming you."

"For the sex, right?"

"Obviously. Aside from the rather astounding sex, it

just feels very easy to be with you. But that also means I can see when something is bothering you and it makes me want to fix it."

"Some parts of me will be broken forever."

"You're a mosaic of all those pieces you've put back together so you can have the life you do now. Nothing is perfect. No one is perfect. We're all messed up and the key is what we do with what we have. You're not the sum of this bullshit with your father. In fact, it's one very small part of the whole of you."

"Yeah, the pain in my ass."

"Certainly. But aside from this annoyance you just got this amazing opportunity for your art. And you're building a wonderful client list at Ink Sisters. You've been absorbed into my family."

"Like the Borg. Resistance is futile. But your branch comes with bread and a love of yummy things. Oh and gross stuff like beets, but whatever. We all have our flaws."

"Beets are good."

"You can say it all you want. Doesn't make it true. That's like saying kale is good. And I guess if you like eating hair, it's fantastic."

"You have very strong opinions about food."

"If you have strong opinions but none are about food I'm not sure I can trust you."

"You have a Russian soul."

As compliments went, it was a pretty good one.

"You can be alone in a room full of people. Alone even when you sleep next to someone else. There are billions of people on this planet and only one you. You fit me." He kissed the top of her head.

She burrowed against his body, toying with the bar in his nipple as they spoke.

"You make me feel beautiful. And strong."

"Because you *are* beautiful and strong. Rachel, you are wondrous. Your existence is magical and you are fucking meant to be right here with me."

She found herself crying. No matter how hard she tried to stop she couldn't.

"Shhh, Rachel, it's all right. You can be scared. I'm scared too." He paused.

Rachel wanted to stop spewing all the things that freaked her out but it was like the tears had loosened the normally high walls she kept around her fears.

Through her tears she managed to choke out, "What happens when you find out that thing, that one thing you don't know about me already that makes you hate me?"

"Are you a cannibal?"

"Don't make fun," she said but she snorted. God, she was probably at the puffy ugly cry snot-face stage so she turned over and fumbled for a tissue to mop her face up with.

"I'm not making fun. You're not the only one who is scared. I'm terrified because you leave me absolutely bare. There's nothing I can do to keep you out of the heart of me. You have free rein. We'll find out things about each other that we don't like, but I know your heart. And you know mine."

She froze. Caught between the urge to roll away—to get out of bed, get dressed and rebuild that distance between them—and the desire to be fearless and let him in.

"Just promise me you won't run. Be brave. Let yourself be happy with me," he told her. "I want to make you happy. I want to help you feel less alone."

What if she had no courage left?

She was quiet a long time as she thought. "Okay. I'll try."

CHAPTER NINETEEN

RACHEL WENT IN to Whiskey Sharp three days later. She got caught up in a hug from her sister before she'd even gotten five steps.

"Hi there," Maybe told her before she left a big red lipstick kiss on Rachel's cheek.

"I'm leaving it because it makes my life look very exciting to strangers," Rachel told her of the kiss print.

"Come sit and have a drink. Vic ran out with Gregori to get food about twenty minutes ago. I like Wren a lot. And she's clearly got very excellent taste in new artists. You're smiling like you have a really good thing to tell me so tell me."

"I don't think you even took a breath during that whole thing," Rachel told her. "I just got a call from the attorney."

Maybe's eyes widened like she was about to open a present. "So? What did she say?"

"The judge dismissed the conservatorship after she looked over the response with all the medical and mental health stuff. I'm free. We're done with them."

Rachel hugged her sister, willing herself not to cry though she was so relieved it made her weak in the knees.

They both sat, holding hands. "Finally." Maybe

locked her gaze with Rachel's. "Will this make him go away?"

"There's a chance he will. That they'll go back to California or Arizona and leave us alone for good."

Maybe arched a brow. "What about that other chance?"

"I spent a lot of time studying all manner of nature's freaky assholes. Dad's flavor is all bound up in me and my choices. What I do. How I do it. There's a chance, a good one, he won't walk away. He might limp off to lick his wounds awhile. Either way I think that'll happen. But he'll be back eventually."

She hated that part. But life sometimes meant you had to deal with people you didn't like. And when he did come back Rachel would defend herself and her sister. Would protect her life in Seattle and not let Richie Dolan ruin what they'd created.

"What's going on?" Alexsei asked as he approached.

Maybe told him before she launched herself into his arms. He buried his face in her sister's hair, eyes closed, a smile on his face and she wanted that from Vic so badly she headed up the block to the entrance to the residential part of the building. Gregori and Wren lived on the second floor in a newly renovated loft that had consolidated the unit across the hall.

They were all set to eat pizza and tacos while watching a hockey game. The cousins were bananas for hockey and it was sort of cute to watch them together. The others often stopped in. Cristian and his fiancé Seth. Nicklaus, who worked at the bakery with Vic. Evie came over from time to time as well, which Rachel liked. Even if it meant Rada came along.

Vic was waiting at the door when the elevator let her

out on Wren and Gregori's floor. "You look like you have something good to share," he said.

Unable not to grin, she hurried along to him, meeting him halfway and climbing up his body and into his arms.

"*Tigryonak*, you're the best thing I've had in my arms since the last time I held you."

"Our lawyer called," she said in his ear before she nibbled on it a moment. "The conservatorship was dismissed."

He squeezed her as he put her down. People got off the elevator at her back so she unfortunately had to stop rubbing on him.

"We have a lot to celebrate then, don't we?"

"Yeah. Hell yeah."

Alexsei came in with Maybe at his side and inside the loft a crowd of their friends already waited.

"What's the good news?" Cora said as she bounced in, her arms full of grocery bags she set on a nearby table.

They sat at the long farmhouse table in the main room, passing food, cracking open sodas and beers and the bottles of champagne always present whenever Gregori was.

Rachel's face hurt from smiling so hard. Something that hadn't happened nearly as much before she'd started dating Vic.

Dating. Ha. A pretty pale word for what they had.

She hadn't grown up around a lot of extended family other than her parents. Her aunt Robbie hadn't been much more than cards at their birthdays and the occasional visit when she'd been in Southern California.

But somehow she had ended up with a full room of intentional family. Friends who'd pulled her and Maybe into their lives and had been loyal and supportive and had filled her life with so much goodness.

She leaned her head on Vic's shoulder.

Satisfied.

SEVERAL HOURS LATER they were alone at Vic's place. She'd retreated a little, settling in a deep club chair with her sketchpad. But she was in his house. Spending time with him and he didn't need her focused on him every moment.

That she was comfortable enough to hang out, not dependent on him to entertain or keep her busy meant a lot.

"Vic? Someone's at the door," Rachel told him with a smirk that said she'd known he was watching her so intently he hadn't heard the knocking.

When he opened up, his sister stood there. "Hi. Feed me," she said as she breezed inside, pulling up short when she caught sight of Rachel. She lifted a hand. "Hey, Rachel. Sorry, I interrupted something. I'll come back later."

"Hey, Evie. No need to leave. You said you were hungry? There's leftover pizza in the fridge," Rachel told her before going back to her sketchbook.

Vic grinned at his sister, who visibly relaxed. "Get me a beer while you're up too."

Evie brought him a beer and a glass of water for Rachel.

"We missed you tonight at Gregori's," he told her.

"I drove Mom and all the rest of the ladies to the casino and hung out with them so I could drive them all back when they were done. And by the way, have you seen how much they can drink? I honestly had to roll more than one of them into the car at the end and threaten to kick anyone out if they barfed. Mom won a few hundred bucks at the slot machines. Tipped me fifty for being their driver she said."

Vic snorted. "Look at it this way, the next few times they go, someone else will play chaperone."

Evie snickered. "To be totally honest with you? They're all a hoot. They've set sail to I-Don't-Give-A-Fuck Island and it's fun to hang out with them."

Rachel laughed. "Your mother and her friends are definitely a hoot. They all know so much and it's spooky and awesome at the same time."

Vic warmed at the words. He loved that Rachel understood how magic his mother was.

"Tonight they were telling me stories about all the men who'd done them wrong and how they'd gotten even. I learned some stuff, let me tell you. If Vic messes up, let me know," Evie told Rachel.

The two had warily been making attempts at getting to know one another not just as neighbors, but much more like family. Now that Rachel was doing Evie's ink, they'd been around one another a lot without Vic around.

It pleased him to see.

Rachel winked at Vic before she thanked Evie for the offer.

Evie looked to Rachel and then back to Vic. There was something she wanted to tell him but didn't know if she could say it in front of Rachel.

Vic tipped his chin to indicate it was okay with him so it was up to Evie.

"Tonight when I stopped by to pick Mom up, I overheard one of them tell her the girl's parents are talking about Danil again. Trying to stir up trouble for Mom and Dad at church," Evie said at last.

Rachel was paying attention, but remained silent.

Danil's old girlfriend had been with him when he'd died. Her family had blamed—rightfully in part—Danil for their daughter's descent into opiate addiction.

"Did you talk to Mom about it?" he asked his sister.

"No. She avoided being alone with me all night long so I figure she doesn't want to talk about it. I thought you'd want to know."

"Did Aunt Klara say anything?" Gregori's mother was Irena's sister and they were very close.

"When I dropped Mom off, Aunt Klara stayed there so I think they were going to talk about it." Evie looked into Vic's eyes. "This is going to open up all those wounds again."

Vic went to her, taking her hands. "I've told you before, this is something they're always going to be hurt by. Something you and I will always be hurt by too. He was our brother and their son. And *that girl* is someone's daughter and sister." He smiled at her softly. "Thank you for telling me. I promise to keep an eye on her. They surface once a year or so. I guess it's time. They'll go away if we don't engage."

His little sister looked sad a moment. She'd been barely eighteen back when Danil had died. Barely more than a kid and for most of her life their brother had been a fuckup of one type or another.

She'd grown up with an addict in the house and it had left a mark. On him too.

"How's the tattoo healing up?" Rachel asked her, artfully changing the subject so Evie would feel better.

"Itchy. But it's all good. I take it we'll have you and Maybe with us this weekend?"

The bakery had a table at a food fair that weekend at Seattle Center and the Dolan sisters would naturally be there to help. His mother hadn't even asked, which Rachel and Maybe seemed charmed by.

His mother had strange and wondrous powers of persuasion.

"Yes you do. I'll see you bright and early Saturday morning," Rachel said.

"Cool. Mom can't stop talking about you. So keep on being good to Vic so she can keep being happy. She's a bear when she's not happy."

That made Rachel chortle a little. "I'll try to keep it up. It's not that hard, your brother is pretty cute and your mother brings me food."

"She bakes for you when she loves you," Evie told her. "Kidding aside, you're good to her. You let her teach you stuff and that makes her so happy."

Rachel shook her head. "It's the other way around. It's your mom who lets me learn from her. She's ridiculously patient with me, though she did crack my knuckles with that flat wooden spoon of hers once."

The three of them shuddered a moment. His mom was small but unexpectedly quick with that spoon if you got out of line.

"It's always wise to stay out of reach when she's got that spoon," Vic advised. "Think of her like a crocodile. She can leap."

The three of them dissolved into laughter.

"Anyway, she's opened her kitchen to me and I know that's the heart of your family. So I'm honored she'd think I was worthy. And she's got great stories."

Before Vic could stop it, his sister piped up immediately demanding to know what stories.

Rachel's glance in his direction told him the story
was going to be about him in some way and he braced
himself.

"She told me about the time there was a kitten in the
big evergreen in your backyard and how you climbed
up to get it and then once you handed the kitten off
you puked all over her because you'd been terrified
the whole time but didn't realize it until you'd handed
your cargo off."

"Did you meet Ashes or just hear the story?" Vic
asked of their fat, persnickety old family cat.

"He came out to hang with me and your dad while
we had our tea. Your mother sneaked little bits of meat
to him when she thought no one was looking."

"She acted like she was going to make us find a
home for him at first. But she's the one who started
calling him Ashes. My dad shook his head at her and
said, 'Now you've done it' and went on with his life."

"Your mom has a crunchy exterior but on the inside she's all goo. Not that she won't cut a bitch who
messes with her or her family, but you know what I
mean," Rachel said.

"What's your mom like?" Evie asked. "I mean, if
you want to talk about it and you probably don't. So no
big deal, let's pretend I never asked."

"The conservatorship was tossed out today. So I'm
feeling free tonight. I can tell you what she was like
for me. But I will also tell you that's not who mothered
Maybe. She was different for both of us in some ways.
Anyway. Compared to your mom, mine is a lot smaller.
She takes up less space. She doesn't have opinions in the

same way. I mean, she's got opinions on everything, but unless it's about clothes or hair, my dad told her what to think and that's how she believes."

"Clearly that didn't rub off on you or Maybe," he muttered, startling Rachel into a laugh.

"She tucked me in every night of my childhood. Put bandages on my scrapes, attended my school stuff like softball games and spelling bees. Took pictures of my dresses on formal dance nights. But her kitchen was perfect when she wasn't cooking. So there was no hanging out and drinking tea in there. There was no rummaging through the fridge for snacks. No thrown-together popcorn-for-dinner night with string cheese and an orange because you were tired or hadn't gone to the grocery store."

"She's like the anti-Irena," Evie said.

Vic exclaimed, intending to rein his sister in. But Rachel said, "Ha! Yes, pretty much. Like for real I get that your mother is ride-or-die for your dad. You can see it in how they are with one another. But she's not his messenger. Not unless she wanted to be. She's got her own opinions. Her own mind. And she might whack you with that spoon but she accepts her kids for who they are and she'd never allow anyone to harm them."

Which was totally true. And why they'd been so utterly devastated when Danil had died. They'd failed to protect their child. It didn't matter that he'd been an adult. It didn't matter that they'd tried time and again to get him help and he'd relapsed every time.

"SHE'LL NEVER GET over the failure she feels about Danil," Vic told Rachel later, after Evie had dashed off home.

"Your mom or Evie?"

"Both probably. God knows we all have guilt about it."

"So his girlfriend's parents go to the same church as your parents?" Rachel asked.

"We all used to go to the same church. They weren't close family friends, but of course we knew them. And when she ended up with Danil they became enmeshed with us. The arrests. Danil stole from them, she stole from my parents. They blamed him and I can't fault that. He assaulted their child. It doesn't matter that she was an addict too. He did what he did. My parents blamed her and I suppose that's true as well.

"When he died, her parents were absolutely vicious. They started rumors, caused more than one person to disconnect from my parents because they were just trying to get away from the drama."

Vic snuggled into the chair with her and she perched in his lap, pulling the blanket over them both.

"My family had lost Danil forever, but their kid was alive. But not returned to them. She's still an addict. Still on the streets. It was impossible for my parents to grieve much less heal when the place they should have been able to receive solace from had become yet another situation they had to navigate. So they left that church and started attending the other in town. It turns out it was a good move. My mom has a home there. Friends. She's active and connected and it's best for everyone that they made the change."

"But they're back? They can't just be satisfied with what they've got given the comparison with what your parents have?"

Rachel was indignant on their behalf and he hugged

her before continuing. "It has always felt to me like if they truly let it go they'll have to admit they might never save their daughter before she too ends up dead like Danil. What parent wants to admit that? So they pop up once a year or so and attempt to make trouble."

"What can I do?" Rachel asked.

What had he done in his life to deserve her?

"She might need a little extra attention over the next week or so. Her friends will circle around her to protect her the best they can. She needs to stay busy," Vic said as he kissed the top of her head.

"What about your dad? I know he likes to make her life easier. It's got to be hard on him. Harder because this must gut your mom and he can't make it better."

Vic was beginning to understand that very thing. He wanted to protect Rachel and her artist's heart and soul and he couldn't. Not from everything.

"He'll want to run interference. Try to be the wall between her and whatever is happening."

His father had been down the darkest hole after Danil's death. Had felt the sting of failure like his mother had. But he felt he'd failed Irena too. Not just Danil, but his wife, the mother of his children.

"And you?" She traced the line of his cheek. "What do you need? You're the big brother. The oldest son who wants to protect his mom and dad from hurt. How can I make it better for you?"

"You do. Every day." He hugged her and they stayed that way for a long while afterward.

CHAPTER TWENTY

RACHEL SLID OFF his lap to put some music on. She felt lighter, a combination of not having this conservatorship hanging over her head any longer and having someone else's troubles to try to soften.

"Pistol" by alxxa played as she held a hand out his way. He got up, slow and graceful like a big cat.

"Can I tell you something slightly embarrassing and I'm really hoping you don't think it's too weird?" she asked.

He got close enough to wrap an arm around her shoulders and pull her close as they started to dance.

"Please do," he teased after she'd been quiet for so long it was clear she was waiting for an answer.

"I made you a playlist," she said, blushing furiously.

His smile widened. "You did? That's...well that's sexy as fuck."

Kehlani's "Do You Dirty" came on and she allowed herself to be pleased he liked it so much.

"A playlist for a music lover is an intimate gift," he said as he nuzzled his way from her temple down to the place where her neck met her shoulder. He blew over the skin there and she gulped in air like a drowning woman. "I'm certain no one has made me one in at least a decade."

How could she explain how silly and light he made

her feel? How stupid in like—it was more, she knew it but she was still dancing around it—she was with him.

"You put an extra lock on your door and you fixed your window latch. For me. So I'd come over here more often. That's pretty intimate too."

He hummed and then licked her collarbone. How he made such a simple thing so ridiculously hot she didn't know. But he just…well he just swamped her with so much pleasure she held on and tried to give as good as she got.

But damn it, she'd started this and he was taking over. Not that it was a bad thing, but she had plans.

She whipped his shirt off and skated her open mouth over the tendons in his neck as she backed him against the wall, dragging her nails up his sides and over his belly.

He snarled a curse as he let her lead.

She licked over his ink, pausing at his piercing. So fucking sexy. The totality of him was overwhelming and all she wanted to do was roll around with him. The beauty of it was that she *could*.

"Mine," she said, nibbling over his ribs.

"Most definitely yours," he told her as he grabbed two handfuls of her ass, hauling her close. "And you, my beautiful tiger, are all mine."

She let her head tip back on a laugh. "Lucky you."

"You'll get no argument from me on that point. I am very lucky."

She was totally sure it was the other way around but it didn't matter. They were together.

And she wasn't going to question it. Not that night.

She wanted to show him what she thought of him. How she saw his sexiness. How much she wanted him.

His intake of breath as she dropped to her knees thrilled her. She knew what it felt like to be the one standing.

Her gaze locked with his, she unbuttoned and unzipped his pants, carefully pulling them past his cock and then once the metal was at his ankles, she drew his shorts down as well, freeing all the bounty she'd just openly claimed just a few minutes before.

It was her turn to hum her satisfaction as she rubbed her cheek against that velvet-soft skin, turning her mouth so she could lick around the head and crown.

She stayed there for some time, simply licking and kissing him, slowly building him up to climax. Rachel loved the way his skin smelled, the way the heat of his body seemed to stir a new scent, one heady, laced with sex.

It made her eyelids heavy, her limbs warm.

Both his hands gripped her skull, his fingers wrapped in her hair. For a moment it was too much. She froze, her muscles locked up. Memory threatening.

He leaned down, gentling his hold. "Come back to me, *tigryonak.*"

"I'm here," she managed to say as she fought her way off the ledge of her memories. "I'm here," she repeated.

He got to his knees to face her. "Tell me what you want. I need you to be right here or we have to stop."

"Stop being so fucking perfect," she said.

He grinned. "I can't. I was born this way."

Rachel reached out to grab his cock. "I'm here. I'm good to go. I want you, Vic. Right now."

He studied her face for long moments. "Not here in the living room. You deserve a bed with soft blankets against your skin."

"Sometimes a girl might want a little rug burn on her knees," she said.

"Jesus. Now who's perfect, eh?" he teased as he pushed her back to the rug she'd been kneeling on. He unbuttoned the front of her sweater and popped the catch to free her breasts.

"The answer hasn't changed from my perspective," she wheezed out as he dived in, kissing and licking her neck and chest and then down to her nipples. His weight—weight he was normally very careful not to rest on her fully—kept her pressed in place, the rough weave of the carpet pressing into her back.

"You asked what I wanted," she said. "I want you to fuck me. No holding back. I want all of you."

The intensity of his expression seared her.

"If I give you all of me, I demand the same of you. No more holding back. I might be easygoing with most things, Rachel, but I love hard, it turns out. Absolutely. You're tough. Strong. You're a survivor. Mine."

He reared back enough to get at her button and zipper while she watched emotions play over his features.

She froze, feeling exposed. Not in fear. But in recognition.

But what really got her was the way he continued to pull her pants and panties free. Gaze still locked on hers.

That trust between them was always there. Time and again he'd only put his strength to use in her defense or in her favor. Never to harm her.

"Okay then," she said at last.

To Vic it seemed sort of perfect that she'd given herself to him with an *okay then*.

Nearly as scorching hot as her comment about rug burn.

She was a continual delight. Surprising him. Underlining what a beautiful, sexy, intelligent creature he'd fallen for.

He teased the head of his cock around her clit as he dipped to kiss her. "Okay then for me too."

He loved the way the light danced in her eyes as she snorted a laugh. A bolt of something pleasant but edged with a bit of terror hit his belly as he had a thought about telling the *Okay Then* story to their kids someday.

When he straightened again, she scooted quickly to wrap her legs around his waist.

Struck with the wanton beauty spread out before him, he paused to take stock of his blessings. A stream of Russian burst forth, lines of poetry about curves, shadow and fog, the bliss of woman.

She still wore the remnants of her sweater and bra, nipples hard and dark, standing out against the pale, unseen skin of the under curve of her breasts. Her eyes had gone glossy with pleasure.

The scent of her desire rose with the heat of her. Tickled and seduced his senses. In the entirety of his life he'd never encountered the like of it.

"Get that condom on, *Vitya*. You have a job to do."

He bent back to dig around in a nearby drawer where he'd stashed some condoms once they'd begun dating. She unwrapped herself long enough for him to get the rubber on.

Then she was back, her long, lithe legs encircling him, holding him in place. The cant of her mouth told him she wanted what she wanted and he'd better deliver. Damn if he didn't adore her.

When he didn't immediately comply and thrust into her, she gave him a grumpy sort of growl, rolling her hips against him. Urging him on.

"Be patient. I want to be sure you're ready," he murmured as he slid the pad of his thumb from side to side over her clit.

She began to argue—naturally—but it died on her lips as she moaned softly instead. Bingo. His lovely Rachel did so enjoy climaxing. And heaven knew he loved to help her get there.

She arched, grinding herself against him as he slowly began to push inside. Even through the latex the heat of her shot up his spine. Moonlight cast silvery fingers over her skin and a fierce need to always keep her safe drove him to settle in to the root and then pull back nearly all the way.

Only to reverse and make that same sweet journey. Keeping time with slow sweeps over her clit.

Again and again as the heat between them built. As his need to come clawed through his gut so he clung by the barest margin. Needing her to come first. Wanting that clasp all around him as she hit her peak.

He craved that blindness that took over her gaze… Ahh, like she had now as she rocketed toward orgasm. All around his cock she superheated.

"More," she whispered. "Harder."

He obliged, adjusting the depth and force of his thrusts. A fire raged through him. The exquisite knife's edge of perfect *just-right* between too much and not enough.

He danced there with her. With her body tightening around his as she began to come on a gasp and a snarl of his name. He waited as long as he could, savoring her pleasure until there was nothing left to do but follow her into climax.

Vic rolled up to his feet and returned shortly with

a throw from the couch. "I'm all over moving to a bed when my legs work again," she muttered as she pillowed her head on his biceps as they lay on his living room floor.

"Just let me know when you're ready," he said, amused.

"By the way, I totally have rug burn. I need to check that off my life list."

"Me too," he told her. "On my knees."

"I'll be checking that off my life bucket list too. Give supremely sexy man some action hot enough to give him rug burn. Boom."

He kissed the top of her head, breathing her in. "Just part of the service I provide."

CHAPTER TWENTY-ONE

RACHEL OPENED VIC'S front door to find him on the porch, his arms full of bags so she moved to the side so he could come in.

"Hi there. What's in those?" she asked, indicating the things he'd just put on his dining room table.

"Look inside and see," he tossed back over his shoulder as he headed into the kitchen to rustle around like a raccoon.

She paused a bit to watch his butt before she poked around and pulled out a beautiful blown glass hummingbird feeder.

"Oh," she said softly.

"Do you like it?" he said as he returned to her side. "I bought several different kinds of feeders for the yard. I figured you'd know best where to put everything but I did some research to see what was best to feed what kind of birds and I checked your shed to see what you use."

She poked through, pulling out the different feeders and feed from peanuts to suet cakes.

Some people liked lingerie, she loved birds. Vic paid attention. He knew what mattered to her. His gifts were quite often like this one and showed how well he listened.

"This is all really amazing." She held up a tray feeder. "Thank you."

"I just want my house to be a place you feel happy in," he said. "And I want the birds to come around. And you like birds. And butterflies too. So I got some stuff the guy at the nursery said butterflies like. That's out in the yard. You could show me where to put it."

Rachel put the feeder down and moved to him. "You're such a catch."

"I know, right?" he asked, imitating her.

She hugged him tight, enjoying how absurdly happy she was at that very moment.

"Let's go and put it all up," he said as he tugged her toward the door.

"Then I'll teach you how to make hummingbird nectar. But only if you're good."

He turned back to her. "But what do I get if I'm bad?"

"A whole different kind of nectar. Though to be totally honest, you can have it either way."

"I am so fucking lucky it's not even funny," he murmured as he bent to kiss her quickly.

Said the man who actually researched to see which birds were native to the area, what types of feeders they needed and what sort of things they ate. All because his girlfriend loved birds.

Rachel reminded herself to tell Pavel and Irena they'd done a great job with Vic. Stuff like that was tricky because of Danil, but it was true anyway. They had done a wonderful job with the two adult children they'd raised.

And that was before he reached into the hall closet and pulled out a hat he plopped down on her head. "Protect yourself from the sun." He kissed her nose.

She showed him how to fill the tall feeder with black oil sunflower seeds and where to put the suet cakes.

"How do you know all this stuff?" he asked. "Did you love birds...before?"

"I've always liked birds. At summer camp they taught us basic bird calls. What to look for. What birds went where. The usual stuff. And then, when there was nothing else, there was birds." She lifted a shoulder. "I'd been looking at bird stuff for a case back when I first started so I knew about East Coast birds too. I had nothing else in that basement but horror."

"I hate that." He shoved a hand through his hair, setting it free. "I hate that you have this thing, this *terrible* thing in your heart and memory and I can't punch it or kick it or scare it away."

He ducked into the house to grab her a throw and came back to the porch swing.

She could tell him it made a difference to her to know he felt that way. But she figured he knew.

"I couldn't turn it off," she said at last. "When I was being held I couldn't turn off being an agent. Everything I heard. Everything that happened and was said I cataloged. I was building a case the whole time. Even when I didn't want to."

There'd been no turning it off. No falling into that place some of the others had. Instead of numb she'd been hyperaware.

He put an arm around her shoulders and she leaned against him.

"Even as I built my case, even as he did the things he did to those other women, I also knew that when I got out I wasn't ever going back to the FBI. Like I got burned out, all those circuits just wouldn't stop working so I'd have to channel something else, be someone else. That's part of what got me through. The idea of surviving just so I could win, so that the new Rachel could survive."

"I'm glad you survived, Rachel."

"So I can make you spend money on making your yard bird-friendly?"

"So my life can be full of the best thing to ever happen to me. And yes, so I can spend money making my yard bird-friendly because then it's also Rachel-friendly."

"I already let you see my boobies. You're being very sweet. Is this to get me to let you do butt stuff?"

The look on his face before he burst out laughing was worth telling him a piece of her past.

"I do have a fondness for your boobies. Butt stuff?" He shrugged. "Maybe on my birthday."

He really was perfect.

IT SATISFIED VIC that she liked to be at his house. That she was comfortable there. Sure the bird feeders were a lure, but it wasn't like he didn't enjoy birds and butterflies anyway.

The change had been happening slowly over the last several weeks. There was a stack of her bracelets on the neck of the water bottle she always kept next to her side of the bed.

She was always cold so there were fleece throws tossed over the back of the chairs and couch. Her Wonder Woman travel mug sat on his counter.

"Every time I see a goldfinch I'm going to think of you from now on," he said, taking her hand.

"When I see a goldfinch I'm always so amazed such

a thing exists. So beautiful. Even with winter plumage they're beautiful. And by the way, your mother has looked out the window of what I think is the guest bathroom at us. Three times now."

He sighed. "But do let me remind you I have a big dick."

Her snicker made him smile. "I think it's sort of cute. She's worried about you."

Vic scoffed. "She's worried about *you*."

"Me? Why?"

"Because that's what mothers do. And she senses the hurt in you and she wants to help with tea and cookies."

"It's what *your* mother does. It's sweet that she includes me. Did you tell her I'm more than capable of putting anyone down who comes at me?" she asked.

"She knows that what has the power to hurt you most isn't always about size. It's about your heart."

They were both quiet awhile, rocking, listening to the rain that fell on and off until a car skidded to a stop in front of his parents' house.

She sat up at the same time he did, the blanket falling to the side as she put her feet down.

"Who is that?" she asked, that soft voice sharpened into what he bet was her special agent voice.

"I don't know."

They both stood and without a word, headed down the yard toward the street.

A woman roughly Irena's age got out of the passenger side. The younger woman in the driver's seat followed, a phone at her ear.

It was the mother of Danil's old girlfriend and if he wasn't mistaken, the driver was the sister.

"Excuse me," he called out to them. The older one

looked over at him and hustled herself in an arc toward the front steps of his parents' house.

"You two, stop where you are," Rachel barked out. Demanded. Ordered.

They both came to a halt.

Rachel's walk had changed. She held herself with a different type of power and damned if it didn't knock him out. So sexy.

He pulled himself away from his dirty fantasies and to the problem at hand. These women were going to make trouble for his parents.

Again.

Rachel strode up and got between the women and the front porch. Vic stood at her side and did his best to look imposing.

"Get out of the way," the younger one said.

"You're going to need to turn yourselves around and leave now. Whatever you're selling, the Orlovs aren't interested in buying," Rachel told them.

At their back, Vic heard his father order his mother to stay inside and call Seth before he came outside.

"They were just leaving, *Pasha*," Rachel said without turning around.

"Murderer!" the mother shrieked and Rachel stepped closer to her.

"I said *stop that right now*."

The whip crack in Rachel's tone seemed to yank all the energy from the other woman.

"You don't know what he's done," the other woman whispered.

"I know he's not the reason your daughter is an addict. I know he's not the cause of your troubles. I know he means a great deal to me and I'm not going to let you hurt him. You're lucky you have a chance, no matter how small. He never will again."

Vic swallowed back the emotion at the way she'd just defended his family as he stepped forward, keeping his father behind them both.

"Go. Tend to your own heartache. I won't allow you to bring any more here," Vic told them in Russian.

Rachel took his hand, squeezing it a moment before she stepped forward, easing the women back a little.

"I understand that you're hurting," Rachel told them in a soft but firm voice. "But you will not be allowed to harass and intimidate this family anymore. Are we clear?" She took the mother's arm and led her down the walk to the curb.

Vic told his father to stay put to keep his mom safe. But really it was an effective way to get his dad to obey while Vic kept at the ready to deal with anything these women wanted to hurl his parents' way.

He overheard Rachel saying, "No. I don't want to hear any more of that. They had nothing to do with Danil's addiction. Or your daughter's. I feel bad for you. I imagine it's a terrible thing to deal with a child who's an addict. But the Orlovs are victims too. They've lost more than you have. They're living your nightmare. You're hurting them and it's not going to make your daughter better. I'm urging you to get the help you need. Even if you can't get your daughter help, you can make sure your other children and you and your spouse are getting assistance. It's not easy loving someone with a substance abuse problem. They can help you learn some coping skills."

"They're bad people. Get away from them before

they do to you what they did to our daughter," the older woman urged.

Rachel said something quietly as she opened the door.

They got into the car and drove off.

"What did you say to get them to go?" he asked her.

"They're in pain. I let them know that mattered to me but also that they weren't going to stomp all over your parents to feel better."

"You made them feel heard. That was some top-notch de-escalation."

"It's nice to use my former job skills in a non-life-threatening way. Come on. Let's go in and let your mom make tea. She's going to be upset after all this." Rachel looked back across the way to his house. "I'll go make sure everything is off and locked up and meet you back here shortly, all right?"

It would also give him a chance to talk to his parents privately, which she knew he needed.

"They're gone. Rachel made them leave," his dad told his mom.

"They'll be back. They always come back."

"Did you call any police other than Seth?" Vic asked as he poured already hot water into a nearby teapot.

"There's no use. They didn't even come to the door. They left without threatening anyone. It just gives them attention when we call the police," his mother said.

A knock sounded on the front door and as Rachel was coming inside, Alexsei and Maybe pulled up next door so he knew they'd be by shortly too.

Rachel gave his mother a hug and made her a cup of tea and another for his dad.

It had been a crappy moment in time, but damn if he didn't love this woman and the way she treated his family.

RACHEL FOUND IRENA in her sewing room. She sat, some mending on her lap as she stared out the window. Rachel put a mug of tea, the kind with a lid so it wouldn't ruin anything the older woman might be working on, on a table near her.

"Figured you might want something warm. I can leave you alone if you'd prefer. Talk if you want. Not talk. Whatever. I just wanted you to know I'm here if you need me."

Irena looked away from the window, smiling a little at Rachel.

"Thank you, sweetheart. Sit. There's a little bottle in that button box on the shelf behind you. Whiskey goes better in tea, I think. And today calls for what I'm told is called a belt."

Rachel dug out the little bottle of whiskey, handing it to Irena, who poured a healthy dollop in her mug.

"Danil died seven years ago," Irena said. "Evie was barely eighteen. Vicktor wasn't too much older at twenty-four. They, the girl, her name is Elizabeta, her parents they do show up about once a year to harass us. But it's usually in the early fall. He died on September 26."

"Why do they come to you when it was your child who died? Was she there too?"

"They say he tried to kill her. That she was fine before that, but his death pushed her over the edge and that's what sent her addiction into a death spiral."

"That was seven years ago? The edge they mean?" Rachel asked. She needed to poke around a little to see what these parents were up to. The mother had muttered something about the Orlovs trying to steal someone's money as she'd gotten in the car earlier.

Rachel wanted to do some research so she could get some basic answers to her questions without making anyone upset. The last thing she wanted to do was make Irena sad.

She wanted to protect the Orlovs and in order to do so, she needed to see more of the big picture.

"I am not a fool," Irena said. "I know what Danil was. Even from an early age he had trouble with limits. He was hard to manage but so good at telling you what you wanted to hear until you believed it. And after a time it was that I was too tired not to believe it. They did the drugs together, you understand?"

Rachel nodded. "Even if he had been a mustache-twirling villain, it's not about you. They don't get to hurt you like this. You've been hurt enough."

"What's enough? When you lose a child what is enough to hurt?"

Rachel fought back her own emotion as she leaned to touch Irena's arm. "It doesn't mean you torture yourself forever. I didn't know Danil, but I know Vicktor and I know Evie and I can't imagine Danil would want you to punish yourself like this."

"What kind of mother's son kills himself that way?" Irena whispered.

"Tens upon thousands of mothers' sons and daughters. Wives and husbands. Sisters, brothers, cousins, neighbors and friends. The opioid epidemic is killing tens of thousands and it doesn't care about how much you loved your son. But you did. You did all you could.

Knowing what you did at the time. You did all you could according to your ability. That's literally all you can do."

"It's one thing to hear it and understand it. It's another thing to believe it in your heart."

"I know. That's the struggle. To believe what you know is true. I'm sorry they upset you," Rachel told her. "I wish I could make it all go away." It tore her up to see Irena this upset. That's when she realized Irena had become a mother to her in a very real way. Rachel was more emotionally connected and invested with Irena than she'd ever been with her biological mother.

Jeez. She was checking off a lot in the life lessons category today.

"When Danil died, everything went dark for a while. I had so much to do, two other kids to love and care for, a husband, a job. But I just…" Irena held her hands up. "It sort of drifted away through my fingers. It was Vicktor who set aside everything in his life to help. He held the bakery together. He takes this very hard."

"I understand about everything being dark for a while. I've lived through similar darkness. As for the rest, well, Vicktor is proof of what an amazing mother you are and how much you love your children. Of course he held the bakery together, that's who you raised him to be." Vic was a *good* man.

Irena's sly gaze was back, which despite being slightly terrifying, cheered Rachel up.

She grinned at Vic's mom. "What are you up to?"

Irena laughed, putting aside her mending to hug Rachel.

"That'd be telling. But I do approve of the way you talk about *Vityunya*. Let's go back into the living room. *Pasha* will be worried."

"Is it all right with you if I look into this whole thing with your brother's overdose and whatever this current attack might be inspired by?" Rachel asked Vic as Evie allowed Irena to cluck over her and spoil her with a BLT, one of her favorite things to eat.

He said, "You don't have to. I don't want to bring more drama into your life." She saw the stress on his features. The helpless worry there. It tugged at her.

The last thing she wanted was for him to feel caught between her and his parents. Especially when she just wanted to help share his load the way he'd done with her.

"I wouldn't have offered if I didn't want to. I can do this. I've got the skills and some good connections and it'll help me get things straight in my head so I can best offer my help for the next step."

For a while he studied her features until he finally sighed and leaned in to kiss her forehead. "Then thank you. Let me know if I can help."

CHAPTER TWENTY-TWO

"So, ANY TIPS about Alexsei's mom you want to give me so I can pass them on all sly to Maybe?" Rachel asked Vic.

It had always seemed to Rachel that Alexsei was far closer to Irena, who'd been raising him since his teens, than his biological mother who still lived in Moscow with her gangster husband.

She always kept the gangster part in her head. But she wasn't stupid. Given the details she'd heard about Polina's lifestyle and the identity of her current husband, it wasn't difficult to put it together.

A simple internet search brought up more than enough to confirm her suspicions.

Rachel didn't feel entirely comfortable about it, but as long as no crimes happened and she didn't became aware of any, she'd keep her opinions to herself.

Unless asked.

She was, however, not above getting some insider dirt on how her sister might impress the woman who would one day be her mother-in-law.

Things had gotten so deep and serious between Maybe and Alexsei over the last few months, Rachel didn't think it would be too much longer before they started to talk marriage.

"Alexsei knows how to handle her better than anyone

else," Vic said as he refilled her wine. They were trying out a new pizza place within walking distance of their neighborhood and so far it had been a hit.

"She and Mom will be happy the first hour and from then on it'll be waves of them fighting. Usually because Polina is a self-centered, selfish bitch who is at best only barely interested in her sons' lives. Sons who know my mother better than their own."

Rachel rarely saw Vic get this worked up and pissed off at someone other than her father and people who put raisins in salad.

"Sometimes it can be complicated between sisters," Rachel said as she grabbed another garlic knot.

He sniffed, indignant. "Yes. And my mother is not always the easiest person to deal with and in Polina's world, she is queen. She comes here expecting that and lets everyone know she's not getting what she expected."

"And your mother is the opposite type of person."

"Yes. That. You met her once when she was here last year. What was your impression?" he asked.

"Generally I share yours. It's difficult for me to imagine what Cristian and Alexsei would be like if they'd grown up with her instead of your parents. Your mom likes to fix things. Likes to help people." Which didn't mean Irena didn't like to be a little martyr sometimes. And like Polina, Vic's mom was queen of her world, though in a totally different way.

Rachel continued. "But my sister is in love with Alexsei and though he holds your mother as number one in his heart, he still wants Polina to approve of his life. Maybe wants that approval too, because it would please Alexsei. She too, in case you hadn't noticed, holds your mother as number one in her heart. And Maybe is my little sister and I want her to have the things that make *her* happy because she always puts everyone else first."

"Make sure Maybe gives her a good gift with some sort of visible brand on it," he said. "And bring flowers to pick her up from the airport. Send flowers to her room too."

"Okay, that can all happen easily enough. Maybe and I had a shopping date tomorrow anyway so we'll grab the present then. Flowers too as she's coming in on a late evening flight." Rachel grinned. "Thanks for all the info. It was really helpful and it'll give Maybe something to do about all her anxiety. She wants to be sure she's not making your mom feel bad either. So I figure I'll give your mom a little extra love, which will hopefully keep the peace a little more. I'll give her a present and some flowers too. Not when we're all together though."

An itching started at the back of her neck. Something was off. She looked up from her plate.

Vic responded to the change in her body language immediately. "What's wrong?" he asked. "Want another slice? They have gelato on the menu if you're feeling like something sweet."

She looked around the restaurant, toward the two doors and the wall of windows in between that looked out over the street beyond. Nothing inside looked out of place.

"Nothing. It's fine," she said, flicking most of her attention away from the world outside and back to him. "I'm just catching movement from outside. Just one of those things. Sometimes that part of me just turns on and I notice something feels off." One last survey of the room and she let it go for the time being.

"It's sexy that you're so capable and badass," he told her as he stole the last slice.

Some might call it paranoid but she appreciated his ability to see everything about her as sexy.

"I know you normally work at least one weekend day, but if it's far enough in advance maybe you could shift your schedule around?"

"Are you asking me to do something over a weekend?" she asked.

"Yes. Not this weekend as we have the engagement dinner for Seth and Cris on Saturday and the welcome party in Polina's honor on Friday. Cristian told me the engagement dinner isn't changing again." Polina had canceled her plans to visit twice now. But this time she'd actually made plane and hotel reservations so it looked like this was the real deal.

"In three weeks. At the end of April. We drive out on a Friday afternoon, stay in a hotel that night so we can hike in first thing Saturday to the campsite. We won't need to pack in tents because we've reserved yurts up there. You and I would have our own, by the way."

"So we don't bother anyone with our midnight games of Scrabble?" she asked.

"Loser has to make the winner come first," he said.

"Or we could skip the board games and just have a lot of sex. In a yurt. Which sounds like the ingredients for a dirty limerick."

"We kayak that afternoon. Something else we don't have to deal with bringing in. Plenty of fish to catch for dinner. We hike out Sunday afternoon and come home that night."

"There should be some excellent birding too. I'm in good shape and all, but a multiple day hike? What's the skill level here?"

"Intermediate. Most of the hike is relatively flat but there are a few inclines. Kayaking is pretty lazy. It's mainly a way to get around to look at all the wildlife around the shore. I think you can handle it no problem at all. And, since I'm being honest here, I'd really like you to meet my friends and they want to meet you too."

She could study the trail map so she was familiar with the area once they arrived. It'd give her some measure of control too.

"I can do that, yeah. It sounds good." She paused.

She'd gone and done what she'd said she was going to do and had looked at the circumstances around Danil's death. It wasn't too hard to dig up the basics. The years of attempts to get clean with times of intermittent sobriety. A juvenile record that'd been sealed but she was able to get the information from Alexsei. The girlfriend had been around since middle school on and off, like the sobriety. She hadn't been with Danil when he'd overdosed as she'd been arrested earlier that same day. Danil had done her share of the heroin too and that's what had been the final nail in his coffin.

"What?" he asked.

"I just wanted you to know I'd done the research into your brother's overdose. I couldn't see any reason for them to feel as if Danil is in the wrong here. She's still alive. Reportedly clean and doing a fifteen-month jaunt behind bars. There's nothing immediately obvious to point to why they've surfaced now instead of their normal time in the fall."

And what assholes these people were to harass Irena

and Pavel when they were the ones who'd lost a child while theirs was still alive.

"I spoke to Seth yesterday about this and he's looking into it as well. It's a positive to have him informed and he adores your parents."

"They approve of him for Cristian. They're both so different, but they fit. Cris brings more whimsy into Seth's life while Seth helps Cris keep his dreams on track. They're both strong. Naturally my mother approves of Seth being a cop."

"While Polina is not so excited?" Rachel said.

Vic snorted. "Consider the source. But, to be fair, there are massive problems with government corruption in Russia," he allowed.

After he finished and they'd settled up the bill he kissed her temple. "Thank you for keeping an eye on my parents."

"And you. Sometimes it's all a matter of finding exactly what the problem is and fixing it. Like is there something one of the parents needs to hear? A word or phrase? Not that your parents should do it or even worry about it because they're the victims here. But if they could just get what they needed and finally fuck off and leave your parents alone that'd be a good option too."

They began to walk back to his place.

"It's helpful because while you obviously care about my family, you have some distance and yes, I know my parents would appreciate bringing a resolution to this," Vic said as he took her hand, tucking her to his side farthest from the street.

His parents had raised him well and just because one of their kids made bad choices and something really awful happened to him didn't undo what an amazing job they'd done with Evie, Vic, Alexsei and Cristian.

And still that itching remained at the back of her neck until they turned down the block his house was on.

At his house—where she'd promised to sleep over that night already—she stayed awake longer than normal. Tucked in a chair, sketching as Vic slept in his bedroom not too far away she'd kept watch on the street outside.

Nothing else had made her feel uncomfortable in the hours since they'd left the restaurant but it was difficult to let go of. She was long past the nights where she'd had the shakes and left the lights and television on and if she got any sleep at all it'd been riddled with nightmares. But real-life monsters prowled the streets which was something she'd never forget.

"WHAT THE FUCK is a yurt?" Maybe asked her the next day as she looked through the wallets at a pricey leather goods store.

"It's sort of a cross between a tipi and a tent. I looked it up online. It has a decent size bed in it. Shared bathrooms but at least they have bathrooms. Even showers though it's still pretty rustic."

"Sounds like hell on earth," her sister muttered. "Naturally you'd find it awesome."

"What about gloves?" Rachel pointed some out. "I lose mine every year so when she wears these she'll think of you as someone who did something nice. Vic got me that pair for Valentine's Day and I think of him every time I pull them from my pocket."

"Unlike that ungrateful Seth who didn't get her a present when she came here the last time," Maybe joked.

"Ha! I'm going to guess he's going to shower her with presents this time. He wants to make Cristian happy and he did mess up before," Rachel said.

"Seven hundred dollars for a wallet. That's beyond ridiculous," Maybe said. "If Alexsei hadn't given me the money and ordered me to spend it all on presents for his mom from this place we'd be out of here."

"I'd buy you a seven-hundred-dollar wallet. If I had that much disposable income. Or maybe if it was your big birthday or a holiday present." Rachel lifted a shoulder.

"Yeah but you love me. I barely even know this woman. I've only spoken to her on the phone for like two minutes. Why should I give her a seven-hundred-dollar wallet just because I'm nailing her son?" Maybe asked, sounding a little hysterical.

"Well, it's Alexsei's money so it's really a way for him to be sure you give her the correct offering and, as it's ridiculous, he's handling it. That's what he should be doing." Rachel took the wallet from her sister and put it back down, settling on a pair of gloves and a scarf with it. "We'll take these. Please gift-wrap them," Rachel told the clerk.

"Things could be worse. I could be Cristian and Seth's party planner for this dinner on Saturday. Or Alexsei at all right now. Because Irena feels like having the dinner catered is an insult to her."

"We need to get her presents too. Not from here. Let's go to that kitchen store across the mall."

Maybe nodded, handing over her credit card and then signing the receipt.

"While we're here, stop by the florist on the ground floor and arrange to have flowers sent to Polina at her hotel while she's here. The last day send her a corsage of some kind so she can wear it while she's traveling. Or not, but you'd be playing dutiful and she can fly with that versus a vase of something. Seth has scheduled a massage for her and if I were you, I'd call over to the hotel and add a facial and a manicure to go with it."

"You are so awesomely sneaky. No wonder the FBI wants you back. How did you find all this out?"

At the kitchen store, they picked out a new baking pan and some utensils. Rachel had noted a certain kind of ladle Irena had used but complained about the handle so she grabbed a replacement for it as well.

All thoughtful gifts that would let Irena know they cared and had truly thought of her. It wouldn't embarrass her by being extravagant or useless either.

"I talked to Seth yesterday. Between you and him, Polina should be happy. Probably. Regardless, I think Cris and Alexsei will be pleased, which is what counts."

"When we stop to deal with the flowers let's go into that chocolate place and get a little something sweet for Irena. I want her to know she's my favorite without making any trouble for Alexsei," Maybe said. "I feel much better. Which is I'm sure what you'd planned from the start."

Rachel rolled her eyes and pretended to be bored.

"I'm not sure what I did to get not just one mother-in-law but two," Maybe grumbled.

"Something to tell me?"

"No. Not yet. I was just bitching. But not really because Irena is adorable and scary and I love her. I'm sure Polina has her pluses. She did get Cristian and Alexsei here, after all."

"Well there you go. Something to be thankful for

and we can just acknowledge the fact that she's got her flaws and move on. If she moves her ass over here we can have a whole different conversation."

"At least she's too fancy schmancy to want to move in."

"Ever the little optimist."

CHAPTER TWENTY-THREE

"AT LEAST MOST of the attention is on Polina or Cris and Seth," Maybe said under her breath.

Vic snorted in agreement.

Right at that moment Polina was trying to get Seth to submit and let her be in control. Seth wasn't giving in though. So, Cris was upset and Alexsei was attempting to soothe their mother and change the subject.

Vic didn't get anywhere near that mess. He had his own shit to shovel in his own ways, but he wasn't sorry it was Alexsei's job to deal with it.

"By the way, I saw the stuff you and Rachel got my mom. Nicely done."

"Your mom has been good to us since the first day we moved in. She and Rachel have become especially close, don't you think?" Maybe asked before taking a shot of ice-cold vodka.

"Does that bother you?" he asked.

"That Rachel and your mom are tight? No, I love it. It makes me happy. I have our aunt and now that our parents are no longer in our lives, she needs that maternal connection. And your mom and I have our own thing too. I adore her and she thinks I'm good for Alexsei. I have a lot of love in my life right now. I'm very fortunate."

Vic smiled at the woman Alexsei had fallen for. In

honor of Polina's visit, Maybe had tuned her blue hair down into a mahogany and the jewelry in her facial piercing was very minimalist. She was still totally herself, but she'd softened the edges for Alexsei's sake.

Polina demanded a tour of Maybe and Rachel's house so they all walked over next door. But at the porch, Rachel stopped and told him she'd be inside in a moment.

As hard as it was, he went in and let her do her thing because that's what she needed to do. Sometimes she just had to walk the perimeter to assure herself all was well and once she'd done that everything would be fine.

"Where did your friend go?" Polina asked Vic as he joined them all in the living room she'd just been complaining about the size of.

"She'll be back shortly." Polina was his aunt and still deserved respect, but she wasn't his mother and he wasn't really ready to tolerate any of her bullshit so he hoped she'd move on.

Which she did. "Why do you want to live here?" Polina asked Alexsei. "This place is as awful as your aunt and uncle's house. No offense," she added, not meaning it at all.

"I can't imagine why anyone would take offense to that," Alexsei said in Russian.

"You were raised better," she replied, also in Russian.

"I certainly was raised better than to be having this talk. What is wrong with this house? It's big. At least twice the size of my old place. Which you never saw anyway, so. It's in a safe neighborhood. Believe me when I tell you this house is probably one of the best defended in the damned state. And Maybe is here. And I love Maybe. So *that's* why I live here."

"This is a cop's house," she said back.

Maybe had been learning Russian, but Vic was pretty sure the speed of the discussion would keep her from figuring out exactly what was being said. But the tenor of the discussion made it clear it was a fight. Given her expression she most certainly had figured it out.

In fact, she appeared to be having a very stern discussion in her head. Probably convincing herself not to punch Polina in the face. That was Vic's thought most often when she was around too so he understood.

Rachel came in the front door, locking up after herself.

"If this is such a safe neighborhood why are there so many locks on the door?" Polina asked.

"Because that's how they want it," Vic said.

"What's going on?" Rachel asked.

"Just giving the tour," Maybe said brightly, not taking the bait like a champ.

Vic smiled, winking when Polina turned her back.

"I'm sure Polina would like it better if we backed off and let Alexsei be her tour guide," Rachel said, eyeing Polina, daring her to make a deal of that too.

Alexsei took his mother's arm and steered her to the side of the house he and Maybe shared.

"You're a professional assassin," Vic told her, approval clear in his voice.

Rachel glared in the direction they'd disappeared. "I don't like that woman at all. She should fall to her knees, grateful for Maybe. The way she pokes at your mother has given me a tic in my eye tonight. What the fresh hell? Can we lock her in the pantry for a while?"

Maybe just threw her arms around her sister and made loud kissing sounds. "The best big sister ever in the world."

"I'm passable." Rachel blushed a little, endearing her to him even more. "I didn't yank her hair and slap her face, so there's that herculean control all for you."

"At least she lives across the world," Vic said. "You won't see her very often."

"There is that. You're an optimist, Vic." Maybe bumped her hip to his before she went into the kitchen to make tea Polina wasn't going to drink.

"We're done with our duty," he said into Rachel's ear. "It's totally okay for us to escape to my house or your room." He'd noted the lines around her mouth. Something was bothering her and he didn't know if it was Polina or something had happened outside.

He did know she wasn't going to show it in front of Maybe so he had to be patient and get her alone before he demanded she tell him what was up.

"When she comes back out with Alexsei. I don't want to leave her without backup with that woman."

Soon enough, Alexsei and his mother returned. He and Maybe escorted her back next door where Seth and Cristian were going to take her to her hotel for the night.

"What's got you upset? I mean, other than the basics of having to deal with Polina," he asked as they settled into her bed a few minutes later.

"I think someone was watching the house tonight."

Her tone was so flat he turned to look at her better. "Did you talk to the cops? What do you think it might be?"

"I don't know what it might be. Let's be real here, Polina comes with her own set of troubles. Having her here could have attracted the attention of a wide host of candidates."

Vic couldn't argue against that. His father hated Polina's husband, who was without a doubt associated with the oligarchs and various connected Russian crime lords back in Russia.

"Or it could be about me somehow. The last three weeks or so I've felt like I was being watched. Not all the time. But enough that after tonight I'm more inclined to think it's about me than Polina."

"If it's about you, who is it? Some monster you helped put in prison? Your dad? What?"

Vic wasn't sure how it hadn't really occurred to him that just because she'd killed Price and left the FBI that didn't mean the remnants of her old life weren't still around. Like all the psychos she was responsible for tossing behind bars.

"If any of the people I've helped imprison were out I'd know. And, if any of them were following me, I wouldn't know it until it was too late. I think it's my father. Which totally pisses me off."

"Better him than some dude who eats human livers with fava beans and a nice Chianti," Vic said, meaning it to his toes.

"Certainly."

SHE HAD TO open herself back up to that part of her skill set, that way of viewing the world that she had as an agent, but that's what it took to overcome whatever her father had in store.

"I don't think he's been on our property. He's all too aware of the rules and how to skirt them. But he's sniffing around which means he wants to make trouble. I just need to figure it out so I can be ready when he makes his move."

"Jesus Christ. I'm going to hell for how sexy I find it when you're tough and threatening someone," Vic said.

That humor helped her let go of some of her anger. She kissed him quickly.

"I imagine if he was watching tonight he got a whole lot of fuel for his foreigners-are-messing-with-my-daughter fantasy."

"Should we ignore it? Report it? What? You tell me what we should do here and I'll make it happen."

So sweet.

She cupped his cheek a moment. "Right now I'm gathering information. Trying to figure out what he might do next. Then I'll know better what to do. I'm not interested in getting into some sort of lengthy legal entanglement. And it's my suspicion that he'd do whatever it took to keep me on the hook somehow."

Vic turned his beautiful mouth into a brief frown. "Okay. Okay. But if he comes back to the bakery I'm going to kick him out immediately. And if he gives me an opening I will defend myself and my business."

"He wants to goad you into a response. That's his MO. Then you're responding and he's making all the moves. Once you see it that way it'll be easier not to let him yank you into something," she told him.

"Yeah, like how you feel guilty that you didn't protect your sister from a situation you didn't even know about until a few months ago?" he challenged.

"I will always feel guilty that Maybe suffered." It didn't matter that she'd been young and away from home. What had mattered was that her little sister had been hurt and her father was still around trying to hurt Maybe to get Rachel to react.

She'd react all right. But in her way. On her terms.

"I get it now. My therapist said something to me last month after my dad came at me outside Wren's friend's building and I've been thinking about it a lot since then. His sense of self has been closely tied to me. Like maybe since I was a really little girl. The more I achieved, the better it made him feel. The more it convinced him that he was a great father and his problems with everyone else were theirs and not his fault. But here I am now. I give tattoos. I live with my sister who has always made him feel like a failure. I'm everything he believes is a failure which in turn makes him one."

She'd had to really delve back into her old self to parse that out and go through it. More in the last few months than she had in years, some of those old Rachel skills had been needed.

And they were right where she'd set them aside as she'd had to work so hard to recover. She wouldn't go back to law enforcement. It was part of her past but not her future. But neither did she feel the need to excise what she'd learned and honed on the job either.

"Right now my approach is to just give him some more rope and see what he does with it. I'm not going to let him lead me or Maybe around anymore."

"All right. I'll do my best not to react. But honestly, Rachel, your father is a prick."

She laughed. "He is. I'm trying to think of him like a suspect. If I keep him at that distance it's not as hard. Can you imagine him and Polina at a wedding together?"

"It's enough to decide to elope."

"Is it terrible that I hope she stays married so she also stays in Moscow? I feel bad about that, but she's not nice and I feel like if she were around she'd spend her time making trouble."

Vic snorted. "If she came to the United States she wouldn't settle here in Seattle. She'd need to be in Los Angeles or New York City. She considers Seattle to be a backwater far beneath her status."

"Whatever keeps her away."

In a totally weird way, she was relieved that his family had its own problems. Not Danil's death, which was a terrible tragedy. But potential mother-in-law trouble? Infighting between Irena and her sister? That was delightfully normally dysfunctional.

"We'll see her more than usual in the next year or so. She'll come for Cristian's wedding and then, eventually when Alexsei and Maybe get married she'll be back," Vic said.

Rachel planned to tell her sister to do all the big things before they let Polina know they were engaged. She bet Alexsei's mother would be a total pain in the ass if she was allowed to get in the middle of any wedding planning.

"I know you've got to get up extra early tomorrow to get to the bakery first thing while everyone else entertains Polina and gets ready for the dinner. Go home and get some sleep," she told him.

"I'm fine here."

"Bull. At your place you can make as much noise as you want in order to get up and out." He was such an adorable little hedgehog in the mornings but he bumbled around and grumped as he got dressed and out the door. He couldn't do that at her house.

"Then you come and sleep over at my house."

Since he'd set about making his house everything

she'd want—new locks and bird feeders included—
she'd found herself at his place more often. She was
comfortable there. Slept more soundly with him than
she did on her own.

"I want to be here." Maybe might need to talk. Or
her dad might pop by. Whatever happened, if it happened she wanted to be there to handle it.

He nodded and then snuggled down into the bed with
her fully. "Then I'll be sleeping here."

"I'm not going anywhere. Tomorrow when you knock
on my door to pick me up to drive me to dinner I'll answer. And I'll look good. I'm not running."

"What if you have a bad dream and I'm not here to
cuddle you back to sleep? What if you wake up at four
feeling frisky and there's no one here to help you out?"
he countered, not moving a single inch.

"I have my own hand if I wake up feeling frisky.
And I haven't had a bad dream in a while. But if I do,
I'll do what I did before you came along. I'll be okay."

He frowned. "But there's no need for that. Because I
have come along and here I am trying to sleep but you're
talking and talking. If you want to keep talking, might
I suggest you give me some details about what you do
with your hand when I'm not around."

CHAPTER TWENTY-FOUR

Vic had been so quiet when he'd gotten up she probably wouldn't normally have even awoken. But it was the loss of his warmth, the solid, reassuring weight of him suddenly gone that had her surfacing enough to say his name.

He moved to her, already dressed, bending to kiss her. "Go back to sleep. I'll see you later tonight."

She listened until he'd gone. Waited for the sound of the keypad being engaged as the alarm was turned off and reset when he left the house. Then the snap of each lock being reengaged.

She let sleep drag her back under and when her alarm went off a few hours later, she woke up glad he'd stayed the night.

Alexsei and Maybe had already left for Whiskey Sharp so she was blessedly alone as she got ready, made herself breakfast, packed a lunch and then headed out to work.

It was raining. It felt like this last winter and early spring had been nothing but rain. But that day she got to avoid the miserable weather because she was going to be so busy she'd drive instead of take the bus.

And it also enabled her to escape if she wanted to as well.

Just after she'd parked, her phone buzzed with a call

that turned out to be from one of her friends back from her Bureau days.

After a slightly awkward hello, Melissa got right down to it. "Your dad has been calling a lot lately. A few people have had to change their personal numbers because of it."

Rachel blew out a long breath. "What is he saying?"

"He's trying to get people to call you and convince you to come back. I'd love to see you back here, but he's pissing people off."

"I'm so sorry. I had no idea. We're not…on speaking terms right now," Rachel said, wishing the ground could swallow her up.

"I had a feeling it was something like that. He seemed a little manic to me. If it makes you feel any better, we all know you have nothing to do with this. We've all blocked him and at the office, his calls go into the kook file. He's also been trying to report some Russian nationals."

They were all citizens, for god's sake! With the exception of Polina, and she was only visiting for four days.

Rachel told her that.

"No one is taking him seriously. But he's annoying folks. Making a nuisance of himself. I thought you should know."

Rachel thanked her and headed in to work.

"I obviously need to tell Maybe," Rachel said to Cora some hours later. "I don't want her to think I'm hiding things. At the same time, she's stressed out about Alexsei's mom being here and this can wait. Don't you think?"

"You're doing this adulting thing hard lately," Cora said, approval in her tone. "I agree that this is a bad time but I also worry Maybe will feel like you're hiding something from her. It's already a sore point between you and she's feeling especially exposed right now. As are you."

"I'm not feeling exposed."

Cora just looked at her.

"I'm just letting someone close. That's not the same as feeling exposed," Rachel said.

"What a bunch of word salad. Anyway. You and Maybe would be better off being totally honest. Even if she is stressed out over this Polina chick. It'll let her focus on something else. And it'll make her feel like you believe she's capable of handling stuff."

She knew Cora was right so she just sighed heavily. "I'll just keep it simple."

"Dad's been snooping around and apparently has bugged so many of my old coworkers that they've all had to block his number," she told Maybe that night as they were getting ready for the dinner.

Maybe gave her a look.

"I was going to wait to tell you until after Alexsei's mom went back home, but after talking to Cora, we figured it'd be best to tell you now. I don't think he's got anything he can do any real damage with. Other than the annoyance factor, that is. I just didn't want you to think I was sandbagging this."

Maybe finished putting her mascara on before speaking. "Why can't *he* live in Moscow?"

"You'd trade him for Polina?"

"Oh. Good point. That's a fucked-up bargain to have to make," Maybe said. "How are you taking all this?"

Rachel shrugged. "Right now I'm not so bugged. I think over the last month I've come to a place where I can separate my emotions from it. I worry about you, naturally. I am horrified that he'd try to hurt Vic's family. To be honest, I'd quake to think about how they feel about this drama with our parents, but they're screwed up too. And I'm shallow enough that it makes me feel better."

"Irena freaking loves your guts. She's never going to hold Dad against us."

"I'm tired of being an impediment people need to overcome because they like me," Rachel said.

"Well, you're not. So there's that."

"I'm sorry. I'm just wallowing."

"You get to wallow. You don't do it very often. You're in love with Vic, aren't you?"

Whoa.

"That was a hit from the side there, wasn't it?" she asked her sister.

Maybe snickered after she finished blotting her lipstick.

"Deny it all you want but I know you," Maybe said in a singsong voice as she left the room.

"Look." Rachel joined her in the living room a few minutes later. She'd chosen a simple, long-sleeved wrap dress. The fabric was soft and warm and hung well on her and the deep blue color accented her skin tone.

Once she'd assured herself Alexsei wasn't lurking somewhere nearby, she began to swap out her handbag to an evening clutch.

"It's not that I'm denying anything exactly."

"No. But you're careful. You think over every step you take. Love isn't something you can control like that. You can't plan it. It's lightning," Maybe replied.

"With Brad," Rachel began but Maybe interrupted.

"Brad cheated on you. It didn't work out. Because you tried to plan it. Handsome guy meets pretty woman, they're both career-oriented but someday will want to have two children and move to the suburbs from their townhouse in the city. That's a thing. People do it every day. But you can't plan for the zing. You can't plan for that, whatever it is when you're seriously so into that other person you're utterly screwed."

Rachel couldn't disagree with any of that but it didn't mean she was just going to let her sister get away with being so wise. Not so easily.

"One could argue that since I've known Vic for over three years now, that it was my plan from day one to get to know him. Become good friends and then shift to love. I mean, I've always thought his ass was great, but wouldn't be sniffing his side of my bed after he left either."

Maybe grinned. "Oh. My. God. You're sniffing the sheets and not to see if they're still fresh. I'll bet you fifty dollars right this moment that you never sniffed Brad's side of the bed. Or wore his shirts or any of that stuff. You would have made a fine combination of genetics for gorgeous, smart kids. But you did not ever really go over for him. That's the stuff that gets you through. The way you get a little lightheaded sometimes when they touch you. It's easier not to be mad at them anymore when you can remember that."

"My little sister is pretty wise."

"Love looks good on you."

"I don't know if I'm at love just yet. But I'm on my way." Rachel knew that was a lie but it was scary as hell to admit she'd been falling for Vic for some time now.

Love was a big deal. Once you said it out loud it changed things.

Maybe rolled her eyes.

"They're going to be here shortly so ixnay on the love talk," Rachel said.

"Like Vic isn't totally head over heels in love with you? Like the whole world can't see it in his eyes every time he even looks your way?"

"Seems to me you've got your own bushel of problems to worry about." Rachel had attempted to sound prim but it was hard to do when your sister knew the right spot to poke your ribs.

She slapped Maybe's hand away as she made a sound remarkably like that cute cartoon dough guy.

"I'm not sure what we interrupted, but if you two want to start a pillow fight, we'd be okay with that," Vic said as he and Alexsei came into the room.

Rachel tossed a pillow at his head. He batted it down to the couch and grabbed her, pulling her into his arms and dropping kisses all over her face.

"What? Did I forget to promise to be on your team?" he teased.

He was so adorable her ovaries pulsed.

"Okay, don't get started with any of that stuff. We're due at the restaurant in half an hour," Alexsei said.

Vic frowned and kissed her once more just to mess with his cousin.

When he stepped away at last, her lips tingled as she took him in. He wore a dark suit with a light gray shirt that was open at the neck enough to show a slice of skin she liked a lot.

The hollow of his throat was a place she loved to nuzzle and kiss. It smelled really good and he was su-persensitive there so it got him all hot. And then it got her all hot because it was pretty amazing to have enough going on to make a man like Vic worked up.

"I don't think it's fair for you to look at me like that before we have to leave," he said in an undertone.

"I can't help it. You look handsome. Dapper."

His hair had been freshly trimmed, along with his beard. He managed to be big and tall but also graceful and very masculine all at once. She'd never seen him look so dressed up and handsome.

"I want you to get started on my new tattoo next week."

He wanted a hand and wrist tattoo.

"Did you decide what you wanted?"

"Birds and sage."

"Is there a story behind that?"

"Sage reminds me of home. The scent of it, the look of it growing in a garden. The way it tastes. And birds, which have become important in my life too."

"Finish making eyes at one another in the car," Alex-sei said as he jingled the keys while standing at the front door.

"I'm surprised your mouth was off my sister long enough to say all that," Rachel said.

"He hates being late," Maybe said, obviously trying to withhold her laughter. "And if we're late, his mom will think it's *my* fault so move it."

"Fine. Fine."

Vic guided her out and to the car where he even held the door and handed her a little square of chocolate.

"You're being so nice to me I'm starting to worry about this dinner," she muttered to him before popping the chocolate into her mouth.

"What bird do you want in your tattoo? One type or a few different ones?" She leaned into him.

"What's your favorite bird?" he asked her.

"Gah! So hard. If I had to pick just one, I'd say a yellow warbler. I love their song. I think they're beautiful."

"I think two birds would be good. A yellow warbler and a blue jay, which is my favorite bird."

"Honestly, it's like I did some dark magic to have you come along."

He grinned.

"Call and make an appointment. I'll work up some sketches between now and then."

"My hot girlfriend is going to give me a tattoo. That's so badass I'm not sure what to do with myself," he said.

She could think of a few things *she'd* like to do with him.

VIC COULDN'T SEEM to tear his attention from Rachel for longer than a few minutes. At the restaurant they'd been shown into a private dining room already full of friends and family.

Rachel's sleek, dark hair framed her face perfectly. Her eyes had been lined more heavily than normal, but it lent her a mysterious air. Her dress was soft and body-hugging and she smelled like sugar cookies.

Even more alluring was the way she protected his mother whenever Polina went in for an unfair swipe. Rachel mainly stayed out of it, but in the times when his aunt had been too personal and too hard-edged, Rachel had smoothly interjected to change the subject or steer them into separate parts of the room.

"This is a really beautiful dinner," Maybe told Polina. The restaurant, one of Seattle's oldest, was owned by a family friend who'd graciously volunteered use of the private dining room that overlooked the Seattle skyline. "Alexsei and Cristian are so proud to have you here visiting."

Vic had to hand it to her, Maybe was bound and determined to charm Polina or die trying. And in doing so, she'd put the other woman in a position where anything but kindness and civility in return looked vulgar.

Not that it would necessarily stop Polina from doing what she wanted, but it was a clever way to approach it and another reason why she was perfect for Alexsei.

"How do you know she can even have babies? If her sister is a spinster too?" Polina asked Alexsei in Russian.

"Stop with this. English from now on, please," Alexsei said gently.

"Hey, I know, how about we all go get a drink and have a little nibble," Evie said, linking her arm with Maybe's, tugging her toward where Rachel was listening to one of his father's stories, laughing.

Vic sidled up to Rachel, sliding an arm around her waist and bringing her to his side. "You can't steal all the pretty women in the world, *batya*," Vic teased his father.

"Lucky for me, you and your cousins keep bringing home all the beauties. That and your mother and I'm set for life."

"You're full of it," Polina said, but she smiled as she did.

He waggled his brows at his sister-in-law.

They all started telling stories from the old days, which always fascinated Vic, but then the candlelight caressed Rachel's skin and he had to dance her off to the bank of windows across from most of the party guests.

"Thanks for guarding my mother tonight," he said, kissing her forehead.

"She really just wants your aunt to say she's done a good job with Alexsei and Cristian. At the end of the day it's about being appreciated by your sister."

He should have known Rachel would see that.

"Or even thank you." He winced at the bitterness in his tone. "Never mind that tonight. You have been good to her. And to my aunt as well."

"Maybe wants to try to have a relationship with this woman. So I sort of feel like she's got to be broken in her own way. Maybe is diabolical. She's not going to give up until she gets what she wants. I'm just on the pit crew," Rachel said dryly.

The words were on his lips before he could stop himself. "You're a miracle to me. I love you, *tigryonak*."

Her eyes widened, but she wasn't afraid or turned off. A light shone in her eyes that felt like it was just for him.

"I'd meant to tell you at a different moment. More romantic. Less crowded with my family," he said.

"What changed your mind?" she asked, a smile lurking on her mouth.

"You were just so you. And it struck me dumb a bit and then I had to tell you."

What was there to argue over with that declaration?

"Okay then," she said.

CHAPTER TWENTY-FIVE

IT WAS NEARLY eleven by the time they came back out to the parking lot and when they did, it was to find several large, dark SUVs blocking them in.

"I'm going to need you to provide your identification," one of them said as he got out of the lead car.

Rachel stepped up, Seth at her side.

"Who are you?"

"Agent Eddie Haskell. ICE."

"I'd like to see some identification, please." Seth slowly put his hands up, palms out. "Seth Andrews, Seattle PD. I'm reaching for my ID."

"No. You there!" He pointed at Pavel who was still standing exactly where he had when they'd been told to stop. "Don't move."

"We'd be happy to comply with whatever directions are legal, sir, when we verify your identity," Rachel said smoothly as she stepped to the side, getting between his father and the guy from ICE.

Everything in the air was very taut and Vic's face was hot with rage and humiliation. His mother stood very close to his back and Vic could feel the waves of tension that seemed to flow from her.

"You don't give the orders here," the ICE guy told Rachel, whose left brow rose slightly. "Noncitizens

don't give orders! Now, everyone on your knees!"
Haskell shouted.

Seth remained standing. "Sir, I'm asking you to provide me with proper identification. We are *not* resisting,
merely asking for your ID."

"You don't have the authority to do that."

"We *all* have the authority to do that," Rachel
snapped, her tone so sharp it gave Vic pause. "Your
identification, please. We have no idea who you are.
Your vehicles don't have government plates and you're
refusing to show us your official identification. Demanding we submit without any assurances isn't acceptable."

At his back, his mother said quietly in Russian, "The
name is odd. Eddie Haskell is a name from an old television show."

"Stop using that gibberish!" Haskell yelled.

Rachel pulled out her phone. "I'm calling the police.
None of this is acceptable."

That's when Richie Dolan erupted from the back of
one of the parked SUVs.

Maybe yelled out but Rachel said, "Alexsei, take care
of Maybe and the rest. Vic, you too." Then she pointed
a finger at her father. "You, old man, stay right the
fuck there."

Vic scoffed as he grabbed her hand to stay her. "If
you think I'll stand aside while this asshole abuses you
and my parents you're out of your mind."

"What I think is that your mother is on the verge
of tears. Your father must feel totally useless, which
would upset him more than most anything else. Polina
is going to start in on your mom and then there'll be an
argument," she told him in a terse voice.

"Fᴜᴄᴋ ᴛʜɪs, Rɪᴄʜ. This has gone too far," fake Haskell told her father. He got into one of the SUVs. Ice-cold rage ran through her veins as she took video of the scene including two of the three SUVs which also took off and then over to where her father stood at the last SUV.

She stalked over, leaned into the car and took the keys, shoving them in that tiny purse so he couldn't escape. And if he made her run in heels she'd kick his ass.

"What the fuck is wrong with you?" she asked her father. "You do realize impersonating law enforcement is a crime?"

"I didn't impersonate anyone."

She poked him in the chest hard enough that he took a step back. "You orchestrated with others, creating a *conspiracy*." He should know better than this.

"These people are poison," her father told her.

"You shut up about that. You don't know a goddamned thing about them."

He started to reply and she held a hand up before she turned and walked back to where everyone else was still standing, agog.

For fuck's sake. Was no one capable of following instructions?

She pulled her authority on as she addressed all the friends and family in attendance who were still there. "Cristian, take your mother back to her hotel. Alexsei, please take Maybe and your parents home. It's late and everyone is upset."

"I'm not leaving you here alone with him," Maybe said.

"She won't be alone. I'm here," Vic said.

She turned to him. "Dude. Go. I'm fine."

"Nope. We already discussed this." He crossed his

arms over his chest as he spoke to his parents in Russian. Which was really getting old.

"You and I are going to have a long talk about you not speaking in Russian to say things you don't want me to know," she said under her breath to Vic before relenting. "Fine. Make sure they all leave. There's no use for them to be here any longer. It's starting to rain. They're all upset."

Of course once she'd gotten rid of Vic, Maybe came scurrying over after they'd gotten Pavel and Irena in the car.

Like herding cats.

Maybe had her stubborn face on. "I'm going to stay with you. He's my dad too."

"Go home, Maybe. Jesus." Rachel pinched the bridge of her nose and took a different approach. "Look. There's nothing you can do here now. In fact, having you all here is a distraction. I need all my wits about me right now. So if you really want to help me, go back and help settle everyone down at home. That's really, truly what I need from you. I've got it handled here. Seth is staying too, so it's not like I have no real backup." And Vic was scowling so hard he could singe paint. "Please, Maybe."

Her sister relented after a hug.

Maybe needed to be protected. Her heart was tender and their father would hurt her more if he thought it might benefit him.

Once they'd driven away, Vic was back at her side with a coat he'd taken from the car. It was huge, but warm and it smelled like Vic, which made her feel better.

Rachel sighed, took a deep breath to center herself and headed back over to where Seth was still on his phone but her father hadn't left. Mainly because she had his keys, she wagered.

"I need to think for just a moment," she told Vic, who left her alone while she pulled herself together and made a plan.

When she was ready, she drew Seth off to the side. "This is between Seth and Rachel right now, okay?"

He agreed and she began to tell him her plans.

When he left, she motioned Vic over.

"Are you cold? Do you want to go back inside? We can use the restaurant to deal with him and you won't be out in the open air."

Why was he always so perfectly sweet at exactly the right moment? Like magic.

"Thank you. I'm good. This is a warm coat and we shouldn't be out here much longer. Look, I think you should leave. At least keep out of earshot."

He raised both brows. "Why?"

"If I told you it would negate the whole idea of having you leave."

"I'm not going so just tell me what you're up to so I can help you," he told her, clearly not planning to give an inch. Which was adorable, but a pain in her ass.

"I'm trying really hard not to make you an accessory here."

"I told you, I love you. Those aren't idle words for me. They're not just things to say so I can fuck you. I'm in. All the way."

She had to be ice-cold so she packed up how warm and fuzzy he made her and put her control back on. She'd keep what he knew up front to a minimum. "Just follow my lead and do what I say."

"Mmm. All right then." He gave her a sexy grin before he kissed her hand and let her go face this mess head-on.

"Thank goodness we aren't on the waterfront, huh?" she asked her father as she finally gave him her attention. Seth had left but would be a phone call away if necessary.

"You can't keep me here," he said.

She ignored the comment. "Conspiracy is one of those things that messes people up every time. I'm disappointed you seem to have forgotten that from your time on the force. I'm pretty sure your friends who drove off are going to be pissed off at you for getting them into this mess. And they *will* be pulled in, Richard. I promise you that."

He began to sputter and she let him for a minute or so.

"Here's how this is going to work."

"He's using you and you're so crazy you can't even see it," her father yelled out, interrupting her.

"Using me for what? You've been bringing up that line for months and months about not just Vic, but Alexsei and the whole family. What are they using me for? His house is nicer than mine. He owns his own business that he runs with his family."

"So he doesn't need money. Yet. The drug dealer your sister is sleeping with will probably need help sometime so don't forget that. But he needs to stay here in the country."

"You must have been sleeping with someone to keep your job as long as you did. You know Alexsei owns a business. You also know Vic and his family are all citizens," she gritted out.

"That visitor they have is married to some scumbag mob boss back home in Russia," her father tossed back.

"If that's so, what's she trying to use me for? More money?"

"I saw you buying expensive things for her at that fancy place at the mall. She comes to visit and gets herself a bunch of pretty presents and some more potential contacts for her illegal activities."

Rachel *knew* someone had been watching!

"*Alexsei* paid for those presents. *She's his mother.* None of them need money and if they did, I'm not the person to get it from. You seem to think I've got millions stashed away. Spoiler alert. I don't."

"They need connections to get green cards and work visas."

She just stared at him. "You don't need a green card if you're a citizen. I've explained to you that they're all citizens except for the one who is visiting now and she has no plans to move here. So. We're back to square one. Just admit it. You have nothing."

"I won't let these people drag you down."

That he'd say that as *he* dragged her down snapped something inside her. "You're going to shut up and listen to me really carefully. You aren't going to contact me again. You aren't going to contact Maybe again. No more following me or any of my friends. No more calls to my old office. No more threats. Nothing. We're done as of now."

"I've already told you, I'm not going to let them hurt you."

"You listen here." She leaned in a little. "Tonight you and your friends committed multiple crimes. I've got video of your little buddy pretend-Haskell and of the license plates of the other SUVs. If you don't care about yourself, think of those jerkoffs you brought out here tonight. You think they want to go down for you? You want to be the cause of them losing everything? Houses, marriages, whatever? All gone because you can't get off on your own merits and you've been riding my coattails since birth. And still you won't control me. I will do what I want with who I want how I want. You get no say. You get nothing but a cup of stay-out-of-my-life."

"You can't be serious." But his tone said he was finally beginning to hear it and understand just how serious she was.

"I've never in my life been more serious. I will turn you in if you continue to stalk, threaten and harass me and my friends. You have no idea what you've awakened so let me be clear. I will destroy each and every one of those guys and knowing it's all your fault as it happened would be icing on the cake. I can do it. I will do it. Your idiotic bullying has given me what I need to get you off my back. Oh, and Rich?"

"Don't call me that."

"Listen carefully. I'm going to track down the identity of those two meatheads who were here tonight. And I'm going to have a talk with them too. Just so they know what's going on. Just so we can all be on the same page and avoid any misunderstandings that could end up getting people in a bad way. You got me?" She snapped her fingers in his face, a thing he used to do to other people when he was being an ass.

She turned her back and took Vic's hand, allowing him to lead her back to his car.

Vic opened her door and got her settled before she remembered she still had her father's keys.

"I'LL TAKE THEM BACK," Vic said.

"I've got him wedged into a place where I've got the upper hand," she said, asking him not to fuck this up.

"I understand." He took the keys she'd handed him and got his breath back under control as the rain let up a little.

He wasn't going to let his ego get in the way of some true peace for the Dolan sisters. And that she achieved it by this nifty bit of badassery only made him love her more fiercely.

But that didn't mean he wasn't going to have his say in some way.

Vic held up the keys as he approached but didn't hand them back right away.

"Before you get on your way, I thought I should properly introduce myself. I'm Vicktor Orlov. I'm the man your daughter Rachel will marry and have children with. You could maybe have been part of it at some point in the future but then you made my mother cry. You made my mother cry and remember a time she crossed the world to escape from a life where she was in fear all the time. I won't forget that. And I won't forget how you tried to cage my Rachel. I'll make sure she never does either."

He tossed the keys and turned his back with a sneer and went to Rachel.

"You let me hold your hand back there. When we walked away from him," Vic said as he drove them back home.

"Of course I did."

What did that mean?

"Are you mad I didn't punch him? Because I really wanted to but then that would have given him leverage against you," Vic told her. "Like I *really* wanted to plant my fist in his face and make him hurt as much as he thought to hurt you and my parents. And Maybe. Mostly you."

"I'm not mad at you at all. You're kind of perfect for me and I'm freaked out. But you're also the aforementioned perfect so I'm working through it. I'm glad you wanted to punch him but I'm also glad you didn't."

They were quiet awhile. "Are you really going to find out who the other guys are?" he asked her. "Hypothetically speaking, I mean."

"*Hypothetically speaking*, someone in my position would want to ascertain who these guys from tonight are. And naturally, understanding who they are will enable said hypothetical person to know all weak and pressure points so they could be exploited." She paused, chewing her lip. "I'm going to track them down, Vic. Then I'm going to pay a visit to the one who made your mother cry tonight just to go ahead and outline the situation the way I did for my father. I don't think there'll be any more trouble after that. My father might think it's totally fine to mess over other people's lives. But those guys he had with him? Pretend-Haskell is going to feel totally differently. He'll provide the incentive for Richard Dolan to keep the hell away."

"You can be stone-cold scary sometimes."

She searched for negativity in the words but found none. All she could hear was his admiration and some of the anger he still had rattling around inside.

He pulled into her driveway with Maybe's car to

the other side. "Go. Check on your parents. I need to... gather myself a moment or two."

"You sure?"

Rachel kept her hands tightly clasped in her lap. "I'm worried about your mother but I have to be totally honest and say if I deal with her face-to-face tonight I might cry and that's the last thing anyone needs right now."

"You have no idea how much control I'm using not to grab you and run for the hills where we could stay in a hotel and hide out awhile. All this is upsetting and you're at the center of it and I worry for *you* more than anyone else. My mother is strong and she's got my dad and aunt and Evie."

"You're her son. She loves you and counts on you. Go on. I'm just going to have to deal with Maybe a bit and then you can come back—if you want—and sleep over. If you don't I totally understand." And she did. Sometimes she had to be alone because it was the only way she could manage to work through something.

"I'll be back. First let's get you in the house and then I'll pop next door to check in on my folks."

Before she could argue, he was out and on his way around to her door.

"Do you think I'm a terrible person?" she asked him suddenly.

Taken aback, he shook his head. "Not at all. What makes you ask such questions? Have I done something wrong?"

"No. Not at all. It's me. I just...well, basically I blackmailed my father. I threatened to ruin other people's lives, Vic."

She'd do it again to protect her sister and the family they'd both made in Seattle.

"And I don't feel guilt about it."

"Why would you? They're the ones who need to feel guilty, Rachel. They're in the wrong. They're trying to hurt you and Maybe and your lives. Don't ever forget that. You're allowed to defend yourself."

Rachel reached up to brush her thumb over his cheekbone.

"More than that, if you hadn't defended yourself I'd have been pissed as hell. He needed to be stopped. You did that. You did absolutely nothing wrong. In fact, you did everything right. You were a warrior tonight."

She managed to quirk a smile at his words. "Thanks."

He kissed her quickly. "Always. I'll be back shortly and most likely with more food." And with one last careful look at her, he dashed off.

Maybe waited on the couch in the living room and she knew she'd done the right thing for them both.

"So, let me tell you what I did tonight," Rachel said as she plopped down next to her sister.

"Cone of silence and secrecy engaged." Maybe made the universal *take a lock to the mouth and toss the key away I won't tell anyone* motion with her hand.

She told her sister everything that had happened after they'd left with everyone else.

JUST A FEW minutes later, after he'd checked in on his mom and found her angry, but fine, Vic approached the Dolans' front porch, not surprised to see Alexsei sitting out in the cold, smoking a stress cigarette. A bottle of beer sat nearby on the porch railing.

"Maybe and Rachel were talking and I didn't want to interrupt," Alexsei said. "How are your parents doing?

I checked on them briefly but I wanted to be around for Maybe. She's been waiting for her sister."

The sisters had a deep, unbreakable connection. They were a force of their own, strong and loving. Anyone who wanted to be with one had to accept the other. Alexsei had learned that and Vic had, in turn, taken that lesson to heart and kept out from between the two.

Vic levered himself around his cousin and found his own place to sit. "Mom and Dad are all right. Worried for Rachel and Maybe. I think for Mom there's some more to it. She grew up seeing a lot of authoritarian bullshit from the Soviet regime. She's lost people. Hell, so has *batya*. Your mom too I'm sure. How is she?"

"Busily making it about herself I'm sure. She really didn't know what was happening other than the general unpleasantness of the confrontation." Alexsei raised one shoulder briefly.

Rachel had done a very good job at stepping between them all and the bullshit her father had put into motion.

"And Maybe?"

"I'm going to be totally selfish right now and say she's doing better because she saw her sister physically step into the line of fire to protect her."

"Rachel *constantly* puts herself between her sister and trouble," Vic said defensively. "You have *no idea* how much guilt she carries for the things that happened to Maybe. *But she was a kid too.* And then she was off in college. She didn't even know the whole of it until a few months ago. She will always feel like she didn't do enough so fuck you for thinking she should feel even worse."

Alexsei glared at him for long moments.

"Like I said, she saw her sister jumping to her defense and it made a difference to her. Don't get so testy about me saying a positive thing."

"It was a backhanded compliment and you know it," Vic said.

Alexsei gave him a bland look—but didn't deny Vic's charge—before speaking again. "Maybe wants to protect Rachel. She's spent the last several years making sure protecting Rachel was the central force in her life. I'm not taking a dig at Rachel. But I *am* all about Maybe. And that she's actually seen her sister jump in the way she has been? The way she did tonight? It goes a long way. And when Maybe is happy, I'm happy."

"Do you know what she did tonight really?" Vic challenged his cousin. "I understand and respect that you're all about Maybe. You should be. But perhaps that's blinded you to the fact that Rachel does more than you give her credit for."

"I never said she does nothing. In fact I said she has been consistently working to protect her sister but you're riled up and you want to start a fight with someone safe."

"Eat shit. Tonight Rachel used every ounce of that protector's brain of hers, along with a spine of steel, and she made a move that most likely will get them out of Maybe and Rachel's life forever so hand over that other beer and settle in so I can tell you about it."

CHAPTER TWENTY-SIX

SHE WAS IN the bedroom by the time Vic came back inside. She'd known he was out on the porch with Alexsei. Had known the two of them also needed to check in and get things straight the same way she and Maybe needed to.

"As predicted, I've been instructed to bring you over some things to eat. My mother claims if you don't eat them it's somehow bad for the world or whatever guilt crap they use. She wants to love you. Food is how she loves."

"Like we didn't just eat for like four hours?" she joked. But she smiled as she spoke because yes, it was Irena's way of saying she loved you.

And it felt like a hug.

"How are they?" she asked.

"They've gone through a lot in their lives. So tonight was upsetting, but mainly because they care about you and your sister so much. To be honest, I do think it did trigger some stuff from when she was young."

His mother had been livid. Outraged on Rachel and Maybe's behalf. Proud that Rachel had stood up for them, protected them. Proud too, that Vic had stepped up, concerned for not just them, but Rachel.

Especially Rachel.

In his emotional reaction that night, his parents had

understood what he hadn't told them yet. He was in love with her.

His father had a different sort of respect in his tone as he'd urged Vic to get back over to Rachel instead of worrying about them. Didn't Vic know Pavel was perfectly capable of handling his wife?

He'd winked behind Vic's mom's back as he'd shooed Vic out.

"My parents are fine. Tomorrow night they can ooh and aah over Cristian and Seth and we can let tonight just be a hilarious story we tell at parties. In a few years," Vic added. "How are *you*?"

She sighed, climbing up onto her bed and tucking her feet under the blankets. "Before you, my greatest fears used to be simple. From 'Will I pass this test?' to 'Will I escape this house of horrors alive?' 'Would I get the job?' After I was held, that fear of losing control, of losing my freedom, that was my main focus.

"Getting better. Moving out here. Doing my apprenticeship time so I could start doing ink on my own. All so I could remain free. Independent. When I got here it was about settling in. Working. Doing art. Having a good life with Maybe and then Cora. And yet, until that first time you kissed me, everything in my life had felt like a reaction."

She paused as she tried to find better words to explain herself. But it wasn't simple. The revolution he'd brought to her life was beyond her ability to put into words to do it justice.

"And then you kissed me. You kissed me and the focus in my life changed. I'd been reacting and surviving. Building a life where I was in total control. And you came along and kissed me senseless and cooked me brunch and made me realize there was more than reacting.

"And then my life began to bloom. This art project and you and work and just so many things. Opening up. My world got larger and I wasn't just looking at surviving anymore. I wasn't just reacting. I was living."

She could tell he wanted to interrupt her a few times. That he'd definitely wanted to reach out and hold her. But he held back knowing she had to speak on her own or she'd lose her nerve.

"I feel safe when you're around. When you're with me. I like being at your house. I don't feel comfortable in a lot of places and yet I've taken naps on your couch. I like the way my skin smells after you sleep next to me all night. In short you changed *everything* for me.

"Tonight my fear was that your family would be hurt. That my father would hurt you all to get to me. To make me submit. My fears were so much bigger because they included the loss of this thing I didn't know I needed and now that I have it I don't think I could get by without it. I know I don't want to. I've had Maybe most of my life. But you, Vic? You're my family too. More? You're my place to belong and I will fight like hell to protect it."

A rough cry came from him as he moved close and pulled her into his arms. "My beautiful, beautiful Rachel. You continue to surprise and move me. I was just this happy-go-lucky guy and you came along and saw me as a man. A man worthy of a woman like you. I was made to be your safe space."

She absorbed his warmth, the steady beat of his heart and the strength of the arms around her.

He wasn't scared. He wasn't going to walk away

and leave her alone. He would get in her business and try to be bossy. He'd be infuriatingly charming as he did it too.

Underneath the charm was a will as tough as hers. A heart unlike any she'd ever known. He was patient and funny and great in bed. But he was a man. *Her man* and being with him was fun and satisfying, but it meant she had to be the same kind of partner to him. It would take work and commitment and drive.

Never in her life had she been more sure about something. He was *it* for her.

She squirmed until he loosened his hold and when he did, she moved, shifting so she could swing around and straddle his lap, facing him.

Emotion was so bare on his face it brought her to a halt for a moment. She cupped his face in her hands and kissed him. Softly at first, just little nips of taste until his hands settled at her hips, yanking her closer.

"Mine," he told her.

She rolled her hips, grinding herself against him in answer.

He reached out and in two deft moves, grabbed and snapped the front of her pajama shirt open.

A gasp tore from her lips as her skin heated in anticipation of the moment when he slid his palms over her breasts to take their weight.

"I'm so glad you changed into pajamas because I wouldn't have ripped that pretty dress you had on earlier," he said right before he bent to brush his lips over the curve of each breast.

She was glad too.

Even more glad when he flicked his thumbs from side to side over her nipples.

Her toes had been pointed so hard she got a cramp in her calf when he nuzzled against her, taking a nipple between his teeth.

"I don't want slow and tortuous," she managed to say.

He pulled back with a pop that sent a shiver through her. "Is that so? What do you want then?"

Leaning in, she pressed her body to his and said in his ear, "I want you to fuck me hard and fast and right now."

He snarled a curse and moved so quickly she was already on her back on the bed as he got out of his clothes, watching her so intently it was hard to find the coordination necessary to get the rest of hers off.

His cock was hard and fierce and it gave her a thrill to recall just how good he was with it. It should have shocked her, the depth of her greed for him. It should have scared her. It *had* scared her.

There he was in her bedroom so big and strong and naked and erect and tatted and pierced and all hers.

All those jagged parts inside seemed to fit against his, clicking into place.

"Don't give me that look. You have some fucking to do," she told him as he raked his gaze over her like he was going to eat her up. Which normally she happily endorsed. But she knew what she wanted and it was to be full of him.

"I'll get to it. I have other plans."

"You always say that and then you go down on me and I lose all sense. Plan to fuck me. Come on. You know you want to."

He looked like he was prepared to put up a fight until she slid her hands all over her upper body and let one of her thighs fall open.

She wanted to laugh with joy when he snarled a curse and pretty much leaped on her.

"You'd better have condoms because I don't know if I've got any in my pants."

"I don't know what kind of man with a big old cock doesn't have condoms when his gal is ready to fuck all the time," she teased him as she stretched to pull one from her side table drawer.

"Just another quality to love about you." He waggled his brows.

"I like your priorities," she said, the last bit ending on a bit of a squeal as he settled on his side and grabbed one of her legs, pulling her to him.

She *loved* that he had the strength to do that so easily. Something she thought she'd never find attractive. Apparently it just took the right big strong dude to do the trick.

With her flat on her back, he pulled her legs up over his hip and entered her that way. That angle enabled him to get deep and left her sort of delightfully helpless to do much more than get fucked.

It was *exactly* what she needed.

She reached up over her head, grasping the side of the mattress for purchase so she could push back at least. That and keep herself from getting thrust right off the bed.

Each time he thrust all the way in, it sent her breasts bouncing. His gaze got caught up each time it happened and it only made her love him more.

"I love to look at you this way. Stretched out, all your ink and skin there for me to see and touch as much as possible. Your muscles flexing. Long and tall and curvy in all the right places," he murmured as he placed a flattened palm against her lower belly and pressed slightly.

That did incredible things to her clit as it also made her tighten around him. "That works," she wheezed out.

His laugh, damn, his laugh was so dark and dirty it sent as much of a shiver through her as when he physically touched her.

"I'm here to serve," he said.

"Thank you," she said, utterly genuinely. Some people's boyfriends made sure they had gas in the car. Hers made her come so hard she saw stars.

And that was before he slid his hand down enough so his thumb brushed over her clit and sent every last thought skittering from her brain.

VIC WANTED TO crow with triumph when her eyes glazed over. Sex drunk. He loved to make her that way. To provide so much pleasure she went pliant. Around his cock, her body tightened around him, her inner muscles fluttering as they did when climax was near.

He hummed his satisfaction as he also focused on not coming. Not yet. No matter how good she felt, no matter how sexy and raw her demand he fuck her was. His personal rule was that her orgasm came first.

Not as if that was a chore. Especially after all the things she'd said to him earlier that night. He may have jumped the gun on his timeline for telling her he loved her, but after everything she'd told him it was clear she loved him too.

And with everything that'd happened *after* he'd told her, he hoped that little bit of knowledge helped her through what was obviously distressing. She'd gone into that confrontation with her father knowing he loved her. Like armor.

He liked that. His love being her protection from all the crap life might hurl her way.

She took a shaky breath as she arched her back, coming in a hot rush that was so good he felt it all the way to his toes.

This was his forever. She was his forever. That was all he thought as orgasm claimed him.

CHAPTER TWENTY-SEVEN

SHE HADN'T FELT this shy around a client since her earli-
est days tattooing. But when Vic slid that damned shirt
free from his body and all those taut muscles, all that
skin she had been delightfully able to grope of late, she
realized how much it meant to her to give him exactly
what he wanted and it wasn't just about ink.

It was more. His opinion mattered. The way he felt
where she was concerned mattered. She was getting
used to it. To the way he'd become central to her life.
To being concerned about his well-being.

He turned, catching her looking at his body like she
was going to lick him and he grinned, leaning down
to kiss her right in the middle of the shop and all she
could do was blush and barely manage not to jump him
right then and there.

They were alone in the shop because early mornings were a time when he could be there around his
work schedule and she liked having him all to herself.
Something she was freely able to admit to herself by
that point.

"Let me get this placed," she said, indicating the
transfer she'd made of her design. Sage and birds. A
blue jay, wings expanded with a yellow warbler perched
in the shelter they made. "Show me exactly where."

He stood in front of her, the heat from his bare torso

blanketing her. He addled her and it was pretty delicious.

"Perfect," he said, looking at the spot from a few angles.

No lie there.

"Straddle the chair for this part. We'll go an hour and see where things stand." She'd already told him a piece as big as the one he wanted with color would take more than one session.

"Your wish is my command. You know I'm high-tolerance." He smirked at her and though it sent a rush of warmth through her, it also relaxed her. Eased that shyness some.

Outlining always felt like a ritual to her. Like the first steps in whatever magic the perfect tattoo came with. That repeated movement, the hum of the tattoo machine, the scent of ink and antiseptic married with the spice of Vic's beard product.

Her hands on him shouldn't have given her such a thrill. She gave tattoos every day, it wasn't as if it was novel to have hands on skin. But this was Vic. And it changed everything.

Sage and birds, he'd said. The sage was for home. The birds too, he'd implied without saying explicitly.

"I had a dream about you last night," he murmured, breaking her free from her thoughts.

"Yeah? Did we do the sexytimes?"

He snorted, but managed to stay still so she kept working.

"It was about birds. And cages. Sometimes I think it takes my subconscious to figure you out. Do you ever want to talk about it? You don't have to. You've already told me a lot. I just…it's a thing you went through and

I'm trying to figure out if I'm doing the boyfriend thing right."

"Doing the boyfriend thing right? What do you mean? You're pretty awesome in that department."

"I want you to know you can always talk to me. And I'm here for you to talk to. I won't judge you. You're safe with me," he said quietly and her heart squeezed a little.

"I *am* safe with you. I never doubt that. I told you I made a mistake. A stupid professional error and that's when he took me. His house, which I didn't know at first, was in the middle of the woods. I don't really remember the physical stuff that happened. I mean, I can recall it, but I try not to focus on that.

"But what I really remember, what sticks with me even though I wish it hadn't was the way I felt. Caged, yes, but more I had no ability to do my job. I could not save those women, the ones he killed while I was there."

"Did he… Never mind."

She knew what he meant. "It's okay. He didn't rape me. Not that way. I was different for him. He *consumed* those others. He used them and hurt them and then when they were empty he threw them out and started on a new victim. He *collected* me. I was a symbol of his power. He'd gotten the drop on me. He had some sort of weird competition with me as I'd been tracking him."

He'd made her watch. Made her listen. Knowing her helplessness would be a form of torture that was designed to weaken her. Break her.

"But you won. In the end, you won," Vic said.

Over the years since she'd gotten free from that basement, she'd heard similar commentary but never once had it felt like it had when Vic said it. Vic understood that the win came with a loss she was still processing to that day. But that she'd endured and that was a triumph. He knew her.

She kept her focus on the lines as she continued, letting the feel of him remind her she was miles away, years away, a lifetime away from that place.

"When I woke up in the hospital I knew I would never go back to law enforcement. I could *not* turn it off. The part of me that was trained to be a special agent kept running in the background. No matter how hard I didn't want to hear it and think about it I was still cataloging things. Still building the case. That focus kept me alive. Stopped me from shattering into a million pieces."

"But you didn't want it anymore. That thing that would always be tainted by what happened in that basement."

How did he always get her so well? And how did she get so damned lucky?

"Yeah. Pretty much. My brain was trained to act in a certain way. It'll always be part of my makeup. I can't deny that. But what I do now uses a different part of my brain. A different set of tools and it's better. If that makes sense. The way my life is now, how I spend my time and with who, it enables me to keep living and being happy. Keep me living without constant anxiety and fear."

If she'd kept her job at the Bureau, the fear would be in her face all day every day. Every case would have something to remind her. Rachel was tired of the fear and in truth, if she'd stayed on it might have eventually broken her.

And she never would have met Vic, which she told him.

"If I could erase that harm for you, even if it meant I never had you in my life I'd do it."

He would. She knew that without a single doubt. And how could anyone matter more to her than he?

"Well, that's sweet and all. But I'd rather have you. So. Up on the table on your side so I can get to your ribs easier."

He stood but didn't immediately lie on the table. First he cupped her cheeks ever so gently and kissed her. "I love you."

He really needed to stop being so perfect or she'd just be a mess of hormones all the damned time.

THREE WEEKS LATER they had just finished a several-mile hike with the sounds of nature all around them as they went.

Birds everywhere. Laughter and chatter from the friends out on the trail. It did make Rachel feel better when they got quieter during the more strenuous parts too.

She hadn't been out on a trail so remote in years and after the first hour when she'd had a few shaky moments, she'd found herself soothed by the clean air, by the sounds of the trees in the breeze, the flap of wings, the scent of warm tree bark and earth.

It had been like a filter, letting her discharge all the heaviness that had come in the time after that last scene with her father.

After the initial elation had worn off, she'd had to do the difficult job of tracking down the identities of the men who'd been with her father that night. Four in all, as it turned out.

And after she'd left Morris Spacer's office—the security firm he worked for had been the registered owner of the SUVs from the scene that night—she'd had to 'fess up to her attorney just what was going on.

Attorney-client privilege was pretty nifty, and it gave her someone to lay everything out for. Someone who'd have effective advice on next steps and that sort of thing.

As she'd figured, her aunt Robbie had called after she'd been the recipient of a nastygram from Rachel's father. He was angry, which wasn't a surprise to Rachel. But he was boxed in. He had no real options without risking the wrath of his dopey friends.

Worse, he knew it.

He hadn't called Rachel or Maybe though. And from what Rachel could tell, there'd been no more surveillance of any of them.

She'd set up like she had in the old days. Had anticipated and erected walls on every single avenue her father could have used to escape responsibility and turn the situation to his advantage. He wasn't better than her. Not a bit. She wanted him to know he was hemmed in. Wanted the sting of it to keep his ass out of their lives if for no other reason than fear that she'd burn his life down and he'd given her all the ammunition.

And at the end, there'd only been one last gambit. One she and Maybe knew was coming.

That had happened just the day prior to the hike, not too very long before she had to leave work to drive up to the hotel with Vic and his friends where they'd stay the night before the hike.

She'd been both dreading and needing that last step to happen and once it had, she'd needed some time to process what she'd heard, said and done.

The miracle of it had been that Vic hadn't been put

off by her need for space to do her thinking. Not that he'd disappeared. Nope, he'd been there at her side. Giving her space, but making sure she knew he was there for the long haul.

Essentially being perfect. Again.

On the trail, he looked at her from time to time. Just keeping an eye on her general state. He seemed to have a trust of her skill level, which was flattering given just how athletic some of his friends were.

The small campsite, run by some friends of friends, sat on a rise overlooking a gorgeous lake. There was a fire pit in the center of a cluster of yurts. Vic had explained they would make their meals. A crude but private outhouse was near, but not too near. Far enough away that she wasn't planning to drink too much before bed so she wouldn't have to stumble out into the cold darkness to pee at three in the morning.

"This is what drew me here to the Northwest," she told Vic as they'd dropped off their things in their yurt. The lake shimmered in the springtime sunshine, a deep—and very cold—blue. She indicated that and the spread of trees all around. More mountains surrounded them. "Stunning natural beauty. I've never been up this way before. It's absolutely marvelous."

He stood next to her, an arm slung around her shoulders. "It can't compete with you, but it does okay."

"Still planning on that yurt sex I see," she murmured.

He laughed, pulling her to his side more snugly. "I'm always planning on sex. As long as it's you, it doesn't matter to me where."

They explored the area with some mini hikes until they found the right place for fishing and set about catching some dinner so they didn't need to resort to the backup dinner they brought in their packs.

Later, alone, they looked up at the sky as they snuggled up under a blanket on the chaise made for two. Out here so far from the city it was clear and dark enough to see so many stars it looked photoshopped.

Vic handed her a steaming mug of tea and she decided it was time. "So. You've been very good about giving me the space and time to work through everything with my parents."

"I told you I wasn't going anywhere."

"How is it you're always so sure about everything?" she asked him.

"I'm not. But I'm sure about you. And I'm sure how I feel about you. I know who you are and I love you." He shrugged.

"My mother came to the shop yesterday afternoon. Well, actually she was waiting for me outside the coffee shop when I came out from a caffeine run. I didn't tell you last night because I had some last bits in my head to tidy up."

"You're telling me now," he said easily.

"She started off with the usual lines about family and love and all that. But then when I reiterated what I'd said to my father, what he'd done to me and Maybe and your family, she got quiet. So I thought, huh, maybe she's actually listening and will see what he's doing and her part in it."

He tried not to snort, she knew he tried, but it was there anyway. And he was right.

"He's the one who went to your brother's ex's family and got them stirred up. He found out about Danil and tracked them down to put all sorts of ideas in their heads about what you were doing to me. That your family was helping you hurt me."

Rachel knew he was seriously angry because his entire body seized up, making him even bulkier. A sex flush worked from her chest up her neck and she was glad it was dark enough that he couldn't see how easy she was for him.

He already knew. It wasn't a secret but she had some pride.

"He and his little buddies won't be doing anything for my dad again," she told him.

"How do you know?"

"I ran an investigation. I found out lots of things and it wasn't super hard. Who the guys were who'd come to the restaurant parking lot that night. Where they worked. Who they dated or were married to. Any sorts of indiscretions they might wish to keep private. Like that time my mother had an affair with the same guy who'd been stalking and harassing Maybe. Turns out she didn't want Richie to know. Go figure. Anyway, it's over. I've spent three weeks blocking every one of his ways into my life. I've learned enough to make sure your family is protected too. If he steps off the approved path he's going to pay. And he's too pitiable to pay and my mother, despite her affair, wants to keep her marriage enough that she'll make sure he leaves us alone."

Vic took her hand so he could kiss her knuckles. An old-fashioned reaction to your girlfriend saying all the stuff she just had. But a Vic reaction. Which warmed her heart.

"A brutally effective way to make sure he can't mess with you. That's really sexy."

"No comment on the fact that my father is the reason those people came to harass and upset your mom and dad?"

He shrugged. "I already thought he was a piece of shit so it's not like finding out another awful thing he'd done was going to make me loathe him more. I'm not even surprised. You'd think he would have found out that I was a citizen though."

"He was lazy with the questions he asked. There's lots of information out there. It's an information age, right? Sometimes there's so much that if you aren't very specific, or if you're too specific you might miss stuff. He just never even thought to see where you were born. He heard Russian being spoken and that's all he cared about. It's lazy. I bet his coworkers thought he was a slacker back when he was on the force too."

"You did all that not just to protect yourself, but everyone. Maybe first and foremost. But me and my parents too. Thank you, *tigryonak*, for taking care of what is so important to me."

"I love you, Vicktor Orlov. I love how you are always able to see the best in me. I love your optimism. Your humor. Your ferocity. I love how smart you are and how much you nurture everyone around you. I mostly love how you look at me. Like I could do anything."

She hadn't said it back to him that night when he first said the words. She'd told him he'd changed everything and made it clear the depth of her feelings. But those three words needed to come at the right moment when she'd handled everything else and could say them with all of her heart.

He burst into laughter, the kind she loved most from him. Delighted, charming, sexy. It was unique to her and it always felt like a gift. "Of course you do. How can you not? I have a big dick and I love making you come."

She chuckled as she pinched him. "Don't forget the bread."

"I will never forget the bread." He leaned over, kissed the top of her head and they went back to watching the stars.

* * * * *

ACKNOWLEDGMENTS

NONE OF THIS would be possible without the help of so many people behind the scenes. Thank you so much to the folks in the art department who shot two completely different cover concepts (all in service to helping this book get as much shelf space as possible).

Thank-yous always go to my editor, Angela James, who truly goes out of her way to help me be the best author I can be.

Thanks go as well to copy and line editors, folks in marketing, the audio books division, the sales team and everyone at Harlequin who makes it their job to help produce a finished product that shows the author at her best and connects with readers.

Thank you to my agent and friend, Laura Bradford, for having my back.

My husband, Ray, is an excellent sounding board. He's also fantastic at helping out with marketing and all sorts of work in the background. Plus he smells good and brings me Peanut M&M's and is a great dad too.

And never least—thank you, readers, old and new. Thank you for the time you give to read my books. Thank you for the kind notes and letters. Thank you all for hand-selling me and talking me up and taking the time to review and all that stuff. It means so very much and I really appreciate it.

*Read on for a bonus, extended sneak peek of
the final book in the* WHISKEY SHARP *trilogy*
WHISKEY SHARP: TORN
Coming Spring 2018 from HQN and Lauren Dane
The deepest love can come as a surprise...

CHAPTER ONE

Pointed west home beckons.
Waits for you like a lover

NOT TOO MANY hours after getting off an airplane, Cora approached Whiskey Sharp—a barbershop and, in the evenings, a bar. The lazily swirling red-and-white candy-cane sign out front was illuminated and the interior lights cast a shine against the gold-toned flourish of the shop's title on the front glass doors.

Inside, it smelled of sandalwood and amber, two of the more popular scents of the products used in hair and beards. Music played loud enough to feel like an embrace but it didn't drown out the low hum of conversation from the people knotted around the bar area.

Alexsei Petrov, Maybe's husband, but also Cora's friend, owned and ran the place that had become another home for Cora. He saw her come in and smiled, tipping his chin to where Maybe stood, working at her station. Giving someone a shave by the looks of it.

Three months before, her friend's hair had been platinum blonde, but currently the tips were a brilliant teal blue that bled into a wash of purple.

It would have looked absurd on most people, but Maybe managed to make it seem retro and futuristic at the same time when she coupled it with high-waisted gray pinstripe pants and a crisp white button-down shirt.

Rachel stood, her hip resting against the table, a smile on her face reserved for who Cora now recognized as Rachel's man, Vic, sitting in Maybe's chair getting that shave.

The weight of the familiar was lovely and bloomed through her belly. This was another one of her places. Full of her people.

"You bitches are still the hottest chicks I know," she said as she approached.

Rachel looked over, her eyes widening in pleasure and recognition. "You're here!"

"I told you I'd come by," Cora said, swallowed up into a hug.

"I know, but you're here now. Yay!" Maybe took over the next hug, smacking a kiss right onto her lips before stepping back.

Laughing, she got hugs from the wild bearded Russians, as Rachel and Maybe referred to their dudes.

"Everyone missed you. Not more than us, naturally, but still," Rachel said after Cora'd been loved up on by all her friends. "Three months is way too long to go without seeing you."

"It's nice to be missed." She was pretty sure she'd just finished her last extended trip with her mother. Yes, it was travel for work and she liked to go new places. But these long stints meant she had avoided getting a dog or a cat. It wasn't fair to have to leave them with someone for weeks and weeks. It meant that aside from one long-distance relationship that had ended two years before, Cora hadn't really seen anyone seriously.

She wanted more roots. And a dog. And maybe someone to go on dates with.

She'd settle for a drink and some food as she hung out with her crew to start.

"Wren said she already invited you to dinner," Maybe called out as she began to clean her station up.

"She informed me that one of their friends is cooking and that there'd be cake. So naturally I'm in."

Gregori—another wild bearded Russian—was Vic and Alexsei's cousin. He also happened to be a hugely successful artist that Cora had known for years through the local art scene. He and his wife, Wren—an artist in her own right—lived in a loft space above Whiskey Sharp.

"There's always cake at their place. It's like a little bit of heaven right upstairs," Maybe said.

"It's like what *I* imagine heaven to be, that's for sure," Cora answered.

"If there's no cake, how can it be heaven?" Rachel said it like a sacred prayer and Cora agreed utterly.

"I can't wait to hear all about your time in London but Wren said she wanted to hear it too and so not to visit too much without her." Maybe hooked her arm through Cora's. "I want to hear it now, so let's get going. I'm also hungry."

"You know how she gets when she's hungry," Alexsei said with a smirk at the corners of his mouth. Maybe rolled her eyes, but smiled as she did it so Cora knew she wasn't offended.

And he was right because Maybe was lovely and sweet, but *not* when she was hungry.

They all headed out and down the sidewalk half a block to the doors leading to the small lobby where the residents of the lofts had their mailboxes and the elevator.

The scent of garlic and onions swirled around her senses as they got out on the right floor. Gregori and Wren's door was painted bright, shiny red and flew open before they were able to use the doorbell.

Wren, wearing a huge grin, rushed at Cora and hugged her tight. "Hi! Come have champagne and eat yummy food while you tell us all how the last three months were."

"I can do that. You look fantastic," Cora told her as they headed toward the kitchen area. "Marriage agrees with you."

Her friends had come back from an impromptu trip right before Cora had left for London only to announce they'd gotten married along the way. After several years of living together it had been the right choice for their relationship.

"I look exactly the same except for the ring part and the way his mom gives me and then my belly a pointed look every time I see her," Wren said.

"Welcome to my world," Maybe said. "Irena has now taken to telling me about all the baby clothes she saw but didn't buy because she had no grandchildren to wear them. I tried to get her obsessing about Rachel's womb, but she's too wily."

"Mind your own womb. You've been with Alexsei longer than I've been with Vic. It's your time to shine, bitch," Rachel said with a laugh.

"I'm so messed up. I missed you all so much." Cora hugged each one tightly.

"You're the perfect kind of messed up," Rachel said, linking her arm through Cora's.

This was good. The best, happiest part of her life.

Her stomach growled as she sucked in the scents all around. "I need food."

"We've got that covered," Gregori called out to them. "Come, I'm pouring champagne."

"No need to call me twice when there's booze involved," Cora murmured to Rachel, who snickered.

Fairy lights and candles made the loft glow. Plus it was the perfect light and her skin would look way better than the jet lag she knew smudged dark circles under her eyes.

"It's all romantical in here and shit," Cora said and then nearly swallowed all her spit when she caught sight of who stood at the stove.

CHAPTER TWO

There is wild joy in recognition.
A leap of faith to let yourself be known.
An old magic.

WELL OVER SIX FEET of hot-ass ginger celebrity chef, former model and childhood poster boy for a cult—and most notably one of her first really hard crushes—Beau Petty had aged really, really well. He had the kind of face that would only get better as he aged. At seventy-five he'd still be searingly hot because it wasn't just that he was chiseled and taut and broad shouldered, his attitude seemed to pump out confident alpha male.

He'd been gorgeous when she'd been sixteen and he twenty-one or two, but seventeen years later, he was magnetic and intense on a whole new level. It made her heart skip a little just looking at him.

Cora had to lock her knees when his gaze flicked from Rachel over to her and his expression melted from surprise into pleasure as he dried his hands on a towel and headed toward her.

And then he hugged her and holy wow it was better than a doughnut. He smelled good and was big and hard and wow, he was hugging her and when he stepped back he said her name.

It seemed as if the word echoed through her, plucked her like a musical note.

Wow.

"It's really good to see you," he said as he stepped back, and she had to crane her neck to look up, and up, into his face.

"What an unexpected surprise," Cora told him.

"We have some catching up to do."

The lines around his eyes begged for a kiss.

"You guys know each other? I mean, duh. Obviously as you just said her name and there was a hug and stuff." Maybe smiled brightly, fishing for details in her cheerful, relentless way.

"First champagne and introductions and then we will hear that story," Gregori said, interrupting Maybe's nosiness long enough to hand out glasses.

HE'D KNOWN BACK then that she'd had a crush on him, but she was still a kid. Then. Now? She still carried herself as if a secret song played in her head. But there was nothing girlish about her now.

Her hair—shades of brunette from milk chocolate to red wine—was captured back from her face in a ponytail, tied with a scarf that managed to look artsy and retro instead of silly. It only accentuated how big her eyes were, how high her cheekbones, the swell of her bottom lip that looked so juicy he wanted to bite it.

"Get started, if you're hungry." He indicated the long butcher block counter where he'd set up some appetizers. "I was down at Pike Place earlier so the oysters are sweet and fresh. That's also where the octopus in the salad came from, caught just today. Just a quick grill with lemon and olive oil and pickled red onions."

"Oh my god, really?" Cora cruised straight over and grabbed a plate.

A woman with an appreciation for food was sexy as hell.

"Update me on your life. What are you doing here in Seattle?" she asked after eating two of the oysters and humming her satisfaction. "So good. This octopus is ridiculous. Is that jalapeno?"

"Good catch. Yes, in the olive oil I used to dress it."

"I like it. What else are you making? Not that this isn't really good, but I'm greedy."

Watching her enjoy his food was a carnal shot to his gut. It set him off balance enough that he focused on the food for a few beats.

"I'm working on a new cookbook so I'm trying out some seafood recipes. Scallop and crab cakes with a couscous salad."

"Yum! Ah, that's why you're in town?"

"I've been in Los Angeles for a long time." Feeling antsy. He had houses, but no home. "I felt a change would be good. A friend who owns a number of restaurants in the area has given me access to his kitchens so I can try my ideas out there as well." He liked working around other chefs, loved that atmosphere in a kitchen where the whole team loved to cook.

It was a good sort of competitive spirit, it pushed him to up his game, to be better. Far better for his liver and heart than all the drugs and alcohol that'd fueled his early twenties.

"That's excellent," she said. "Sometimes a change in surroundings is what you need to hit the reset button. Congratulations on your success. Every time I see your face on a cookbook or on television it makes me smile."

Back when he'd met her he'd only been out of what his father called a religion but the rest of the world called a cult for three years. Barely more than a legal adult. Modeling and wasting his money on drugs and private investigators, trying to find his kids.

Seventeen years and it had been more than one lifetime. And he still hadn't found his kids, who were already adults.

He shoved it away, into that well-worn place he kept his past inside. "Thanks. What are you up to these days? I know your mom is still working because I listen to her stuff a lot when I work."

"I'm still with her. Just got back from three months in London as she finished up a project."

Rachel wandered over to them. "*And* she helps run the gallery. Plus she holds the tattoo shop together. *And* keeps Walda out of trouble. And she writes poetry and takes amazing photographs. Oh and she's an amazing knitter."

"I keep books for my sister from time to time. That's hardly holding the shop together," Cora said with affection clear in her tone.

"And the marketing. You set up the new network too. So, yeah, holding things together. It's what she does. How do you and Cora know one another?" Rachel repeated Maybe's earlier question more firmly, clearly taking his measure.

"At first glance you think it's Maybe who's the pushiest. But Rachel is way sneakier," Cora told him with a shrug. "Beau and I met when he and Walda lived in the same building in Santa Monica. I was fifteen or sixteen at the time. He was a model so Mom kept herself between us. As if he even noticed me when he was surrounded by gorgeous models."

He hadn't noticed Walda getting between him and Cora, but Cora had been correct that he hadn't seen her in that way. For a whole host of reasons, chiefly that she was simply too young.

Then. Not so much now.

"We were there a year so I had a tutor, which, if I recall correctly, Beau *definitely* noticed." Cora snickered.

Beau hadn't learned algebra until he was an adult. Hadn't read a single classic literary novel until he was twenty-one. Education was a tool, something to dig yourself out of a bad spot—especially if you didn't have the face and fortune to be a model while you got your education—so he was glad Walda snapped to it when it came to being sure her daughter got what she needed.

He honestly couldn't even remember the tutor, just the sweet kid who'd grown up well.

"Anyway, that's how we met and in the intervening years he's been a supermodel and now a celebrity chef and cookbook author." Cora smiled at him. "Go you."

"How do you know Gregori?" Rachel asked once they'd settled in at the long table in the main room.

"He and I were young men with more money than sense in the art scene," Gregori said. "He was one of the first friends I made here in the US. We've been in contact on and off since. I had no idea of the connection between him and Cora."

"It was a pleasant surprise," Beau told them with a shrug. "I know many people. I'm friends with very few, so those I like to keep around."

"I didn't even know crab and scallop cakes were an

actual thing. I vote yay," Cora said as she put another two on her plate.

In addition, there were brussels sprout leaves roasted with parmesan and walnuts, fruit and cheese with honey, wine, champagne and, at the end, not just one cake, but two.

Not a lot satisfied Beau more than seeing people enjoy food he'd made. Cooking was his way of pleasing others. Of being worthy.

As fucked up as he was, he'd managed to substitute out the most harmful ways of feeling worthy and pleasing others at least. His life was his own now. No one made his choices. He owed no one anything he didn't want to give.

"You're having a very intense conversation in your head," Cora said quietly.

He shrugged. "Not really," he lied.

She sniffed, like she wanted him to know she saw right through him. Defensiveness raised in his gut, warring with fascination and no small amount of admiration that she would not only see the truth of it, but also let him know she got that he was evading.

A few hours in, Vic and Rachel peeled off. Gregori explained that Vic worked in a bakery, the same one that had provided some of the sweets they'd eaten that night, and had to be up by four thirty.

He realized, as they cleaned up, that he didn't really want his time with Cora to end. Which was…unusual. Unusual enough that he paid attention to it. She was a gorgeous, creative, interesting woman and an old friend. That was it. Probably.

Still, when she headed to the door, he followed. "Hey, where are you off to?"

"Home. I've been up well over twenty-four hours at this point and the travel has just sort of smacked me in the head. Now that my belly is full and I've been loved up on by my friends, I'm going to head back to my place and sleep for many hours."

"Where are you parked? Do you need a ride home?" Wren asked and then Gregori sighed. Clearly he'd noticed the chemistry between Cora and Beau all night.

Cora hadn't seemed to notice Gregori's sigh as she replied, "I'm just right around the corner at the lot near Ink Sisters. I'm good. Thank you, though." Cora hugged Wren and then tiptoed up to do the same with Gregori.

"I'll walk with you," Beau said, grabbing his coat. "If that's cool with you."

Cora shrugged. "Sure. You don't have to. It's not that far."

"And then you can give him a ride," Gregori told her. "He's staying in a flat in the Bay Vista Tower so he's on your way home anyway."

Gregori gave him a very slight smile. Beau owed his friend a beer for that little suggestion that allowed him more time with her.

"Ah! Yes, that's totally on my way home. I can easily drop you off as a thanks for walking with me and defending my honor in case a drunken Pioneer Square reveler gives me any guff. Not that they would with an eleven-foot-tall dude, but you know what I mean," Cora said.

"There are perks to being tall. And I'd appreciate the ride as I walked over earlier today." And he'd get to be alone with her in the car where he planned on asking her out.

He shouldn't. He usually kept himself clear of get-

ting involved with a friend or anyone in his social circle that he might have to see regularly in the wake of
something unpleasant.

But she felt like home to him in a way that he couldn't
really put to words. And he really needed home after
drifting for far too long.

CORA LIKED WALKING with Beau. When she stopped to
peer more closely and then photograph a wet leaf, he
didn't get impatient. When she wanted to look in a window or pause to stare up at the lights, he paused too.
He meandered like she did. Which was something she
found herself charmed by.

Certainly there was no denying the way people
tended to get out of their way as they came along. Even
sauced up patrons who'd poured out of bars and onto the
sidewalks parted to let them pass. He was big. Sturdy
and broad shouldered. As a short girl, it was pretty
freaking nice, she had to admit.

So she told him. Or, well she thought it out loud and
then just went with it because it was too late to do anything else.

He leaned closer and the heat of him seemed to
brush against her skin. "It's a novel thing to imagine
the world from your perspective," he said in his voice
that wrapped around her and tugged.

"You have a great voice. I figure I should go ahead
and tell you that." She pointed at her car as they came
upon the lot where she'd parked. "That's me."

Cora didn't think herself overly concerned with things.
But this car—named Eldon—was her not-so-guilty
pleasure.

A gift from her mother—because Cora never would

have done it for herself and because Walda loved giving extravagant gifts.

It was low slung and sporty and when she got in and closed the door, the world drifted away.

He came to a startled halt. "That?"

Cora was glad it was dark enough he couldn't see her blush. "Okay. I know. It's an extravagance. My mom decided I should have it. And I tried to turn it down or talk her to a less, uh, over-the-top choice. But she's Walda and she does what she wants."

"I'm jealous. I nearly bought a TTS last year."

Oh. Well, that was nice. She clicked the locks and he waited for her to get in before he followed suit.

"You're really tall and I was worried you'd have to bend like a pretzel to fit in the passenger seat. So I'm glad that didn't happen because you have those jeans on and I don't want you to have to cut off circulation or whatever."

Jesus, she just made a thinly veiled joke about his dick getting bent in an uncomfortable way. She'd been hanging out around the Dolans way too long.

He snorted a laugh. "I've never been as entertained by a conversation," he said as she pulled out of the lot.

"Oh. Well. Good because I'm entertaining that way so I'm delighted you can see the benefits. I'm glad you're in Seattle, Beau. I hope we'll see one another again before you leave. And wow, this whole segment of our conversation is really just me wandering all around. I'm normally better at this. Really."

"Still entertaining. Five stars," he said through laugher. "I'd love to see you again. Me and you. What does your kitchen look like?"

"Uh. It's a nice kitchen. I like to cook well enough.

I decided to take the space from a third bedroom and make the kitchen and the master bigger. Gas stove."

He nodded and she felt a little relieved that she'd passed a test of some sort.

"Are you free tomorrow night? I'd like to make you dinner and catch up on the last seventeen years."

He just asked her out. She *hadn't* imagined the chemistry between them. This day was pretty fucking great so far.

"Totally free. I'll be home by six and I can handle the dessert."

"I'll be there by six thirty with everything I need."

A wave of heat washed through her. There was no misunderstanding the way his voice had that husky undertone. That was maybe "I'll be putting my mouth on you at some point during this date" tone and she liked it. It left her drunk with delight.

She gave him her address as she found a space to slide into across the street from his building. "Okay. So. Um. I'll see you tomorrow night then."

He unbuckled himself but before he got out, he leaned close and surprised her when he laid a kiss on her lips.

Just a casual kiss. Quick but not so fast he didn't slowly drag his teeth over her bottom lip as he pulled back.

"See you then."

Still tasting him, she watched as he jogged across the street and then made his way into the building.

Cora wasn't entirely sure what she was getting herself into, but she liked it.

CHAPTER THREE

In a flurry of wind a red leaf skitters
Dances on the air
As summer dies
And autumn puts on her fiery crown

"WHY AM I NOT SURPRISED?" Cora asked.

Rachel and Maybe stood on her porch with a pink-and-white box holding her favorite doughnuts and bearing big grins as well as coffee.

She opened up. "Get in here before you let out all the warm air."

"You're not surprised because we're predictable and nosy. And because we come bearing coffee and doughnuts." Rachel kissed Cora's cheek before she put her things down and hung her coat in the front closet.

"We were sort of bummed to find out you're alone this morning," Maybe told her as she popped the lid off the doughnut box and carried it, along with her coffee, to the living room.

Cora snorted. "Don't you two have to be at work or something?"

"My first appointment isn't until one," Rachel said as she chose a chocolate glazed.

"I'm sleeping with my boss," Maybe told her. "What is the deal with you and sexy chef guy? I know I wasn't imagining it. Especially when he just about shoved Wren out of the way when he got the chance to walk you to your car."

"He's making me dinner tonight." Cora sipped her coffee.

Rachel grabbed one of the throw blankets Cora kept everywhere and tucked it around herself before saying, "I googled him this morning after Vic left for work. He pretended like he didn't know I was going to. We like to pretend I'm nicer than I really am. It's why we've stayed together for two years." Rachel continued after another bite of her doughnut, "But you know Beau's had quite the colorful life. I mean. Wow. Also the modeling shots alone might have made me pregnant."

Cora nearly choked on her coffee as she laughed. "Now imagine seeing that when you were sixteen."

"Dude, I'm absolutely convinced I'd have had no idea what to do with a guy like him when I was sixteen. All the tattoos and the piercings. Super hot."

"We saw the tasteful nudes. He's quite gifted. And a natural redhead." Maybe toasted Cora by holding her doughnut aloft a moment.

"You're going to have to Heimlich me if you make me laugh like this while I'm eating," Cora said between fits of giggles. "I missed you two. A lot."

"We missed you too. When you're done telling us about Beau, let's talk about you not leaving for so long again." Maybe reached out to squeeze Cora's leg a moment.

"He's got a complicated backstory, to say the least. But there's something, I don't know, genuine about him. He's…" Cora raised her hands, not finding the right words for how she felt. "Aside from being gorgeous, he's interesting. It was easy being with him last night at Gregori and Wren's. And then after. He kissed me. Just a fast thing. Not a peck. No tongue, but he gave me some teeth when he broke the kiss. And he used the sex voice on me. It worked. I mean. Every part of me heard it, like a tuning fork."

"Zing." Rachel nodded her head and Maybe echoed the action. "You have zing. I have zing with Vic. Maybe's got it with Alexsei. Zing is good if it doesn't, you know, cloud your head because your *other* parts are too dazed. If you know what I mean."

Cora batted her lashes and leaned toward her friend. "No. What do you mean?"

Rachel started to reply before narrowing her gaze and flipping Cora off.

Laughing, Cora said, "It's been a while since I've been dazed with zing. It's not underrated." She hadn't had that sort of delicious sexual chemistry with someone in years and she hadn't realized until then how much she'd missed it.

"Seems to me your priorities are in the right order," Maybe told her. "Get some."

Rachel rolled her eyes before adding, "He could get it, no lie. I mean, if I wasn't head over heels in love with Vic. Literally over the weekend. I need to start stretching before sex."

Cora and Maybe both burst into giggles. This too, *sisterhood*, was a sensation she'd missed. The ability to be totally who she was, bumps and scars and flaws aplenty, with these two women in her living room filled her with happiness. Made her more confident.

"Now I'm going to see that every time I see him.

Which is often, in case you haven't noticed," Maybe managed to say.

Rachel just shrugged. "So you're going to let Beau get all up in your space. I also found out some details about his personal life. He's got a reputation. Or maybe had? Anyway, he likes the ladies. And a few gentlemen too. But not for very long. He used to be a favorite on all the gossip sites. Partied. A lot. But you know, some of those pictures from back in the day were with Gregori and we know he's changed. He's had the same core group of friends for years. Gregori and Ian Brewster, the restaurateur friend he mentioned both live here in Seattle. Another lives somewhere in Europe. That shows something good about him, I think. He's loyal once he, uh, commits."

Cora clapped her hands over her ears a moment, blushing hard. "Oh my god. I should have stopped you sooner but let's be honest, I wanted to hear it." She waved a hand, took a bite of her doughnut and thought a bit before she spoke again. "I knew about most of it. I've followed his career here and there over the years. I'm going to let him make me dinner. We'll catch up and have—hopefully—great conversation and then if there's anything else—smooching, groping, what have you—that's all good. At some point he'll take his new recipes and that chiseled jaw away from Seattle. So why not enjoy what I can now? It's not like I want him to move in or be my boyfriend or whatever. I just want some fun and to hang out with an old friend. Hopefully excellent sex. Also I'd like a dog. I'm really thinking of getting a dog. Not a big one because my little yard isn't really good for a big dog. Small and smart and not yappy. I don't like yappy dogs and the neighbors would complain."

"This conversation is moving at the speed of light. I'm here for it. And another doughnut. We need to start our walks again so I can have more than one doughnut without guilt," Maybe said and then started to snicker. "Just kidding. I love having more than one doughnut and feel zero guilt about that. But I do love our walks too."

Rachel said, "Okay, now that you've told us about your romantic life, why don't you tell us the rest. Seeing you so happy about this Beau thing has underlined for me I've seen that Cora less and less over the last eighteen months or so. You've sounded less and less happy, more and more tired. Don't you think it's time to seriously re-think your job situation?"

They knew her so well.

"I love to travel. A few weeks away is one thing, but three months and more? Too much. And, to be totally honest? It's a lot harder on my mother than it used to be. But she won't admit it and she doesn't have an off switch. So things go left and I have to clean up the mess. Then she gets mad at me because she's not forty anymore. More often than not what I do is make excuses for some terrible thing she's done to make someone cry and keeping her out of jail or worse. It makes me tired."

"Fair enough. She's a big personality. But you're not her keeper." Maybe used what was left of her doughnut to stab Cora's way.

"Ha! I totally *am* her keeper. It's turned into a family joke. I'm the Walda whisperer, the keeper of the creative. It's fucking exhausting and I don't think it serves her. Not who she is now. Her career is different. The world is different." Cora shrugged. "Anyway, I used to be content wandering the globe whenever and wherever she needed me. It was wonderful while it was wonderful. I've learned a lot. I've had a relationship with my mom that is totally unique and wonderful. But it's also… *I'm* the mom most of the time."

"I think it's absolutely fair that you want to reevaluate the situation now. Yes, she's getting older, more frail. Especially in the last two or three years." Rachel paused, looked Cora square on. "Even if none of those things were true it's still okay even if it was just about what *you* want. It's okay even if it's only about you. You get that You want to build a life that will take you into your future. You want to shift gears, sink roots and make a life that entails a different sort of work," Rachel said.

"It should be all right for a while. She's done, except for promotion, which won't start for three or four months. And even then it shouldn't take her too far from home. I should encourage that." Cora grabbed her notebook and jotted a note down to do more radio and podcast interviews and to have them done in a local recording studio instead of traveling.

Rachel looked pointedly at the notebook before focusing on Cora again. "You're still taking a few weeks off though, right?"

"Well. I won't be traveling anywhere nonrecreational. In fact I was thinking of leaf peeping and could probably include some birding. Perhaps cap it off with a stop at Samish Cheese? Something for everyone." Cora grinned at them.

"I'm in."

"Me too," Rachel said. "Now, getting back to the question, which was about you taking a few weeks off."

"Yes I am. From my mother. But I'll be at the gallery. There's a new installation coming up so I want to be there or who knows what they'll do?"

"So now you can finally quit being the Walda-keeper and shift to the gallery full-time. But you can still take a week or so. I mean, what did they do for the last three months without you there?" Maybe asked.

The gallery was her baby. Sort of. Cora had spent a lot of time and effort in creating a space that had a voice. A unique voice in a very rich local art scene. "Call me fourteen times a day?" She'd pretty much done the job over the phone and online anyway. But that? That'd felt like it should have. She'd *wanted* to be involved. It fed her creative hunger in a way few things did.

"Okay then," Rachel said. "Over the last several years you've mentioned here and there that you want to run the gallery full-time. Why not finally make that shift now? Then someone *else* can handle your mom." Rachel's severe look had Cora's denials dying in her chest. "It's unfair that they'd expect you to keep on like this indefinitely. Oh sure, they all thank you for doing it—and they should—but none of them has stepped up to help you out. Not on this. Plenty of people can be your mom's personal assistant/manager/keeper. For the right kind of money," Rachel added at Cora's expression. "You're irreplaceable because no one will be as perfect as you. That's a given. But Walda's not the only diva in the world. We can help you find the right solution."

Maybe leaned over to squeeze Cora quickly. "You want to defend your family. But I promise you we aren't attacking them. We're your best friends and it is our god-given right to take your side. And to tell you the truth."

"So let's skip the part where you tell yourself you're selfish for wanting something for yourself. Who but you knows Walda works better when lightbulbs are this or that wattage? Or that she likes nutmeg in her coffee? And so what if you do? She's a grown woman, not a toddler. She can express her wishes to someone else. It's not like she's shy," Rachel said, deadpan.

No, Walda wasn't shy. But beneath all the feathers and bright colors and whatever else she did, her mother wanted to be loved.

Of course Cora felt selfish. And guilty.

"It's on the list of things I'm thinking about," Cora told them both. "Thank you for caring about me enough to make me face this stuff. But I'm done with facing it for now. Let's talk about something else. Tell me what's been happening. How was your show last weekend?" she asked Maybe, who played drums in a punk rock band.

As Maybe excitedly filled her in, Cora leaned back, tucked herself under a blanket of her own and let being with her friends wash over her.

CHAPTER FOUR

That time you walked in
And the universe shifted...
I've been falling ever since.

OF ALL THE things from his childhood, Beau had come to terms with the way he'd been raised when it came to a usual lack of nervousness. A natural sense of ambition and ability.

But as he wrestled the box with all the ingredients for dinner out of his trunk, he realized the butterflies in his belly were all about her.

It was fucking delicious.

He didn't even have to look at his phone for the number of her town house because once he entered the circular courtyard he knew immediately which porch was hers. It just had the most life around it. An overflowing planter on either side of the steps framed them artfully.

And on each step, words had been painted.

I am the light of a thousand stars
I am cosmic dust made human.

As he got to the top step, he caught sight of her through her front window. She stretched up to light candles dotted across a mantelpiece. He couldn't see anything but the grace in the movement, lost his other senses for a bit as his heartbeat seemed to thunder in time with the blood pounding in his cock.

He managed to hit the doorbell and when she opened up to him, her smile lightened his nervousness. She looked at him like she knew him. And wanted to be with him anyway.

"Come in!" she said as she stepped aside to admit him. "You can put the stuff on the table." Cora indicated a stout, round table in the nook just to the left of the kitchen.

He managed not to rush, no matter how much he wanted to hug her. Beau even managed to get his coat off and slung over the back of one of the chairs before he said hello and pulled her into an embrace.

She hummed, low and pleased and a shiver rode his spine.

"Good evening," he murmured as he brushed a quick kiss over her brow.

"You smell good. What are you cooking for me tonight?" she asked him as she started to poke through the crate.

"Thank you. You not only smell good, you look good." She wore a bright yellow sweater with faded blue jeans and thick socks. Cora looked like a fucking flower. Pretty and fresh and sexy all at once.

She blushed and he found it incredibly appealing.

"So I, uh, do you like pasta? I was thinking linguine with clam sauce for the main. Some bruschetta with mushrooms and parsley and another with roasted and marinated red peppers and garlic."

"Yum! I like all those things. I have a feeling I'll be overeating. I grabbed some wine, red and white and some prosecco just for giggles. I wasn't sure what you'd be making and it's not like a bottle of wine won't find another use if I don't drink it tonight. Oh and there's beer too.

"I didn't know what you'd be needing, so I just made sure the counters were extra clean," she said with a shrug. "Cooking stuff is in the cabinets and under the stovetop there." She pointed. "Use whatever you find, ask if you don't see something."

"Perfect." He washed his hands while she poured them both a glass of red wine.

"I'm a rebel. I wear white after Labor Day and drink red wine whenever I please." She toasted him, clinking her glass to his.

"I like a little rebellion. We can have white later with the pasta, if you like. Red would be fine as well. Basically, anything you want because I aim to please." He tied on an apron and began to get to know her kitchen, setting the oven to get the bruschetta started.

She cleared her throat before speaking. "Can I help in any way or just watch you prepare a feast for me and fantasize about you kissing me?"

He didn't stop himself from bending down to kiss her. Intending it to be quick but once she sighed softly, he couldn't keep it quick. Instead he backed her to the counter and settled in, tasting, teasing, sipping at her until his skin felt too tight.

Cora slid her tongue along his as she pressed herself closer, her hands at his waist, fingers hooked through the belt loops of his pants to hold him there.

She was sexy. Sweet and hot. Like nothing he'd experienced.

It rattled him enough to break the kiss, but in two breaths he had to go back for another kiss.

Because he needed it. Her taste was dark and rich and utterly irresistible. He wondered if the rest of her tasted as good.

With a groan, he pulled away when the oven pre-heat timer dinged.

Cora cocked her head, her smile gone feline and satisfied. "Well, okay then. You can find me available for kisses anytime." The slight slur of pleasure in her voice was a caress along the back of his neck.

"Now I'm ready to get back to work. You just sit there, keep my wine glass filled and be available for more kisses in case I can't get along until I have another."

"Right-O." She hopped up on one of the stools facing him across her kitchen island.

He sliced mushrooms thin as he tried not to stare at her mouth but she made it difficult because she talked a lot, smiled a lot, laughed a lot.

It was really only the fear of slicing into his finger instead of the veggies and herbs that kept him from drooling over her like a cartoon dog.

That made him snort, catching her attention.

"Do I amuse you?" she asked, a teasing note in the words.

"Absolutely. So what did you do today? What have you been up to over the past seventeen years? You only hit the highlights last night."

"Today I had coffee and doughnuts here with Maybe and Rachel and then I went into the gallery for a few hours."

"I need to stop by the gallery and check it out. I'm

curious and always looking for something new. Up until now, my art guidance has come from Gregori. Fortunately, he knows my taste so he rarely steers me wrong."

Her eyes lit as she beamed at him. That was when her dimple came out and had him licking his lips for another taste of her.

"That's such a mistake to reveal to someone who runs a gallery." She sipped her wine. "I had a meeting with a new artist today. She's got a show coming up with us and I'm amazed at the stuff she does. We like to focus on regional artists, give them space and a voice. She came here with her family from Cambodia when she was an infant so her stuff, which is mixed media, has this sense of roots and ownership of gender and identity that blows me away. She used to be a chemist for the state department of fisheries and one of her kids encouraged her to take early retirement and give her art more time. And she did. That was three years ago."

He liked the way she talked about art. A lot like he suspected he sounded when he talked about food. As she described the pieces she planned to put into the show, the passion for what she did seemed to flow from her.

"Sounds fantastic. I'll definitely cruise by the opening."

"Oh gosh, please do. Not only do I think you'd like her work, it's nice to be supported by your friends. The opening should be pretty fantastic, if I do say so myself. Which naturally I do because I'm speaking. Anyway, I throw a good party. I'll make sure you get an invite."

Her kitchen was well stocked, but not overdone. The town house wasn't huge, like the condo he was in. But it was comfortable. She'd made excellent use of the space she did have.

It was warm and accessible, a lot like her so that wasn't really a surprise.

He found all the tools he needed—which meant he could leave all the stuff he'd brought just in case in the trunk of his car. She kept his glass filled and did an excellent job of rubbing garlic on the bruschetta when he asked it of her.

By the time they settled in at her table, it was nearly eight but he was warm from the wine and the exertion and though he'd snacked as he'd worked, he had quite the appetite for the pasta.

"Would you be weirded out if I took a picture of this? I mean it looks like art," she said.

Pride filled him. "Not at all. I'm flattered." And he was.

She went to grab her phone, took a few pictures and then put it away again, giving him all her attention once more.

Mesmerizing.

After she ate and moaned with joy at whatever it was she tasted, his ego was about to explode. That and his dick. He was grateful his lap was hidden by the table.

"Tell me about the words on your porch steps," he said. "Where's the quote from?"

"Do you like it?"

He nodded. "Very much."

"It's mine. I've been writing snippets of poetry since I was a kid. That's part of a poem called 'Star Stuff.' I change it up from time to time."

"Lots of layers to you, Cora Silvera."

"Like an onion."

He stood and began to help her clear the table and clean the kitchen, over her protests that he'd cooked so she would clean up. It also enabled him to be close enough to brush against her as they moved around, wiping counters and filling the dishwasher.

"Come through to the other room for a while. Tell me how long you're going to be in Seattle." She took the bottle of white wine along with her into the living room where he joined her, settling on her overstuffed couch.

"I'm here for…well, for the next while. At least a year. Likely more. Love the weather and all the stuff to do outdoors. My friends live here—including you. It's a food culture I really like. And I'm done with New York and LA. Not for visits—I still love both cities. Both were great for my career. But it's time for something else. Seattle seems a good place to be somewhere to land. Finish this cookbook."

"Well, I'm glad to hear it. There's a cherry walnut cake for dessert but I'm pretty full," she said, voice lazy as she leaned against the cushions.

"We should do something else until we digest dinner." He took her hand, threading his fingers with hers and tugged her toward him. "I can think of a few ways to spend some time."

"Yeah? I think maybe we have some of the same ideas on that."

"Let's compare notes."

Before he knew it she was on his lap. And like he'd figured, she fit him.

Perfectly.

"Let me know when I get too heavy," she said, her lips so close to his, the heat of her made him a little light-headed.

"When that happens, I'll get on top. I like being on top."

With a laugh, she nipped his bottom lip, tugging it sharply. "I'm not surprised by that."

Look for WHISKEY SHARP: TORN
by Lauren Dane
Spring 2018
wherever HQN books are sold

HARLEQUIN® *Desire*

Family sagas…scandalous secrets…burning desires.

Save **$1.00**

on the purchase of ANY
Harlequin® Desire book.

Available wherever books are sold,
including most bookstores, supermarkets,
drugstores and discount stores.

✂

Save **$1.00**

on the purchase of any Harlequin® Desire book.

Coupon valid until July 31, 2018.
Redeemable at participating outlets in the U.S. and Canada only.
Not redeemable at Barnes & Noble stores. Limit one coupon per customer.

Canadian Retailers: Harlequin Enterprises Limited will pay the face value of this coupon plus 10.25¢ if submitted by customer for this product only. Any other use constitutes fraud. Coupon is nonassignable. Void if taxed, prohibited or restricted by law. Consumer must pay any government taxes. Void if copied. Inmar Promotional Services ("IPS") customers submit coupons and proof of sales to Harlequin Enterprises Limited, P.O. Box 31000, Scarborough, ON M1R 0E7, Canada. Non-IPS retailer—for reimbursement submit coupons and proof of sales directly to Harlequin Enterprises Limited, Retail Marketing Department, 225 Duncan Mill Rd., Don Mills, ON M3B 3K9, Canada.

52615607

U.S. Retailers: Harlequin Enterprises Limited will pay the face value of this coupon plus 8¢ if submitted by customer for this product only. Any other use constitutes fraud. Coupon is nonassignable. Void if taxed, prohibited or restricted by law. Consumer must pay any government taxes. Void if copied. For reimbursement submit coupons and proof of sales directly to Harlequin Enterprises, Ltd 482, NCH Marketing Services, P.O. Box 880001, El Paso, TX 88588-0001, U.S.A. Cash value 1/100 cents.

5 65373 00076 2   (8100)0 12351

® and ™ are trademarks owned and used by the trademark owner and/or its licensee.

© 2018 Harlequin Enterprises Limited

HDCOUP0418